SAM

"This—this is an outrage!" she stormed

SAM

BY

E. J. RATH

ILLUSTRATIONS BY

WILL GREFÉ

NEW YORK
GROSSET & DUNLAP
PUBLISHERS

CONTENTS

S A M

SAM

CHAPTER I

SAM, THE BOAT PERSON

MISS CHALMERS stood on the wharf at Clayton, poised upon one foot, while she employed the other in executing alternate tap-taps, denoting impatience, and vigorous stamping, by which she registered rage. Even the half-grown boy who had volunteered to find her a boatman knew that she was angry.

Her free foot beat upon the rough flooring of the wharf with increasing vigor. The wharf did not care; it was old and stout, and did not pretend to be ornamental.

Miss Chalmers's shoe might have protested, had it possessed a voice, for it was new and spotless, and of delicate constitution. With its mate, it had cost Miss Chalmers twenty dollars, a fact which is set down to obviate the necessity of describing what else the lady wore. Her whole costume was in complete financial and artistic harmony with its twenty-dollar-shoe foundation.

It was dark and clear and warm —somewhat after nine o'clock of an August night. There were gleams of light upon the St. Lawrence, some in motion, some merely shimmering restlessly as they lay fixed upon the rippling surface. It was an evening for poetry and romance and beauty — if only the last steamer had not departed.

The boy came back and confirmed his previous impression that no other boat would stop that night at Witherbee's Island.

"It's absurd — inexcusable!" exclaimed Miss Chalmers sharply.

"Yes, ma'am," said the boy.

"How am I to get there, then? Well? Answer!"

"I got a man who'll take you."

"Where is he?"

"Down that way," replied the boy, nodding his head toward the end of the wharf.

"A reliable man?"

"Yes, ma'am."

"You know him?"

"No, ma'am."

Miss Chalmers stamped her foot again.

"How can you say he's reliable if you don't know him?" she demanded so imperatively that the boy winced and shuffled his feet.

"Well, he's got a power-boat, and his name's Sam," said the boy defensively. "He ain't ever been wrecked 's fur as I know."

Miss Chalmers made an eloquent and helpless gesture with both arms, then surveyed her light field-equipment — six trunks and a grip.

"Show me the man," she spoke abruptly.

The boy made off in haste, with Miss Chalmers at his heels. He led the way among bales and boxes and barrels, stopping presently under a dim oil lantern set upon a post.

On the string-piece of the wharf sat a man, smoking a pipe. He looked up at Miss Chalmers casually, yet speculatively, then arose and nodded amicably.

"Looking for me?" he asked.

Miss Chalmers was annoyed at the phrasing; never yet had she "looked for" a man. But she swallowed her annoyance.

"I must go to Mr. Stephen Witherbee's island — to-night," she said.

"Yes, ma'am."

"You know where it is?"

"Oh, yes!"

"How far is it?"

"Something like fifteen miles."

"Can you take me there at once?"

"Well," said the man, removing his pipe from his mouth and regarding Miss Chalmers with solemn interest, "it all depends on what you call ' at once.' I can take you there, but I'm no speed-king."

"Take me, then!" exclaimed Miss Chalmers. "And get my trunks."

The man went up the wharf at a leisurely gait, accompanied by the boy. Almost immediately the boy came back.

"He says he can't take all them trunks, and for you to pick out two."

Miss Chalmers strode back to her trunks with no improvement of temper. She found the boatman surveying them placidly.

"Which is the emergency-kit?" he asked pleasantly. "I'm not running a freighter, ma'am."

"They've all got to go — every one!"

The man shook his head doubtfully.

"Swim?" he asked presently, looking Miss Chalmers evenly in the eye.

"Why, cer— Oh, how ridiculous! Will you or will you not take those trunks?"

"Oh, I'll take them — only maybe the boat won't. Anyhow, we'll make a stab," he said cheerfully, shouldering the nearest trunk.

The boat took them, but not without wabbles of warning and an ominous loss of freeboard. The boatman dumped them aboard with easy nonchalance, while Miss Chalmers shivered in solicitude. But she made no comment; she was in a hurry, and she did not purpose to descend to argument with a 'longshore person.

"Well, I guess we're ready," said the boatman as he gave the last trunk a final kick into place and reached a hand up for his passenger. Ignoring the hand, Miss Chalmers stepped swiftly aboard, unaided.

"Here, boy!" she called, tossing a quarter back upon the wharf.

The boy fell upon the coin and was off.

The six trunks of Miss Chalmers occupied three-fourths of the cock-pit, so that she found herself crowded far aft, in close and unpleasant proximity to the bearded and greasy-shirted master of the launch. She wrapped her skirt close about her knees — not a very difficult task as skirts go — compressed her lips tightly, and stared out upon the river.

There was an interval of several minutes, during which the launch coughed, gasped, and volley-fired, while the boatman panted and heaved at the fly-wheel. Five times the engine started, and five times it stopped with a sob. The man arose from his knees, fumbled about for a candle, lighted it, and examined the gasoline contraption curiously. Then he spun the fly-wheel again, which produced more coughing and another wailing sob of despair.

Miss Chalmers turned abruptly from her survey of the river.

"For Heaven's sake, prime it!" she snapped.

The boatman twisted his head and regarded her with undisguised astonishment. He not only looked at Miss Chalmers, but he studied her hat, her gown, and her twenty-dollar shoes. He also resurveyed the six trunks. But Miss Chalmers had again turned her attention to the lights upon the river, and was unconscious of his scrutiny.

"That's a good tip," he observed, after satisfying his eyes.

Whereupon he primed the engine, and the boat buzzed away from the wharf.

Miss Chalmers was but partially relieved in mind when she found herself being borne out upon the St. Lawrence.

The day on the railroad had been hot and cindery, and the train was hours late at Clayton. To cap that misfortune, she had loitered to purchase some stamps and write some telegrams, and arrived at the wharf in time to get an excellent view of the disappearing stern-light of the last regular boat that would stop at Witherbee's Island that night. It seemed easier to get to Europe, she reflected.

Well out into the American channel, the boatman shifted his helm and headed the launch down-stream. He was smoking again, leaning back comfortably against the coaming, his long legs stretched out so

that his feet were braced against the nearest
trunk.

Occasionally he glanced at the lights that shone
cordially from the islands and the mainland, and
now and then paid brief attention to some passing
craft; but most of the time he appeared to be studying the back of Miss Chalmers's head. Several
times he smiled, and once his silent reflections
brought forth a soft chuckle.

An hour passed. The launch still voyaged in midstream, making irregular détours where islands
loomed out of the channel. Miss Chalmers extended her hand close to a flickering lantern that
stood on the floor of the cock-pit and examined the
dial of her wrist-watch.

" How far have we gone? " she demanded.

The boatman studied the shore for a few seconds.

" Oh, seven or eight miles," he answered.

" And you say it's fifteen? "

" To Witherbee's? Oh, all of that."

" You mean to tell me this boat cannot do better
than seven or eight miles an hour? "

" She has done better," sighed the boatman.
" She did eleven once. But she was new then, and
her bottom was clean, and her cylinder wasn't full
of carbon, and she didn't leak, and her carbureter
didn't have asthma, and she didn't have six trunks
on board, and —"

Miss Chalmers interrupted the apology with an
angry exclamation.

" It's nearly eleven o'clock," she said. " It's
beyond endurance! I wish I hadn't started."

" Well, we can turn around any time," remarked
the boatman mildly. " But she won't do better than

eight miles an hour at the outside. You can play that bet to win."

Miss Chalmers devoted to the boatman a swift and stormy glance. He irritated her even more than his atrocious boat. The easy, almost familiar style of his speech was something to which she was unaccustomed — from the lips of common persons. It seemed to her that he assumed a position of equality.

A boatman — a grimy-handed, hatless, whiskered boatman! A person who hired out!

She set her jaws tightly and resumed her unsatisfying study of the river. Her dignity checked upon her lips a withering rebuke.

More islands were passed and the channel widened somewhat. The passenger observed with growing annoyance that there were fewer lights ashore. The summer folks were going to bed. High time, she thought; she was tired herself.

Nearly half an hour more elapsed, enlivened only by an astonishingly swift movement on the part of the steersman, who uncoiled himself like a spring, flung himself forward, and rescued, with a long and lean arm, the grip that belonged to his passenger just as it was about to slide quietly from the narrow deck into the hospitable St. Lawrence. Unceremoniously he jammed it into a safer place under the gunwale. Then he resumed his lolling posture at the tiller. Miss Chalmers made no comment.

Then, after a little, the rhythmical wheeze of the engine was supplanted by a series of irregular choking gasps, then a sharp popping at broken intervals, and then — silence.

The boatman sat up lazily, reached for the lantern, and held it close to the machinery. The launch carried her momentum for a minute, then swung broadside to the current and drifted contentedly. Miss Chalmers bit her lip.

Very deliberately the boatman studied the engine, poking the lantern about and, when it failed to illuminate dark recesses, lighting the stump of candle. Then he spun the fly-wheel.

There was no answer. Again and again he spun it, but the engine remained inert. After a while he resumed his placid and apparently purposeless examination of the gasoline monster.

"Well, what is the matter now?" demanded a cutting voice.

"Engine stopped," said the boatman, putting down the lantern and beginning to refill his pipe.

"Thank you for the information," said Miss Chalmers icily. "Why has it stopped?"

"I couldn't begin to tell you — ma'am."

There was something about the "ma'am," drawled out at the end, that peculiarly exasperated her; it seemed to lack the servility that was familiar to her from the lips of servants.

"Do you know anything about engines?"

"Not much that's good."

Miss Chalmers's temper was rising rapidly. She looked at her watch, then at the dark shores and islands.

"How dared you bring me out here if you didn't — Oh, it's — it's — perfectly outrageous! It's —"

She left the sentence unfinished, seized the lantern, brushed her way past the boatman without so much as a scornful glance, and dropped to her knees in the bottom of the cock-pit.

The floor was oily and dirty, but Miss Chalmers paid no attention to that. She devoted the next five minutes wholly to an examination of the engine. The boatman watched and smoked.

Item by item, she inventoried the one-cylinder pest. She peered into the oil-cups; she smeared her gloves on the cam that operated the timing-lever; she fussed with the tickler on the carbureter; she did a score of other things, while her audience watched in silence. After she got through with the engine she turned her attention to the batteries, tightening a wire connection here and there.

"Now, where's your socket-wrench?" she demanded.

"Socket-wrench?" repeated the boatman. "That's a new one on me. I don't remember —"

"Haven't you ever taken out the spark-plug?"

"Oh, you mean that funny thing that screws it out. Sure! I've got one somewhere."

He fumbled under a seat and drew out a box that contained a disorderly array of tools. Miss Chalmers dived a daintily gloved hand into it and brought forth what she sought.

"If you want me to do that —"

He did not finish the sentence, because she already had the spark-plug in her hand and was holding the points close to the light.

"Dirty, of course," she commented disgustedly. "Have you any sand-paper?"

He found a bit after more fumbling, and watched her while she scrubbed the metal points until they were bright. Then she replaced the plug and screwed it into position with a vigorous twist of the wrench.

The boatman had settled back in his place. After that she found a screw-driver and removed the cover from the float-chamber in the carbureter. A brief inspection of this mysterious compartment satisfied her.

"Now spin that fly-wheel," she said abruptly, rising from her knees and moving aside to make room for him.

The boatman spun the fly-wheel, not once, but many times. Twice the engine started, only to stop after a few revolutions.

"It's abominable!" exclaimed the passenger. "What do you propose to do?"

"Nothing, I guess," replied the boatman. "You've done more things now than I ever knew could be done. Don't suppose you damaged anything, do you?"

She glared at him, then turned her scorching glance out upon the river.

"Here comes a boat!" she said suddenly.

The boatman followed the line of her pointing finger and discerned the lights of a craft that was bearing rather closely toward them.

"Do you think they will help us?" she asked.

"Might," he admitted.

"They must! I can't stay here all night. Hail them!"

He put two fingers between his lips and sent forth a shrill whistle.

"Do you call that a hail?" she exclaimed, rising to her feet. She made a miniature megaphone of her hands and flung a vigorous " Ahoy! " across the water.

The boat was closer now.   Presently there was an answering voice.

" Any trouble? " said the voice.

The question affected the boatman like a shock of electricity.   He started from his seat, leaned over the gunwale, and squinted through the gloom.

" Breakdown," called Miss Chalmers.   " What boat is that? "

" Yacht *Elizabeth*.   Want any help? "

Before Miss Chalmers could answer a voice at her ear boomed out:

" No-o-o, thanks!   All right in a minute."

She turned in amazement upon the boatman, who was now on his knees in front of the engine, his face hidden from her.

" Why — you — you —"

The jingling of a bell from across the water interrupted her.   Then she heard the churning of a propeller, and the dark outline of the yacht began to move again.

" Ahoy! " screamed Miss Chalmers.

" Never mind! " roared her boatman.

She whirled upon him furiously.

" How could you!   How *dare* you!   Are you mad?   Do you think —"

She broke off and sent another hail in the direction of the yacht.   But that craft had disappeared in the night, and there was no answering call.

She looked down upon the kneeling figure, a tempest of wrath upon her lips.   The boatman was fussing aimlessly with a wrench.

Miss Chalmers fought for self-control.   She had

a passionate desire to slay, but she lacked a con-
venient means. Besides, she could not see that
homicide would speed her way to Witherbee's Island.
And even in her stormiest moments, Miss Chalmers
never quite abandoned her grip on things as they
were and problems that had to be met.

But she was bewildered, even alarmed. She did
not fear the consequences, however unpleasant, of
an all-night drift on the river. It was the boatman
who furnished cause for dismay. She wondered
if he was insane.

" I would like to know," she said, struggling to
quiet her voice, " why you did that."

" Did what? "

" Sent that yacht away."

" Reasons," he responded briefly.

" Reasons! What reasons? "

His only answer was a shrug.

" I demand to be told why you sent those people
away."

There was another hunch of his shoulders.

" Do you mean deliberately to keep me out here
in this boat all night? "

" Oh, not at all! " he said easily.

" Then why did you —"

" Sorry. Can't explain."

Miss Chalmers sat down with a gasp and tried
to consider the situation.

It was past midnight. The launch was slowly
drifting down-stream in a steadily broadening channel. The boatman was unable to operate his engine, and had refused an offer of help. He was
probably mad. She wondered if he was dangerous.

For several minutes she sat in silence, watching

him as he fussed about the machinery in an amateur-
ish fashion. Then she gritted her teeth and aroused
herself to action.

"Get out of the way!" she commanded.

He moved to make a place for her, and once more
she knelt on the greasy flooring. Very patiently,
considering the state of her emotions, Miss Chalmers
went over the engine again.

She shook her head, puzzled. Nothing seemed
to be wrong with it. Suddenly she turned to him.

"Where's your gas-tank?" she demanded.

"Forward. But you needn't look there.
There's plenty. I filled it —"

She seized the lantern and began climbing over
the trunks; she was not going to take the word of an
incompetent. Her white gown suffered dismally as
she scrambled in the direction of the gasoline-tank,
and she had a sinking sensation that the spectacle
afforded to the boatman was lacking in dignity. But
she was determined, and tried to comfort herself
with the thought that it was quite dark.

She located the tank and unscrewed the cap. The
aperture was large enough to admit her hand and
arm; in she plunged them resolutely. The tank
was nearly full. She replaced the cap and crawled
aft again.

Then the boatman did a strangely considerate
thing. He turned his back and pretended to be doing something to the engine, while Miss Chalmers
slipped down from the trunks and shook her skirt
about her ankles. She made a mental note of it.

"Where does your gas-line run?" she asked
briskly.

"Gas-line?"

"Oh, the pipe that connects the tank with the engine!" she cried in exasperation. "Don't you know *anything?*"

The boatman grinned cheerfully.

"I'm learning," he said. "It runs along under the gunwale on the port side, I think. I never paid much attention, but —"

"Hold the lantern here," she ordered, now on her hands and knees, with her head poked under the gunwale.

The boatman obeyed.

"Now move forward," she directed.

He moved the lantern as she directed, while Miss Chalmers explored the gas-line, beginning at the carbureter.

Presently they arrived at an obstacle in the shape of the passenger's baggage.

"Move that grip," was her next order.

He yanked the rescued bag from its place of safety, and she craned her head into the opening. A few seconds later she withdrew it and bestowed upon the boatman a look of unutterable contempt.

"Get down here," she said.

He knelt beside her.

"Poke your head in there."

He obeyed. Miss Chalmers also poked her head in, so that wisps of her brown hair brushed his unshaven cheeks.

"Now, do you see that little handle there?" she inquired.

"Yes, ma'am."

The boatman's voice was meek.

"Do you know what it is?"

"No, ma'am."

" Well, it's the cut-off in the gas-line."

" Never noticed it before," he commented blandly.

" And it's cut off now," continued Miss Chalmers.

A gentle swell rocked the boat, and their heads bobbed together. She paid no attention.

" You cut it off when you jammed my grip under there," she said tersely.

" There! Now I've turned it on again. The idea is that a gasoline-engine always runs better when supplied with gas. Now spin that fly-wheel! "

The boatman went aft and obeyed. The engine started joyfully. The launch moved. Miss Chalmers resumed her seat and surveyed her costume by the yellow light of the lantern.

" Now you take me to Witherbee's Island as quickly as you know how — if you do know," she observed.

The boatman made no answer. When the launch had obtained headway he altered the course, and presently they were passing through a series of narrow channels, between darkened islands. He seemed to know where he was going, but Miss Chalmers had no confidence in him. She was merely relieved to observe that they were going somewhere.

Presently they headed in toward a wooded island that was dark, save for a tiny light that flickered at the water's edge. As they neared the shore the boatman made his first remark since the engine had resumed wheezing.

" If you don't mind, I'd like to know —"

" I haven't run a six-cylinder car for nothing," interrupted Miss Chalmers sharply. " Is this the dock ? "

For answer he stopped the engine and guided the

boat alongside a low wharf, at the end of which burned the lantern they had seen.

"Witherbee's Island," he said as he reached to help her ashore.

Miss Chalmers sprang upon the wharf without aid and demanded her trunks. The boatman heaved them out methodically. He paused for an instant to study an inscription on the end of a particularly bulky and heavy one, and, when he had difficulty in deciphering it, reached for the lantern. He read:

ROSALIND CHALMERS, N. Y.

Then the trunk followed its mates.

"Anything more I can do?" he asked pleasantly.

"I should say not! I owe you something, I suppose?"

"Well, rather."

"How much?"

"Ten dollars."

"Ten dollars!" cried Miss Chalmers. "For what happened? After all that — Why, it's —"

She snapped her purse open and handed him a bill with an angry gesture. In fact she flung it at him. Anything to be rid of him, she thought. He pocketed the money with a chuckle.

"My name is Sam," he remarked as he stepped back into the boat. "Any time you need a launch, why —"

"I'll know whom not to engage," said Miss Chalmers, finishing the sentence.

The boatman laughed, started the engine, and headed across an open space in the river. Miss Chalmers glanced about her with a sigh of weary satisfaction. It was one o'clock, but she had arrived!

CHAPTER II

THAT particular insular possession owned by
Mr. Stephen Witherbee was, indeed, a
dark corner of the earth. It was also insistently quiet and lifeless. Just which one of the
insufficiently enumerated Thousand Islands it was
did not concern Miss Chalmers in the least, any
more than it concerns the reader. All she sought
was shelter and a couch.

She walked the length of the little wharf and
stared in among the trees that came down to meet it.
Somewhere beyond was a house she knew — a house
that contained Mr. and Mrs. Witherbee, Miss
Gertrude Witherbee, perhaps Mr. Tom Witherbee,
and various other persons who constituted a Witherbee house-party.

There was not the least doubt that they were all
asleep. Miss Chalmers could not hear a sound save
the ever-diminishing *thump-thump* of the one-cylinder launch.

"Asleep they are, certainly," she observed aloud.
"I've done a ridiculous thing, of course. It serves
me right for coming a day ahead of time. That
boatman — ugh!

"Where the house is I haven't the least idea.
But I can't stay here. I *must* find a place to sleep.
Perhaps — just perhaps — somebody is up, after
all."

She returned to the end of the wharf and surveyed her six trunks. "They'll do until morning," said Miss Chalmers as she picked up her grip and started in search of the Witherbee house.

There was a gravel path, beginning where the wharf met the shore, and Miss Chalmers followed it. Even in the gloom of the trees this was not difficult, for the gravel was white, and lay before her like a ghostly streak. Besides, it crunched under the twenty-dollar shoes.

Miss Chalmers was displeased with herself. She felt foolish. Something had gone wrong with her poise; something seemed to have been subtracted from the considerable sum of her dignity. The world was not playing flunky as usual. Her old austerity was there, perhaps, but it lacked confidence and authority.

The path forked, and Miss Chalmers paused to consider. The house was still invisible.

"Why does a strange path always fork when one is alone and in a hurry, and particularly at night?" asked Miss Chalmers aloud.

There was no answer; so, after an instant of indecision, she took the fork that led to the right. Naturally it was the wrong fork. It simply had to be, under the circumstances. It brought her back to the shore of the island, where a summer pavilion was erected on a rocky point.

She retraced her steps back to the fork and took the left branch of the gravel path. In not more than two minutes it guided her to the edge of a lawn. Beyond this she could see the house — a large, solid, black mass against a background of trees.

" Not a single light! " she exclaimed impatiently. " It's positively —*uncouth!* "

She crossed the lawn and paused again at the foot of a flight of steps that led to a broad piazza.

" It's almost as if the place was closed," she commented as her glance roved upward toward the windows. " But of course it's not. Oh, well! "

She ascended the steps, crossed the piazza, and found a push-button in the framing of a closed door. She pushed and waited — but not long; she was too impatient for dalliance.

Several times she pushed the button in rapid succession, holding her thumb upon it for extended periods. Nobody came to the door, which angered her anew. Then she realized that she herself could hear no ringing of a bell.

" Out of order, of course," she said bitterly.

She rapped smartly with her gloved knuckles upon the paneling of the door time after time until they ached. Then she dropped her grip, went back to the lawn, and looked up at the house again. It slept calmly.

Miss Chalmers made a circuit of the Witherbee dwelling. Not a ray of light filtered out of it from any side, not a sound — not even a snore. She returned to the front door and rapped again. Then she seated herself in a porch-rocker and frowned.

" I absolutely will not shout," she told herself. " I am sufficiently absurd as it is. I will *not* be laughed at! "

She placed particular emphasis upon the last thought, as if somebody, somewhere, was displaying amusement at her plight. If there was one thing Rosalind Chalmers would not for an instant endure

it was mirth of her own unintentional provoking.
She was not a lady to be laughed at.

In the first place, she was too dignified, even to the
point of a certain severity in manner. Where she
lacked severity she substituted condescension. In
the second place, she was too coldly handsome, too
tall, too slimly erect. In the third place, she was too
old — twenty-five. In the fourth place, she was a
Vassar graduate. In the fifth place, she was too
rich. In the sixth place —

Oh, why continue? It is already plain that under
no circumstances was Miss Chalmers a lady to be
laughed at, even by equals — to say nothing of a
common river-man.

Yet she knew exactly what would happen when
she succeeded in arousing the sleepers on Witherbee's Island. First, they would grumble and stum-
ble and rub their eyes. Then they would shuffle
to a window or a door and discover her. Then
there would be surprise and hurry and a scene.
And then — then, when everybody was thoroughly
awake — would come the laughter. She reasoned
it very logically and found no flaw in her conclu-
sions.

" I will not wake them," she decided. " I will get
into that house somehow, find myself a couch down-
stairs, and get my sleep. It's not that I mind waking
them up; not a bit. But I won't be —"

She left the murmured sentence unfinished, arose
from her chair, and walked briskly to the nearest
window. The sash was either securely locked or
thoroughly jammed, like a parlor-car window. She
could not move it.

She tried the next window; the result was the

same. A third window gave her no access to the dark interior of Witherbee House. She vented her annoyance in a sharp exclamation and turned the corner of the porch. The next window rattled encouragingly in its frame. It moved half an inch. She slipped the tips of her fingers under the sash, drew a deep breath, and heaved valiantly. The window ascended abruptly and with a clatter. And then —

A great bell clanged!

No decent, friendly, hospitable bell, but a raucous, brazen, mocking gong, pounded upon at the rate of a hundred or so strokes to the minute by a fiendish electric hammer.

The sound of the bell echoed in the gloom of the house and flung itself boisterously through the open window into the astonished and dismayed ears of Miss Chalmers. She fell back a step and raised her hands protectingly in front of her.

" A burglar-alarm! " she cried.

The din was appalling. It seemed to grow steadily in volume. Miss Chalmers was not truly frightened, but she was thoroughly amazed and startled. She was incontinently hurled from her pedestal of calm assurance.

For five seconds she hesitated. The bell boomed on. She stepped close to the window, placed her hands upon the sill, and leaned inward. From somewhere above she heard a heavy footstep, then a medley of sleepy voices.

She turned and ran.

She was dimly conscious in her precipitate retreat that, mingled with the clanging of the gong, there was another sound — a rattling of something on the porch floor.   But it was not a propitious moment for investigation.

Around the corner of the porch she fled, upsetting a wicker table and scattering its burden of magazines.   From its resting-place at the front door she scooped up her satchel.   Down the steps to the lawn she leaped recklessly and then across the space of level sward.

Her skirt was not fashioned for running.   With one hand she swept it up to her knees, a maneuver which added perhaps a knot to her speed.   Give her a fair chance and Miss Chalmers was an excellent runner.   She could even invest running with a certain stateliness and dignity — but not on this occasion.

Somebody had left a rocking-chair on the Witherbee lawn.   She had not observed it when she approached the house, but now she fell over it.   It bumped her knee cruelly, in addition to depositing her at full length upon the grass.

Within a second she was on her feet again, flaming with anger.   She groped for her fallen satchel, recovered it, and ran on toward the shelter of the trees.   At the edge of the trees she paused and looked back.   Lights were moving in the windows of Witherbee House.   She heard voices, some shrill with alarm.   Again she turned and fled.

Just why Miss Chalmers ran away from the haven of refuge she had been so long in reaching she could not clearly have explained.   She was flurried in mind, yet not to such an extent as to dim the fact that her conduct was quite illogical.   For fifteen minutes she had been trying to rouse the house; now that she had succeeded, she was in flight.

In among the trees she hesitated again.   The

simple and obvious thing to do was to walk straight back and announce herself. After that she would be in bed in ten minutes. But they might laugh. In fact, it was a certainty they would laugh. The alarm, the silly panic of a resolute lady, the chair on the lawn, her gown — oh, it was impossible. She ran once more, dodging among the trees and praying that she might find a path.

Presently she felt the gravel under her feet and followed the trail until it brought her back to the wharf, where her trunks crouched like black monsters in the faint light of the lantern. Here she paused to recover breath while she listened.

Through the little wood that had once seemed so dense she saw a glimmering of lanterns passing to and fro.

"I am *not* frightened!" panted Miss Chalmers hotly. "I am merely a fool! Yes — a complete fool! But they'll not find me — not now! Not for anything in the world! I'll go back; I'll find some way. I *won't* stay on this island. The whole thing is perfectly beastly and absurd!"

The moving lanterns among the trees seemed to be coming nearer. Men were calling to each other. She could hear footsteps on the gravel path.

There was no concealment on the wharf, yet Miss Chalmers was determined to be concealed. There could be no backing out now. She looked quickly about her.

Close to the wharf, at the very edge of the water, she now observed what looked like a boat-house. She sprang toward it and stepped out upon a small float that was anchored in front of it to find herself barred from refuge by padlocked doors.

The lanterns were now close to the wharf. Miss
Chalmers had no time to waste picking a lock,
even if she knew how. She slipped around the
corner of the boat-house and flattened herself
close against it, trying desperately to breathe noiselessly.

A moment later there was a shuffling of feet on
the wharf, then an exclamation of surprise in a man's
voice. Her curiosity urged her to risk a peep.
Very cautiously she advanced her head beyond the
corner of the building that screened her.

What Miss Chalmers saw shocked her. Three
men in pajamas, each carrying a lantern, were standing upon the wharf. Their feet were shod in bedroom slippers. Two of them carried walking-sticks
gripped tightly at the wrong end, evidently intended
to perform service as clubs. The third had a revolver.

She was shocked, not because she regarded pajamas and bedroom slippers as improper, but because
they seemed so utterly common, so plebeian, so lacking in anything that approached character or smart-
ness or form — in short, to the eyes of Miss Chalmers they were sheer vulgarity, even though of possible utility. She shuddered a little.

One of the men she recognized; it was Mr. Witherbee. She was well aware that Mr. Witherbee
was stout, but not until now did she realize that he
actually bulged. It was the first time she had ever
seen a fat man in pajamas, and she was impressed
with the fact that the effect was more robust than
artistic.

One of the other men was tall and blond, with a
drooping mustache. His pajamas were far too

short in the legs and his bare ankles were inelegant.

The other man had his back toward her. She thought he might be Tom Witherbee. He looked more fashionable than the others. It was also he who held the pistol, which, perhaps, gave him just a suggestion of devil-may-care.

The three men were gravely regarding the six trunks. Miss Chalmers caught her breath.

Too late now! She could never disappear from Witherbee's Island and explain those trunks. Yet she knew this, too; she never, though the heavens might fall upon her otherwise, would step forth and proclaim herself to three men in pajamas.

Mr. Witherbee advanced to the nearest trunk and inspected it by the light of his lantern.

" Well, what do you know about that! " he exclaimed.

" 'Pon my word, I know nothing whatever about it, my dear fellow," said the tall one.

" These are Miss Chalmers's trunks," declared Mr. Witherbee in a voice of wonder as he examined another.

The young man with the revolver made an inspection of his own and avowed that Mr. Witherbee was right. The tall one stroked his mustache and said nothing.

" But she's not expected till to-morrow! " cried Mr. Witherbee. " How the deuce did her trunks get here? "

" Must have sent them on ahead," observed the armed one.

" But who brought 'em? When? The boat didn't stop here to-night."

Mr. Witherbee stared at the trunks in succession

and juggled one of them as if to assure himself that it was real. All the time he was muttering.

"Well, this isn't finding the burglar," remarked the man with the pistol. "He's probably gone by now, anyhow. Ah-h-h — I'm sleepy."

Mr. Witherbee pondered the trunks again.

"I've got a theory," he said presently.

"Shoot."

Miss Chalmers winced, divining that this was slang.

"Why, it's like this," said Mr. Witherbee, putting down his lantern and diagraming his remarks with his cane. "There's a prowler about these islands — you know of that, of course.

"Well, Miss Chalmers sends her trunks on in advance. Some boat brings 'em down, probably after we're all in bed.

"This chap cruises around and spots the trunks. Then he comes ashore. He finds the house dark. He makes up his mind that everybody has gone away and that the trunks are waiting to be taken aboard the morning boat. So he makes a try at the house. Burglar-alarm goes off — he gets scared — runs like the Old Harry — hops into his boat — *au revoir*. How's that?"

"By Jove, it's wonderful!" said the tall man. "By the way, old man, are your ankles cold? Mine are."

"Accepting your theory, then," remarked the man with the pistol, "whoever rang the burglar-alarm has already escaped, so we can all go to bed."

"Clever as the deuce!" said the tall man.

"I don't suppose there is much more use in looking," admitted Mr. Witherbee reluctantly.

(His ankles were not cold.)

"You don't guess he could have hid in the boat-house, do you?"

Miss Chalmers shivered.

"It's locked," said the armed one. "He wouldn't bother with the boat-house. You can bet he's not on the island now. What 'll we do with the trunks?"

"Leave 'em until morning. It's not going to rain," Mr. Witherbee observed. "But, by jingo! I'd like to get that fellow!"

"So would I. But what's the use now? Listen! The folks are calling. I guess we'd better go back and tell them it's all over."

"All right," sighed Mr. Witherbee, picking up his lantern.

The trio in pajamas turned back toward the path. Miss Chalmers put her head forward cautiously for another glance. She was just in time to see the figure of the tall man disappear, his pajamas flapping disconsolately about his ankles, his lantern swinging listlessly.

"They're worse than the boatman," she commented.

Not until the last sign of a light had disappeared, and only when she could no longer hear sounds from the direction of the house, did Miss Chalmers venture from her seclusion. She went back to the dock and sat down on the string-piece.

"This is a fine state of affairs," she reflected. "Now I've *got* to stay. I never thought about the trunks.

"But how will I ever explain? I'll die before I admit I set off that burglar-alarm. I'll not only die, but I'll lie. I'll die lying. Some time to-morrow morning I've got to announce myself.

"But how? I'm an idiot — but I won't admit that either.

"Why did I run? That's what I should like to know — why? I've been behaving like a child."

Presently she shuddered, but it was not because there was a chill in the air. She was thinking of pajamas.

"I shall never wear them again," she murmured. "Thank Heaven, I brought —"

At this point her thoughts very naturally drifted to a consideration of some place to sleep. She had no liking for camping out under the stars if she could help it. She wanted a roof over her head.

Sneaking back to the open window in the Witherbee House was out of the question; anyhow, it was probably shut and fastened by this time. She wondered if there was a way to get into the boat-house.

Back she went, armed with the dock lantern, and began an inspection of the lock. It was a solid-looking padlock, but Miss Chalmers thought the staple through which it was passed showed signs of weakness. She looked about for an instrument and finally found a stick that seemed as if it might do.

The stick broke several times during the process of prying the staple loose, yet she made headway. Under most conditions an impatient and somewhat imperious young lady, Miss Chalmers was curiously persistent when she set her hand to any mechanical task. She labored uncomplainingly at the staple for fifteen minutes, and gave a satisfied little nod when it fell loose from the woodwork.

The interior of the boat-house was not inviting. A rowboat and two canoes were piled along one side, with a lot of loose gear, a collection of ill-smelling paint-pots and some oars and paddles.

At the farther end was a pile of canvas. She tilted her nose slightly, but did not retreat.

"It's a roof at any rate," she observed. "I'll sleep on the canvas. Nothing can hurt this gown now. It's gone."

She put down the lantern, sat on the canvas, and slipped off her twenty-dollar shoes. Then she lay down and attempted to convince herself that the bed was comfortable.

It was an entirely laudable effort at self deception, but quite useless. The bed was anything but comfortable. It had some pulley-blocks under it, for one thing.

Nevertheless she became drowsy. This ordinarily delicious sensation crept upon her with unwelcome quickness. She wanted time to think about to-morrow morning. It might require considerable planning, she feared.

"Oh, well," she murmured in a resigned tone, "I guess it will come to me better after I sleep a little."

Then she almost slept. The reason she did not quite sleep was an abrupt volley of shots. She sprang to her feet with an angry exclamation.

"Haven't they stopped hunting me yet?" she snapped.

CHAPTER III

HER initial impulse was to dash out of the boat-house, confront her pursuers, and visit them with a merited rebuke for having disturbed her rest. Not for an instant did it occur to Miss Chalmers that anybody else's rest had been disturbed by her.

But she remembered that she was not yet announced upon Witherbee's Island; that she would not, in fact, arrive until morning, so far as the official statement was concerned. So she checked her rush and occupied a wise half-minute in putting on her shoes.

Tiptoeing across squeaking boards to the open doorway, she looked out and turned her head in either direction. Silence had followed the shots. She could see no lights on the island. Everything was as restful and somnolent as a lecture on metaphysics.

She stepped out on the little float, from which she could obtain a better view of the wharf and the beginning of the gravel path. There was neither sign nor sound of the pajama squad, facts that contributed greatly to her satisfaction. Not a glimmer came from the direction of the house.

The shots puzzled her. She was wide-awake now, and she was quite sure she had not dreamed a volley. Pausing for a couple of minutes on the float,

31

she made her way noiselessly to the dock, where she stopped to listen again.

"I know perfectly well I heard shooting," she remarked. "I'm not given to imagining things. There!"

Four shots there were this time; she had not counted the first group. Instantly she ran to the end of the dock and looked out across the water. As she stared into the darkness there was another shot, preceded some three or four seconds by a yellow flash.

"It's on another island," she told herself rapidly. "Can it be possible that there *are* burglars about? Heavens! Suppose they really did come here!"

She listened for more shots and watched for more flashes. Presently a light showed again, but it did not come from the muzzle of a gun.

She knew it to be the white, steady beam of an electric torch. A moment later another showed. Then they began moving in opposite directions. A little after that she heard the faint bark of a dog.

She glanced behind her into the woods of Witherbee's Island. Nobody else seemed to be paying the least attention to what was going on across the water.

Miss Chalmers's curiosity was unleashed and stalking from its lair. It was possessed with a consuming desire. She found it dragging her along, with little or no effort on her part to hold it back. Its enthusiasm infected her. She, too — all the rest of her — wanted to know what was going on out there in the river.

Curiosity is a subtly cunning creature. Almost before she knew it, it guided Miss Chalmers to a St.

Lawrence skiff, the existence of which she had not noticed before. The skiff was moored to the wharf; it did not take her more than two seconds to lower herself into it, cast off the line, and pick up the two light oars that lay in the bottom.

"I might just as well," she remarked in extenuation. "It's out of the question to sleep. Nobody will know anything about it. And — well, it cannot be much more than half a mile."

She fitted the oars to the swivel-locks, swung the skiff around, took her bearings from one of the electric torches, and fell into a long, steady stroke. The boat moved lightly and easily. She found something exhilarating in the exercise. She could not remember having touched a pair of oars since she rowed with her class-crew at Vassar.

She rowed well. That, of course, was characteristic of Miss Chalmers. Things that she could not do well, she did not do at all. For instance, holding her temper; almost invariably she bungled that, so she had given up trying. Besides, there is no particular reason why a rich, handsome, and imperious lady should hold her temper if she happens not to want to.

For a quarter of a mile she rowed without pausing, then made another observation over her shoulder. She was holding her course admirably, for the lights on the land ahead of her were much nearer. Now she could hear voices, particularly that of a man, who cursed a barking dog and then did something to it to make it yelp.

"It's another island," commented Miss Chalmers as she rested a second time, now not more than a hundred yards from the shore. "It's another burg-

lar-hunt, too. Oh, dear! I suppose it means pajamas."

It did. Somebody struck a match to light a cigar,
and the brief illumination revealed two men who
were most palpably dressed for bed. She allowed
the boat to drift quietly while she listened. The
match burned out and the figures were hidden again,
but she could hear their voices distinctly.

" The dogs aren't worth a hoot," growled one of
the voices.

" Seems like they ain't quite as noticin' as they used
to be, sir," admitted the other.

" I gave them the scent, right where we found
the footprints in the flower-bed, but they didn't even
seem excited."

" No, sir."

" Did you see him at all? "

" Not a sign, sir; nor heard him either."

" It's a deuce of a note," complained the first
speaker. " I've got watch-dogs and servants and
locks on my doors and windows, and yet I can't
keep thieves out of my house."

" If only Mr. William was here, sir, we might —"

" Confound Mr. William! He's not here and he
won't be here, so we've got to do without him —
Listen! What was that? "

" I think that's James and Eliza hunting along
the other side of the island, sir."

" Eliza! Is she at it, too? "

" She stopped to dress, sir," explained the voice
apologetically and hastily. " She's awful particular
about James, sir. She don't want nothing to happen
to him unless she's —"

" Never mind that. If she wants to make a fool

out of herself, she may, so long as she continues
to get the washing done.   We'll go on up the shore
until we meet them.   But I suppose it won't be any
use."

"Probably not, sir."

"Here, Duke!   Where's that blooming dog now?
Oh, well; let him go.   I suppose he's eating out of
the burglar's hand."

The torch carried by one of the speakers began
moving along the edge of the island.   Miss Chalmers was slightly bored.   Being a watcher was not
nearly so exciting as playing the quarry.   But she
decided to follow.

One of the oars rattled in its swivel, and she heard
the two searchers halt.

"He's in a boat!" exclaimed the one in authority.

"I don't think it was that, sir.   It sounded more
like —"

"I tell you I heard it perfectly.   Don't stand
arguing.   Come on!   It's too late; but we'll finish
the round, or at least until we meet James.   Ouch!
Great —"

The remainder of the sentence was blurred, yet
high-pitched.   A minute later Miss Chalmers heard:

"If it was Patrick who left that lawn-mower
standing out I'll ship him off to-morrow.   Why in
blazes didn't you throw a light on it?"

"Sorry, sir.   But you've got the torch, sir."

"Shut up!   Come on!"

The men began moving again.   Miss Chalmers
calmly reached down and tore a large piece of ex-
pensive goods from the bottom of her skirt.   This
in turn she tore in halves.   Then she carefully
swathed the swivels.

When the oars were replaced they made a sound so soft that it could not have been heard a dozen feet. Keeping her distance from the shore-line, she followed the searchers.

The man who seemed to own the island began to talk again:

"He'd have had the silverware and the whole works if it hadn't been for me. It's a pity I have to do all the hearing for this house. I don't see why my servants can't have insomnia once in a while. What are they paid for? *I* have it, so I suppose everybody else thinks it's all right to imitate the *Seven Sleepers*. You're quite sure he didn't take any of the silverware?"

"Almost certain, sir. But I'll look again when we get back. Nothing on top of the sideboard had even been touched."

"Well, it's mighty queer; that's all I've got to say. Except that I've a good mind to shoot a couple of dogs to-morrow morning."

"Oh, sir — please — I wouldn't, sir. They'll probably do better next time, sir."

"Next time! How many times do you expect this is going to happen, I'd like to know? I tell you I'll shoot 'em!"

"But they're not mad, sir; and I think —"

"Mad! I know they're not mad, you idiot! But they'll be darn-well provoked if I plump a couple of bullets into 'em."

Miss Chalmers rowed on slowly, her lip curled slightly to indicate her contempt for the conversation. It seemed to her that the evening had furnished nothing save a series of revelations of the incompetence of man. Not a thing that any man had done within her ken that night but she could have performed more efficiently herself, she reflected.

This was the stronger, the dominant sex, was it? With her shoulders she made an eloquent gesture, which was lost upon the night.

Almost at the point of returning to Witherbee's Island was she, when a yell from the shore caused her to turn her head swiftly.

"There he is now, by George! He's got a boat. Run! Head him off, before he gets away!"

A dog began to yelp excitedly.

"Sick him, Duke! Sick him! Stop that yawping and grab hold!"

She heard a soft patter of footsteps along the shore, then the staccato note of a gasoline engine.

"Lord! It's a motor-boat! There he goes! Hang that dog, he missed him!"

A fresh volley of shots came from the island.

"Get the launch! Quick! We're almost at the boat-house now! We'll get him yet!"

"Yes, sir, I'm after it."

The motor-boat that Miss Chalmers heard was exploding gasoline in boisterous fashion. She leaned as far as she dared across the gunwale of the skiff and tried to discern objects in the gloom.

It was difficult to distinguish anything save the dark bulk of the island. But the gasoline motor was whirling furiously. Then there were voices again.

"Got her cast off?"

"N-no, sir; not yet."

"For the love of Mike, hurry! He's under way now."

"There! All right, sir."

" Get forward and keep a lookout. Tell me which way to steer."

A second engine burst into action with a defiant roar. Miss Chalmers, resting upon her oars, knew that a chase had begun.

It was rather exciting now. A burglar was being pursued, but she could see neither the burglar nor the pursuers. Two engines were trying to smother each other's din, with the result that their voices mingled in a discordant bedlam.

Then a dark object passed within fifty feet of her skiff, ran on for a hundred feet more, suddenly slowed down, and ceased firing. In closer to the island, but still beyond her vision, the second boat was clattering truculently, and the voices rose even higher.

" He's stopped! He's stopped! Spot him now! It's our chance! "

" Can't see him yet, sir."

" You've *got* to see him! If you miss him you're fired! Why the blazes do I have to be near-sighted? "

Miss Chalmers edged her skiff closer to the boat that had abruptly paused in flight. She had a suspicion. A moment later she knew. A half-suppressed exclamation reached her ears. The voice was one of recent memory.

For several seconds she was irresolute. Far be it from her to interfere with the long arm of justice or retribution, or whatever it might chance to be. It was no business of hers to trip Nemesis. And yet —

Well, perhaps she would not have acknowledged that it was sporting blood, but it was something

singularly resembling it.   She cared not a whit for
the burglar; he deserved his fate.   Contrariwise,
she cared nothing whatever about the pursuers.
They were entitled to no better than they could
achieve.   But she *did* care about something
else.

A stalled engine was a perpetual challenge to her.

To some persons the joy of battle lies in overcom-
ing fellow men, to others in conquering the forces
of nature, to still others in achieving hard-won
triumphs over poverty or riches or other forms of
adversity or perversity.

To Rosalind Chalmers, by some queer twist of
her brain, it lay in starting a balky engine.

She hesitated no longer.   What she did was without reason; but she was past that.   Her fighting
mood was uppermost.   She laid to her oars and
put herself alongside the motionless launch with
such violence that the skiff rocked threateningly.
Another instant and she was aboard.

The crouching figure of Sam, the boat person,
arose from the cock-pit.   Simultaneously a long arm
whipped out with all his weight behind it.   Miss
Chalmers dodged.

" You fool! " she exclaimed wrathfully.   " Here
— hold the painter of this skiff."

The boatman whistled shrilly, then chuckled.

" Well, if it isn't the master mechanic! " he said.

Not far distant in the darkness, the second launch
was plunging furiously onward, the man in the stern
anathematizing his lookout.

" Thief! " hissed Miss Chalmers.   " Strike a
light here."

She was already bending over the silent engine.

"They'll see me if I do," said the boatman. "Best lie quiet for the present."

"A light!" she commanded.

He obeyed, holding the match low in the boat as he lighted the candle-stub and shielded the flame with his hand.

"You burglar!" she muttered contemptuously. "Where's your wrench?"

He reached under a seat and handed it to her.

"Hold that light closer — thief! Give me a hammer, too."

Fresh shouting reached their ears. The light in the cock-pit had been seen by their pursuers.

"Starboard! Starboard, sir!" beseeched an anxious voice.

"I see him. Shut up! You ought to have spotted him before. Stand ready now to make fast to him."

The boatman turned a glance in the direction of the voices and whistled again.

"I guess I'd better swim for it," he observed complacently.

"You quitter!" cried Miss Chalmers. "Get that light closer. There — hold it so! Oh, how helpless you are!"

The boatman's ears told him that pursuit was steadily drawing closer.

Miss Chalmers was doing something swiftly and mysteriously — just what, Sam had no idea. She gripped and twisted something with the wrench, then struck something else two smart blows with the hammer. A second later she seized the rim of the fly-wheel in both hands and gave it a vigorous turn. The engine buzzed noisily.

She stepped quietly out upon the wharf, advancing to the nearest of
her trunks and seating herself upon it

" There — you house-breaker! " she cried triumphantly.

The boatman took the tiller and blew out the candle.

" Much obliged," he remarked.

She dropped, panting, to a seat, and began to wonder what irresponsible act she would next commit.

There were cries of dismay from the stern boat when the quarry was off again, but there was no abandonment of the pursuit. In fact it was enlivened by a pair of bullets, which struck the water not far from the rejuvenated launch.

" Better get down on the floor," advised the boatman.

Miss Chalmers held her place.

Very calmly the boatman reached out, laid a hand upon her shoulder, and twisted her off the seat with a single motion, so that she landed with a bump on the floor.

" How —"

" Dared I? " he inquired. " Oh, I don't see any sense in running a chance of getting plugged. That fool back there just might hit something."

She was in a white rage from the touch of his hand and for the moment speechless. But she did not climb back on the seat.

Another shot sounded, but it went wide. The boatman took a knife from his pocket and cut the rope from which the skiff trailed in their wake. Miss Chalmers uttered a cry of despair at his action.

" We can't tow dead wood and expect to get away — not in this tub," explained the boatman.

" I — I don't want to get away! " she exclaimed.

" You don't? " There was genuine astonishment in his voice. "Then why in Sam Hill did you start that engine?"

She felt there was no fitting reply, so said nothing.

Soon there was a new sound from the rear, or rather a jumble of sounds — a shout of warning, a crash, a splintering of wood.

"There goes one of Mr. Witherbee's skiffs," commented the boatman. "They ran it down."

The lady who sat on the floor made no comment. She had no compunctions concerning the skiff, but she was suddenly alarmed over her own plight.

How would she get back now?

"He's gaining some," observed the boatman after a short interval. "I told you I wasn't a speed-king."

Miss Chalmers's mind once more detached itself from her predicament. She rose to her knees and stared out over the stern.

What the boatman said was true. The launch behind was now clearly visible.

"At this rate he'll get us in about five minutes," added the boatman after another inspection.

She made a dive for the engine and began tinkering with the spark. They *must* escape! It would be too humiliating, too utterly beyond explanation to be caught now. She coaxed a few more revolutions out of the engine.

It did not trouble her that she was trying to cheat the law of its prey. She was wholly solicitous for the reputation and the dignity of Rosalind Chalmers.

"We're doing better than eight, now," she said defiantly.

"We haven't got the trunks," he explained. "But I'll bet she can't go nine."

Couldn't she? Miss Chalmers purposed to see. She mothered the engine again, touching it here and there deftly and tenderly, adjusting a screw, listening, adjusting again, doing a dozen things that the boatman would not have thought of doing. The engine responded gallantly.

"That's the first time I ever heard it purr," he said, in admiration. "You don't happen to be the inventor of that engine, do you?"

She ignored the question. She was too busy trying for that nine miles.

But still the stern boat gained — not so rapidly as before, yet consistently.

"I can't do any more," she said desperately. "You've got to do the rest. Do you understand? You've *got* to!"

"Yes, ma'am," answered the boatman. "Will you take a chance in a mean channel?"

"Anything!" she cried.

"That's funny," he chuckled, "for a lady who doesn't want to get away. I was going to take the chance anyhow. Sometimes I make it and sometimes I miss it. I've been aground there six times. This is the first time I ever tackled it at night."

Miss Chalmers looked over her shoulder and saw that they were rapidly approaching land.

"You're running straight ashore!"

"Maybe — if I don't hit it."

By hitting "it" he meant a channel, into which they plunged a moment later. It was very narrow and very dark, and it served to make two islands where the casual observer thought there was only one.

"If we don't pile ourselves up this is going to be about as clever a thing as I ever did," remarked the steersman genially. "If we do hit anything you'll find a life-preserver under the starboard seat. In any event I'll lay you three to one they don't follow us."

She did not take the bet; she was too intent upon watching the rocks that rushed by almost within reach of her arm.

"I said it would be a pretty clever stunt," observed the boatman a moment later. "Here we are in open water again. No fear; they won't try it."

He swung the tiller sharply. The launch swerved and began to follow a new course.

"Is that Mr. Witherbee's Island?" demanded Miss Chalmers, pointing.

"That? No, indeed. We've been going away from Witherbee's."

"Take me there at once."

"You mean to say you really want to go back?"

"Take me there! Do you hear?"

"Why — yes, if you say so. Only, I took you there once and you wouldn't stay put. What brought you out, anyhow?"

"My own affair," answered Miss Chalmers shortly.

"Meaning I'm not to ask questions. All right. I'll take you back. You needn't worry about that — ma'am."

"Worry!" she flashed. "Do you think I'm

worrying?   Do you think I'm afraid — just because you are a burglar? "

" Well, to tell you the truth," answered the boat-man slowly, " I've got an idea you're afraid I'm not a burglar."

" But you are! "

He shrugged his shoulders and devoted his attention to the course.   It was a roundabout way to Witherbee's Island.   The voyage was finished in silence.   She did not know whether she was sorry or pleased when she set foot upon the lonely dock for a second time.

" No charge this time," observed the boatman. " It's on me."

She turned upon him fiercely.

" Let me warn you," she said, " that if you are caught —"

The boat was under way again.

" Well, good night — or rather good morning — Miss Accessory-after-the-fact," he called back.

CHAPTER IV

QUESTIONS — AND A CLUE

DAWN gently touched the eyes of Miss Chalmers and awakened her. She sat up briskly and surveyed the interior of the boat-house, at first with bewilderment, then with quick understanding.

"I remember," she nodded.

Then, glancing at her gown, she added:

"It's not likely I could forget. This is the day I arrive. I must hurry."

She reached for her grip, opened it, took out a ring full of keys, and arose from her canvas couch. A brief reconnaissance from the doorway of the boat-house assured her that Witherbee's Island was probably sleeping late, making up a lost hour.

She ran swiftly to the wharf, selected without hesitation one of her six trunks, unlocked it, and spent two minutes with its contents. Then she retreated to the boat-house.

Fifteen minutes later she reappeared with a bundle under her arm, returned to the trunk, stowed her burden away, shut down the lid and locked it again.

Miss Chalmers was a different lady. Her gown, her gloves, her hat, her shoes were all spotless. She carried a sunshade. Her hair was smoothly gathered in a low and luxuriant coil. If a Fifth Avenue shop had suddenly appeared in the background you would have wagered she had just stepped out of it.

46

" I think I'll take a little walk," she said.

She did not seek the path, but chose to follow the line of the shore in a direction opposite from that of the house. The morning air was virile. She breathed slowly, deeply, purposefully. She was a very healthy young woman.

" I have just arrived," she told herself. " I came down on a very early boat. I wonder if there *are* any early boats — regular ones. If not, I hired one.

" And it's all perfectly true, too. I did get here this morning; it was past midnight. My trunks came ahead of me. How they came to be sent down last night I don't know; I'm not supposed to know.

" H-m! That's not quite so truthful. However, it will have to do. Of course, I know nothing about anything else — if they mention it. Particularly the pa-pajamas. I never saw them; I never heard anything; I never went anywhere.

" I don't think it's lying — exactly. If it is, so much the worse for the truth. It's necessary."

She followed the shore for several minutes and then, when the walking became difficult, retraced her steps. Out across the river she could see the island where the second burglar-hunt took place. Occasionally she scanned the water in other directions, half expecting to see her boatman engaged in futile fumbling at his engine. But there was no sign of him.

" To think — a thief! " she exclaimed. " I employed a thief! I might have known he was a thief when he charged me ten dollars! And twice I started the engine for him! I can't imagine why I did it — except the first time. I wouldn't be here

now if I hadn't done that. It cost me a new gown,
but — Oh, well! What's a gown?

" Such a brazen thief, too — he accepted what I
did as a matter of course! Bah! A dirty spark-
plug! The thing is without excuse."

Miss Chalmers had reached the wharf again.
Now she paused hastily and stood rigid, watching
a figure that stood on the end of it. The man, who
was tall and rather square in the shoulders, was
dressed in white flannels. He was standing on the
string-piece, his back toward her, his eyes searching
the river through a pair of field-glasses. From
right to left his vision ranged, while he stood with
the military erectness of a bronze statue.

Once, as his head turned, she glimpsed the end of
a tawny mustache. Then she knew him for one
of the pajama trio. Involuntarily she looked at
his ankles, and breathed a soft sigh of comfort when
she saw that they were well covered.

Eventually, becoming tired of watching the
watcher, she stepped quietly out upon the wharf, advancing to the nearest of her trunks and seating herself upon it. She was still studying the observer,
wondering whether to speak first or to wait for him
to turn, when there came a swift change in the
tableau.

A bell rang loudly.

The tall man on the string-piece dropped his
glasses into the river and whirled about. Then, remembering the glasses, he reached for them, a full
second after they disappeared.

He reached too far for the purpose of equilibrium
— not far enough to retrieve his loss. His body
swayed outward. He clutched at the air; it slipped

easily through his fingers. Then, folding up like
a jack-knife, he disappeared from Miss Cnalmers's
vision.

The last thing she noted was a pair of surprised
blue eyes, looking at her with unblinking steadiness.
She was not at all astonished that the splash was a
loud one, considering the manner in which he made
his plunge.

The bell still rang blithely.

Miss Chalmers sprang down from her trunk and
seized her grip, which lay almost at her feet. She
had had enough of bells. Snatching it open, she
turned back the alarm lever on a nickeled clock, then
snapped the grip shut again. After that she resumed
her seat and waited.

Over the string-piece a head appeared. Its owner
observed her solemnly.

"I — er — I beg pardon, you know," said the
head. "But — er — by Heaven! did you hear a
bell, madam?"

Miss Chalmers shook her head.

"Odd as the deuce!"

His shoulders came into view and his arms
gripped the string-piece.

"Odd as anything in the world," he added, as he
continued to stare at her. "I could swear there was
a bell, you know."

"I don't hear it," she said.

"Nor I, madam. It — er — seems to have
stopped, you know. But there was one — oh, I'm
sure! Unless, of course, you say there wasn't. I
may have been mistaken. But — oh, it's frightfully
odd!"

Miss Chalmers chewed her under lip until the

pain made her wince. She had never before seen a
long, yellow mustache drip water at both ends, and
she was amazed at the quantity.

"If you've finished tubbing, why not come completely ashore?" she inquired presently.

"Why —er — thank you. I believe I will."

The rest of him appeared above the string-piece.

"Did you get your glasses?"

He stared at her for half a minute longer.

"I supposed, of course, you were going after
them," she added gravely.

"So I was, by Jove! I quite forgot."

The tall man in the wet flannels turned around,
stepped upon the string-piece again, poised himself,
and then shot head downward into the water, cleav-
ing it as cleanly as an arrow. Miss Chalmers was
too surprised to move. She merely waited.

A quarter of a minute, then half a minute elapsed.
Then, just as she was minded to run to the end of
the wharf and look for him, a hand containing a
pair of field-glasses appeared, followed immediately
by its owner.

"Awfully good of you to remind me, don't you
know."

Miss Chalmers was thinking swiftly.

"I don't know whether he is a fool or not," she
told herself. "I'll be careful."

The tall man stroked his wet mustache and looked
down at his flannels.

"Hope I didn't frighten you, I'm sure," he observed.

"Not in the least. You — interested me."

"Awfully kind of you to say that — awfully
kind, Miss — er — er —"

" Chalmers."

" Ah — Miss Chalmers! We were expecting you
— but not so early."

" I took an early boat."

" Why — er — the first boat down doesn't get
here before ten, I believe," he said, staring again.
" And it's not more than —"

" Not more than three minutes after six," interrupted Miss Chalmers. Then she flushed and
frowned.

The man took out his watch and held it to his
ear. He looked at the dial.

" Still going and — By Jove, you're right, Miss
Chalmers. What amazing guesses you Americans
make! "

It was not a guess, however. Miss Chalmers's
alarm clock, now ticking softly in her grip, had been
set for six exactly. But she could not explain.

" We came so early," she said hastily, " that I decided to wait until somebody was up. I've been
walking around the island, Mr.— Mr.—"

" I beg your pardon. Morton is the name."

He bowed deeply.

" As I was saying, Mr. Morton, I took a short
walk after the boatman put me ashore, and —"

" Boatman, you said? "

" Why, yes; certainly."

" A chap with his own boat, was it? "

" It seemed to be his own boat," answered Miss
Chalmers. " It's not very much to own, however."

Mr. Morton appeared to be interested.

" Now — if I'm not too inquisitive, you know —
would he be a man with a beard? "

" He would; in fact, he was."

" Hum ! "

Morton fell silent for a little, then turned to the
river, raised his glasses, and made another survey.
Miss Chalmers was becoming curious. Mr. Morton faced her.

" If you'll pardon me again, Miss Chalmers,
would his name be Sam ? " he inquired.

" He said it was. But why ? "

Mr. Morton was silent again. Once more he
scanned the St. Lawrence, now shining under the
risen sun.

" Um — er —" said the dripping one as he abandoned his scrutiny. " Why ? Did you ask why,
Miss Chalmers ? Why — er — really, no reason
at all, you know. I've seen him — that's all. Just
occasionally, you know. Really no reason at all, I
assure you."

Miss Chalmers was assured there was a reason.
She did not, however, pursue the inquiry. She told
herself that it would be unseemly; what she meant
was that it might be embarrassing.

Mr. Morton seated himself on the string-piece
and allowed his glance to encompass her baggage.

" We saw your boxes last night," he remarked
after a study.

" Indeed ? "

Miss Chalmers spoke cautiously.

" Quite a surprise, you know, to Mr. Witherbee
and all of us. We were looking for a rascal — a
scoundrelly thief, by Jove — and all we found were
your boxes. They're tremendously prompt with lug-
gage in this country, aren't they ? Why, they get it
there ahead of you ! "

"Sometimes," she admitted. "Did I understand you to say something about a burglar?"

"A burglar," he confirmed. "He rang the alarm, you know. Woke us all up. Rotten nuisance. Hunted all over the island. Found nothing — except your boxes. The bally bell woke the whole house."

He looked rather fixedly at Miss Chalmers.

"Awfully odd about that other bell, wasn't it?" he observed. "Quite startled me, you know. Made me drop my glasses. Must have been thinking of burglar-alarms."

"It was probably an echo of the alarm," she suggested.

"Really now, could it have been? Odd idea that. And you might be right, you know. You might be terrifically right, Miss Chalmers. They say your echoes travel tremendous distances in this country."

Miss Chalmers was vaguely uneasy. She felt that she was suspected as to the six-o'clock bell. She could not be sure, but he stared rather hard. Nor was she reassured when Mr. Morton coupled it in his memory with the ringing of the midnight chime in Witherbee House.

Perhaps it was natural enough to make the association; they were both bells, and both were abrupt and startling. But — well, she wondered if the man in the wet flannels was really a clever person.

"Are there many burglaries here?" she asked.

"I can't speak for the other islands, of course," he replied. "But this was the first for Mr. Witherbee. Fine chap, Mr. Witherbee. I'm just a guest, you know."

"Was anything stolen?"

Miss Chalmers asked the question perfunctorily.

"Upon my word, not a thing! Rather a joke, you know, too, because he left a clue."

"A clue?"

She sat up straight on her trunk.

"Seems like a clue, at any rate. You see —"

There was a heavy crunching on the gravel path, and the voice of Mr. Witherbee called:

"Well, Rosalind Chalmers! And at this hour of the morning. You and your trunks seem to make a specialty of mysterious arrivals."

Mr. Witherbee greeted her effusively and surveyed her from head to foot.

"Same girl, same girl," he commented admiringly. "Style — class — eh, eh, Morton? Oh, I beg your pardon! Have you met Mr. Morton?"

Miss Chalmers indicated that an introduction was unnecessary.

"I was so early, I thought I'd better wait down here for a while," she explained.

"Nonsense! Why didn't you come up at once? Ring the bell — bang on the door — do anything. We don't mind. Do we, Morton? Why, man alive, what's happened to you?"

Mr. Witherbee was regarding the white flannels with wide eyes.

"Mr. Morton dropped his glasses overboard and went to recover them," said Miss Chalmers.

The man on the string-piece shot a swift glance at her, then nodded confirmation.

"Huh!" said Mr. Witherbee, as he marveled at the wetness of his guest. "Just for a pair of glasses, eh? You're a queer cuss, Morton. By the way, Rosalind, did he tell you about the burglar?"

"He's just finished telling me."

"Fine note! Tell you all about it by and by. This is your grip, is it? You must come straight up to the house. Mrs. Witherbee 'll be delighted."

He lifted the grip, grasped Miss Chalmers cordially by the arm, and started up the wharf. Then he stopped suddenly. A perplexed expression came into his face. Suddenly he cocked his head on one side and listened.

"Hear anything?" he asked Miss Chalmers.

She shook her head.

"I do," he affirmed. "Something clicking."

He listened again, then raised the grip and applied his ear to it. Miss Chalmers flushed.

"Please let's hurry," she said, urging him on.

Mr. Witherbee laughed.

"Clock, eh? I couldn't make it out at all."

She did not venture a glance at the guest, who remained behind, even when Mr. Witherbee called back:

"Better change those clothes, old man. Early breakfast to-day."

Mr. Morton remained sitting on the string-piece, looking after them with expressionless eyes.

Mrs. Witherbee was a sunup riser, like her husband, and she greeted her new guest with open arms.

"Everybody will be down presently," she said. "My, how wonderfully fine you look! How do you manage it — at such an hour? I suppose I'm a fright. Well, no wonder — this morning. Did Stephen tell you — the burglar? Oh, it was a terrible scare! I'm so glad, my dear, you were not here. It would have upset you frightfully."

Miss Chalmers, standing on the porch, glanced across the lawn and saw an overturned chair.

"Things like that do upset one," she murmured.

"I should say they did!" exclaimed Mrs. Witherbee. "I'm afraid I'll never feel safe on this island again. I'll always be lying awake, waiting for that alarm to go off. Really, I'd feel safer with it taken out, Stephen."

"Nonsense," said Mr. Witherbee. "Why, it scared him away, didn't it?"

"And scared the rest of us almost to death. I can't see any economy in that, I must say. I suppose, though, we should be thankful we're alive. Shall I show you your room now, Rosalind, or will you wait until after breakfast?"

"I'll wait," said Miss Chalmers.

Mrs. Witherbee stepped into the hall and called: "Gertrude!"

"Yes, mother," answered a voice from above.

"Rosalind is here."

"I'll be down in a jiffy."

"And, Gertrude!"

"Well, mother?"

"Bring down what we found after the burglar left, dear."

"All right."

Mrs. Witherbee returned to the porch to find Miss Chalmers staring at her apprehensively.

"We've got a clue," she bubbled. "It's the strangest thing in the world. I suppose if you simply have to have a burglar, the next best thing is to have a clue. Stephen thinks it may lead to a capture. Do you still think you'll send for detectives, Stephen?"

" We'll see; we'll see, my dear."

Miss Chalmers walked to the porch-rail and steadied herself.

A clue!

It seemed she had never heard a word that sounded so sinister. A clue to the burglar! She shivered a little.

" Rosalind, you're positively chilly! " exclaimed Mrs. Witherbee, slipping an arm around her. " Run, Stephen, and tell Mary to hurry the coffee. It's this morning air, my dear. You'll get used to it in no time."

There was a quick step in the hallway, and Gertrude Witherbee rushed out upon the porch. Miss Chalmers returned the embrace, rather perfunctorily. She was thinking of clues.

" Here it is, mother," and Gertrude tossed an object to Mrs. Witherbee.

" Our clue! " said the lady of the island, holding it up for inspection.

Miss Chalmers was looking at her own bracelet.

CHAPTER V

"WHY — why —"
She checked herself and reflected swiftly. She must not — she could not — claim it.

"Why," faltered Miss Chalmers weakly, "what a curious bracelet!"

"Isn't it, though?" exclaimed Mrs. Witherbee, holding it up so that the light played upon the dull gold. "That's what all of us said. We're having a time trying to decide who will keep it — that is, of course, if nobody claims it. Gertrude is crazy about it; Polly Dawson wants it; I fancy it tremendously myself."

"May I see it?" asked Miss Chalmers.

She gazed more sadly than curiously at the bauble Mrs. Witherbee dropped into her palm.

"Notice the carving," urged Mrs. Witherbee. "Did you ever see anything so odd?"

"It's very odd," assented the owner dully.

"And not a jewel in it!"

"Not a jewel," echoed Miss Chalmers, shaking her head.

"Gertrude and I have been wondering where in the world it was purchased. We both want one. But there isn't the sign of a maker's mark; it doesn't even say how many carats."

58

The artistic soul of Miss Chalmers was in revolt. Maker! Carats! There was something shockingly coarse in the suggestion. How little they understood! Nobody in the whole world knew the name of the artisan who fashioned it, nor ever would know. He went to his peace five thousand years ago. There were no carats in those days; not for this workman. For he made the thing for a princess, and he made it of pure gold.

Nowhere, unless in some undiscovered tomb in Egypt, was there anywhere its mate. Weighed in the scales of trade, it might have brought fifty dollars as metal. To Miss Chalmers it was a thing beyond price.

She knew little of its history save this: Only two women in the world had worn it. One was a princess, daughter of some forgotten Pharaoh. It was upon her wrist when they opened the tomb. The other woman was Rosalind Chalmers.

Just how Reginald Williams came into possession of it Miss Chalmers never knew, but he had brought it to America for her. And she had worn it with a pleasant sense of satisfaction in the fact that the bracelet had merely been transferred from the arm of a dead princess to a living one. Miss Chalmers, rightly enough, had an excellent opinion of herself.

Reggy Williams thought she wore it for him. It was neither kind nor worth while to tell him his mistake. The reason she wore it had partly to do with the Egyptian princess and partly with the fact that it was unique and beautiful.

Now, as it lay in her hand, she experienced a sense of dismay. She could snap it about her arm, of course, and then explain — explain that — Of course she could *not!*   No; that was out of the question.   Not after all she had told them that morning.

Into Miss Chalmers's mind flashed the memory of a sound that had reached her ears, even in the tremendous din of the Witherbee burglar-alarm. She recalled it as a rattling noise, but had given it no second thought in her panic.   The discovery of her bracelet in the possession of her hosts supplied an exasperating explanation.   She asked absently:

"You say the burglar dropped it?"

"Right on the porch where he had opened the window," said Mrs. Witherbee.

"Tom says it was quite a little distance from the window, mother," interrupted Gertrude.

"It was on the porch, at any rate," continued the hostess.   "We think he had just stolen it from some other island.   It's not likely a man would be carrying a thing like that around for any length of time.

"Tom found it while they were hunting with the lantern last night.   We're going to make inquiries, of course; but, to tell you the truth, dear, we're just hoping a little that the owner won't be found.   In that case we'll keep it."

"You mean *I'll* keep it, mother," said Gertrude.

"Well, Polly wants it, too, my dear.   Probably the best way will be to send it to the city and have copies made.   Then we can each have one."

Miss Chalmers shuddered.

"We've all tried it on, but I think it fits me best," asserted Gertrude.

The owner felt dizzy.   It had been tried on — defiled!

"You can wear it for a while, if you like, Rosalind," said Gertrude generously.

"No, thank you," answered Miss Chalmers as she returned the bracelet to Mrs. Witherbee.

Her voice was flat and faint.

After that Tom Witherbee joined the group and the tale of the midnight alarm was spun again. Then came Polly Dawson, short, plump, and light-headed — both ways, for she was blonde — and Polly told it all over, but in such different fashion, and with such a completely new set of facts that it became quite a new story.

Afterward a few others came straggling down — the two Winter girls, Fortescue Jones, and a dull-looking youth named Perkins, of whom Miss Chalmers had never heard. And presently Mr. Morton, rearrayed, made his second appearance that morning. He bowed again very formally to the new guest.

It was a dull breakfast for Miss Chalmers. Everybody except herself babbled incessantly about the burglar, the bracelet, and the hunt by lantern-light.

The trinket of a princess was now upon Polly Dawson's arm, she having beseeched Gertrude to let her wear it during the forenoon at least. The owner eyed it gloomily and made plans. Even though it had been desecrated, she did not propose to abandon it to utter vandalism. She did not even intend that any vulgar modern craftsman should make copies of it.

When the moment was opportune, Miss Chalmers proposed to steal it. Of course she could never wear it again in the presence of the Witherbees or any of their guests; but she would possess it at any rate.

Breakfast was served on a broad porch at the rear of the house, which was the Witherbees' dining-room for all meals when the weather was fine. It was not yet finished when Miss Chalmers saw something as she glanced beyond the railing that fascinated her.

She stared fixedly, then brought her glance suddenly back to the table and furtively examined the faces of her hosts and fellow guests. After that she looked over the railing again. If she grew a shade paler, nobody appeared to observe the fact; nor did any one notice she had become restless.

After a minute or two she rose and walked toward the steps. They descended to a lawn that was broken with shrubs and flower-beds and paths.

"Where away, Rosalind?" called Gertrude.

"I want to see the garden," she called back.

But instead of making directly for the garden she followed a course closely parallel to the porch, which brought her to a pathway that led from a rear door of the house to a small outbuilding that served as a summer kitchen.

"Wait! Stop, Rosalind!"

She did not seem to hear, but stepped upon the path.

"You'll ruin your shoes!" cried Mrs. Witherbee. "That concrete was just laid yesterday. It's soft."

Miss Chalmers looked down at the path, then took a step forward as if to verify. Still unsatisfied, she tested the path once, twice, thrice, with her immaculate shoes. Then she turned and looked up at Mrs. Witherbee.

"Why, how stupid of me!" she exclaimed. "It *is* soft, isn't it?"

She moved toward the porch, treading again upon the slightly yielding surface. Then she stepped back upon the grass.

"I'm so sorry," she murmured. "I'm afraid I've marked your path."

She paused to study the footprints. There were nine distinct impressions in the concrete. One was slightly deeper than its mates.

"They won't notice that little difference," she reflected. "But I hope to Heaven nobody took the trouble to observe that I stepped on the path only eight times."

Then she wandered off into the garden, with a remark upon the unexplained magnetism that wet paint, particularly when so labeled, exercises upon meddlesome fingers.

(*Moral:* In order to cover your trail be the first to discover it — and then multiply.)

"It's rather exacting work," thought Miss Chal—

Wait a minute! This eternal "Miss Chalmers" is tiresome. We've known her for at least twelve hours; we're going to know her much better. Nearly everybody else is calling her "Rosalind." Why stand aloof?

"It's rather exacting work," thought Rosalind, "this business of arriving at unconventional hours and then making believe that everything was thoroughly conventional. If they don't stop talking about clues I shall go mad."

If there was one thing that particularly bored Rosalind it was discussion of a topic plunged into with undisguised relish by Mrs. Witherbee, when that good lady joined her in the garden and deftly maneuvered her beyond the hearing of the others.

"Is it seventeen now, my dear, or eighteen?" asked Mrs. Witherbee with a knowing little chuckle.

"Seventeen — or eighteen?" puzzled Rosalind. " I don't understand."

She did, however, because Mrs. Witherbee always approached the subject from the numerical angle.

"You know very well, my dear. Do not pretend. I thought the last one was the seventeenth, but Gertrude is sure he was the eighteenth. It was Mr. Williams, wasn't it?"

"Oh, please!" protested Rosalind.

"Oh, please?" echoed Mrs. Witherbee, hugging Rosalind's arm. "Oh, shucks, you mean! Why shouldn't we talk about it? Everybody else who knows you talks about it. Why shouldn't I?"

"But — but it's so intimately my own affair," said Rosalind, annoyed.

"It's more than your affair, dear. It's the affair of seventeen or eighteen perfectly nice young men — I wish to goodness I could remember the exact count! Seventeen or eighteen eligible men — all ready to marry you if you say the word."

"All!" exclaimed Rosalind in a shocked tone. "Why, Mrs. Witherbee!"

"Well, you know what I mean," declared Mrs. Witherbee. "Of course you wouldn't marry them all. But it could be any one of the seventeen or eighteen. Now, couldn't it, Rosalind?"

Rosalind sighed, not because she was either romantic or pensive, but out of sheer despair.

"I presume it could be," she admitted.

"Oh, you heart-breaker!" chided Mrs. Witherbee confidentially.

"I'm not!" declared Rosalind stoutly. "There
isn't a broken heart among them. Their hearts are
all perfectly sound and serviceable. They're not
only air-cooled, but water-jacketed, and not one of
them ever had a misfire on my account."

"Rosalind! What in the world are you talking
about?"

"Oh, well, please let's not talk about it any more.
I can't stop them from asking me, can I?"

"No, but — Why, some of us wonder if you
ever will be married!"

Rosalind shook her head wearily.

"Oh, I suppose I'll be married some day; most
women are. Meantime, what's the use of considering and plotting and planning, or even bothering
about it? When a girl wants to get married she can
do it — any time. There's nothing mysterious or
unprecedented about it. It's been done several
times, I believe."

"You're so cynical, Rosalind."

"I'm not — not in the least. I'm merely sane.
Listen, now! Whose voice is that? You seem to
have callers."

"It sounds like Mr. Davidson," said Mrs.
Witherbee, listening. "He's one of our neighbors.
Shall we go and see?"

They walked to the front of the house, where a
group of persons stood in a circle around an elderly
man who talked volubly.

"Come and listen to this," advised Mr. Witherbee, beckoning. "Davidson had a thief last night,
too. Same one, probably. Miss Chalmers, let me

present Mr. Davidson — one of our island neighbors."

Mr. Davidson bowed briefly, then resumed his
recital in a voice that Rosalind remembered quite
well.

"We thought he was all alone at first. He
started up his launch, and then he had a breakdown.
Thought I had him sure then. But, by jingo! Do
you know there was another fellow lying out there in
a rowboat? He was keeping watch, I suppose.
The second chap climbed into the launch, and they
managed to get things started again.

"Even then we'd have had 'em in a fair race.
He cut loose his rowboat after a while, and we
smashed into that; we didn't stop to pick up the
splinters. That delayed us a little, of course.

"But he put one over on us by slipping through
that channel that splits Houghton's Island. I
wouldn't take a chance on it. By the time we went
around the island he wasn't in sight."

"A pair of them, you said?" asked Mr. Witherbee.

"A whole gang, likely enough; but we saw only
two. Don't know whether I hit any of 'em or not."

"Anything stolen?"

"Now, there's the queer part," affirmed Mr.
Davidson. "Not a blessed thing, so far as we can
discover, unless it was something out of the library
that we haven't been able to locate as yet.

"He seemed to have spent all his time in the
library, as nearly as I can find out. He had a lot
of books out on the floor. Perhaps he thought we
hid things behind them. We can't find that he did
anything except mess with the books."

If Rosalind was afire with curiosity she did not betray the fact. Outwardly she maintained the frigid poise that had been the despair of the seventeen or eighteen.

"Well, from your story," commented Mr. Witherbee, "he got to your place after he visited us. He had hard luck here; he lost something. Who's got the bracelet? Here, Polly! Show it to Mr. Davidson."

Polly held out her arm.

"If he hadn't visited us first I would have thought probably he stole it from your place," said Witherbee.

Mr. Davidson glanced at the bracelet and shook his head.

"Haven't got any junk like that in our house," he declared. "Never saw it before."

Rosalind flamed with resentment, but remained silent. Junk!

"We've got to organize; that's all," declared Witherbee.

"It's a cinch something's got to be done," growled Davidson. "I tell you, there's funny goings-on around this place. Earlier last night, for instance. We were coming down the river in the yacht when somebody hailed us from a small boat. One of 'em — sounded like a woman, too — wanted help. The other one — a man — didn't want any help. Seemed to be having a row among themselves, so I didn't butt in."

Rosalind was too bewildered to analyze the relation of this episode to what happened later. She merely made a mental note of the facts for future consideration.

A man in overalls approached Mr. Witherbee and touched his cap.

"One of the skiffs is gone, sir — the new one," he said.

"Then he did steal something, after all!" exclaimed Witherbee. "Isn't that the devil now? I suppose that was the skiff you ran down, Davidson."

"I suppose so," said Davidson gloomily. "Sorry."

"Oh, that's all right. Don't bother. But, say, Davidson, you ought to do something for your own protection. Put in a burglar-alarm like ours, for instance."

"Burglar-alarm!" snorted Davidson. "What do I keep dogs for? And what good are the dogs, either? I threatened to shoot 'em last night. I'm not sure but I will, even yet. That rascally nephew of mine spoiled those dogs. They've been mooning around the place ever since I shipped him off to New York. By Judas! I'd bring him back if it wasn't for the fact that I'm getting good reports about him. Witherbee, he's actually making good! Had a letter from Hastings & Hatch only this morning. He'll be a regular banker some day, they tell me. Would you have ever thought that?"

"I never would," admitted Witherbee.

Rosalind wanted to slip away and think. She wanted to be undisturbed, so she might put together the pieces of the puzzle, which seemed to have been jigsawed into hopeless confusion.

What she wanted most to know was just where she fitted into it. If there was to be serious burglar-hunting, if clues were being scattered about indiscriminately, she was considerably concerned as to where they might all lead.

When Mr. Davidson had apparently arrived at the end of his facts and was turning to comment and speculation she detached herself from the group and wandered off to the summer pavilion, which she had first found during the course of her exploration in the dark hours.

But she was not to be left alone. Mr. Morton, stroking his blond mustache, strolled in pursuit.

"Funny, by Jove! Isn't it, now?" he said. "Everybody chasing somebody, you know, and nobody catching anybody. I say it's confounded strange. What's your theory, Miss Chalmers?"

"I never theorize," said Rosalind shortly.

"Oh — ah — I see. Hum! Not a bad plan, that, either; not at all bad. Saves one a whole lot of bother, I should think."

"Decidedly."

"Oh, yes, a lot of bother," he went on aimlessly. "But we can't all do it successfully, you know. Deuced difficult not to think about anything."

Rosalind's caution was uppermost. This drawling Morton person was somewhat enigmatic. She could not tell exactly why, but she was ill at ease.

Presently he seemed to remember something, for he turned toward the river, of which the summer pavilion commanded a sweeping view, took his field-glasses from his pocket, and devoted himself to another of those surveys at which she had surprised him in the early hours. Rosalind watched in silence.

"Not a sign," he observed after a long scrutiny.

"Of what?"

"I — Oh, I beg your pardon. Did not know

I had spoken — really.   Nothing at all, Miss Chalmers; nothing at all."

"Do you commonly look for nothing?"

"Had me there!" he exclaimed.   "I suppose one doesn't really look for nothing, even if one expects nothing.   Why — I — I was just looking for a boat; that's all.   Nothing of importance, I assure you."

Rosalind's thoughts reverted to Sam, her burglarious boatman.   What did this man know about him?   Why had he questioned her so down on the wharf?

She was framing a guarded inquiry when Polly Dawson gurgled into the pavilion.

"Oh, Mr. Morton!   I thought we were to play tennis this morning," she cried.

"Right you are!" he assented — with surprising alacrity, Rosalind thought.   "Upon my word, I'd forgotten, Miss Polly.   Awfully kind of you to look me up.   You'll excuse me, Miss Chalmers?   Or will you join us at the courts?"

"I think I'll excuse you," said Rosalind, deliberately.

He stared for a brief instant.

"Why, yes; yes — of course.   Awfully kind of you, too."

Polly Dawson had him by the arm and was insistently urging him in the direction of the courts. As they passed out of the pavilion Rosalind caught another glimpse of her bracelet.   She gritted her teeth.

"Now, let's see just where I stand," she murmured to herself, and began checking off her thoughts on her fingers.

CHAPTER VI

" PALS ! "

A DIRTY gray boat, quite too large for a skiff was being slowly propelled against the current with the aid of a pair of oars. The man who furnished the power was talking torridly to himself, to the boat, and to the oars, with occasional digressions in which he addressed himself to the river, the waning day, and the Goddess of Luck. He perspired a great deal more than he progressed.

Once he paused to wipe his forehead, an occupation which gave him opportunity to survey a nearby shore. Upon that shore he observed a lady walking. The lady was alone. The boatman smiled. He believed he could easily understand why the lady was alone, provided her tongue had not been paralyzed. He remembered it as a tongue that fended people off.

As he looked at the slowly moving figure it came to a halt. At the distance and in the dusk the boatman could not be sure that she was looking at him, yet he rested on his oars, waiting.

He saw something wave — a scarf or a handkerchief perhaps. He smiled again behind his shabby beard. Then he headed his boat toward the shore.

Not until he was close to the island did he turn his head, and then with the remark:

" Did you call me, ma'am ? "

"What's the trouble now?" she asked sharply as a rejoinder.

"No trouble at all that I know of."

"Why are you rowing?"

"Oh! You mean about the boat? Why, my batteries have gone dead."

"How long since you replaced the cells?"

"I don't know. Maybe a year."

Rosalind Chalmers uttered an exclamation of disgust.

"I wish to be taken somewhere," she said. "It's important."

"I'll do my best to row you. How far is it — Europe?"

"I do not care to be rowed," she said. Her tone would have frozen mercury.

"Well, I'm headed for Clayton," he observed. "To buy some batteries. It's a long, long way; but if you'll be here until I get back I'll be at your service."

Rosalind considered briefly.

"If I find a set of cells for you," she said, "may I employ you for an hour or two?"

"Surest thing you know, ma'am."

"You'll wait here?"

"I'll not budge."

"Don't come to the dock," she warned.

"No fear."

She disappeared among the trees at a brisk walk, while the boatman edged his craft closer to the shore, made fast to a shelf of rock, and prepared to smoke. Twice he chuckled, once broke into a low laugh, as he sat in the stern of his launch, and waited.

As the dusk thickened he lighted a grimy lantern.

Its dim, yellow rays illuminated the cock-pit, and his eyes fell upon a book that lay on the floor. He reached for it, and picked it up, and began a casual study of its pages.

There was one page, however, to which he reverted at frequent intervals, finally devoting his undivided attention to a study of it. He was thus engaged when a light footstep caused him to drop the volume.

The lady was standing within a few feet of him, a bundle in her arms.

" Catch it! " she commanded.

It unrolled itself as it reached his arms, and half a dozen dry cells clattered to the floor of the cock-pit. The wrapper that contained them was a light silk shawl. Almost simultaneously with the bundle Rosalind herself was aboard.

Sam, the boatman, picked up the nearest cell and examined it.

" Where 'd you get them? " he asked, looking up at her.

" None of your business," said Rosalind calmly. " I suggest that you put them to work at once."

He turned to the box that contained the dead batteries, disconnected the wires, and tossed the useless cells overboard. Then rather clumsily he began wiring the new cells into place.

Rosalind, seated opposite, watched the performance with impatience, but said nothing until he had nearly finished. Then it was:

" Don't you know better than to connect two positive poles? There — see — between the fourth and fifth cells."

He grinned without meeting her eyes and made

the necessary change. Very quickly after that the
launch was headed into the river, moving without
the aid of oars.

"Nothing like having the master mechanic
aboard," observed Sam as he refilled his pipe.

"Never presume to address me in that manner
again," said Rosalind, turning swiftly upon him and
drawing her skirt closer to her ankles.

"All right — Miss Chalmers — ma'am."

They ran on for several minutes in silence. Then
he inquired indifferently:

"Which way did you say you wanted to go?"

"I didn't say. But "— her arm pointed across
the river —" you may take me in that direction until
I tell you further."

"That's Rockport, on the Canadian side," he observed as he altered the course. "That place where
you see the lights."

"Very well; head for it."

The launch moved onward for fifteen minutes,
only the steady exhaust of the engine breaking the
silence. The boatman smoked steadily and devoted
the chief part of his time to a study of his passenger's profile. She seemed to be thoroughly oblivious
of his presence.

Abruptly, when Witherbee's Island was a good
two miles astern, she leaned forward and switched
off the spark.

"This will do," she said.

Sam made a cursory observation of their position, which was midway in the broad Canadian channel. The nearest island was probably a mile distant.

"I desire to talk to you," she remarked, turning

a calculating pair of eyes upon him. "The reason why we came here is that I did not care to be interrupted."

He nodded.

"I think I may as well tell you," she added, "that I have a pistol with me."

"Well, it might come handy if we meet anything," he admitted, not a trace of surprise in his voice.

Having reached this initial point in their conversation, Rosalind paused. She was perplexed as to the best way to begin. She was a little worried; but he must never suspect that.

A long afternoon hour of study over certain events in which she had been an actor since her embarkation at Clayton the night before had convinced her that it was highly desirable to know something more concerning this common person, who made such poor work of his avowed occupation as a boatman. Yet that was not exactly it, either; what she most wanted to know was something concerning the plans and intentions of this person in case certain contingencies arose."

"Your name is Sam, I believe?" she asked suddenly.

"Yes, ma'am."

"Sam what?"

"Oh, Sam anything. Whatever you say; I aim to please."

"You live here?"

"Hereabouts, ma'am."

"Of course you are a thief."

"You've said that before," he remarked placidly. "You said I was a burglar and a house-breaker, too."

" But you are! "

" Am I? "

Rosalind had no patience with people who fenced, but she checked her temper for the moment.

" After what I observed at an early hour this morning," she said, " I cannot see that there is any doubt of it. You entered and robbed — or attempted to rob — Mr. Davidson's house."

" Well," he said slowly, looking up at her, " I don't happen to be on the witness-stand. But I might remark that I didn't enter or attempt to enter Mr. Witherbee's house at any rate."

She flushed angrily, but she had learned something.

" Then you spied," she said.

He made a non-committal gesture.

" It's a matter of no importance," she added hastily. " I believe you understand that I am a guest at the Witherbees'."

" Of course," he assented. " I expect you explained the whole thing to them this morning."

She looked at him narrowly, but his face was impassive behind its beard. Nevertheless, she had a disquieting feeling that he suspected she had not explained anything — and did not care to explain.

" But you were simply a plain intruder at Mr. Davidson's," Rosalind went on.

" I haven't admitted it, ma'am."

" Oh, why quibble about it? " she exclaimed.

" All right, then; we won't quibble," he answered, after a second's thought. " We'll go to it a little bit straighter. I'll say this: I did land on Mr. Davidson's island. That 'll be enough for a while — except this: I wasn't working alone."

" You mean, there was somebody else who —"

" Always," remarked Sam confidentially, " when there's a house-breaking to be pulled off — that is, 'most always — a man doesn't work alone. He has to have one pal. If he does the inside work, his pal sticks around outside, doing lookout duty, and to help make the getaway. It's one of the most important parts of the job. Now, whatever I did or didn't do at Davidson's last night, the fact remained that I needed my pal a whole lot when it came to making a quick duck."

He paused and studied her, a faint twinkle in his dark eyes.

" You mean —"

Rosalind's voice was trembling.

" I mean that my pal started an engine that I couldn't have started in a year," he added, complacently.

" You — you villain ! "

" Ma'am ? "

" You unspeakable scoundrel ! "

Rosalind had risen to her feet. Her hand crept to a pocket in her sweater.

" You hit on a new name that time, ma'am."

" You dare to say," she exclaimed in an unsteady voice, " that I was in any way associated with — with — whatever you did at Mr. Davidson's ? "

" Well, now, I haven't said so exactly. Only just try to look at it from the jury's angle."

Rosalind choked and sat down. Her fears—fears that she had been trying to smother all afternoon — were realized. This was blackmail!

The boatman continued to smoke, unruffled. There was silence for a full minute.

" I suppose we're all through talking," he observed finally.

" We are not! "

Rosalind's tongue was loosed again.

" What you have just hinted at is despicable, wicked — depraved! It's beyond belief. You are contemptible enough to take advantage of an entirely innocent situation to make trouble — for a woman! Of course, with you it's entirely a question of money. Therefore, how much? "

" How much for what? " he inquired mildly.

" For what! As if you didn't well know —

" Never mind; I'll put the thing plainly, if you wish. Through a series of unfortunate circumstances, I engaged you as a boatman last night. Through a second series of circumstances it became impossible for me to announce my arrival at Mr. Witherbee's in the usual manner. Through still another series I had the misfortune to become involved in an affair which you very well know was none of mine.

" You are a thief; I am not. It happens, however, that I cannot afford to have my name in any way, either directly or indirectly, connected with the escapades of a burglar. The probability is, if you continue to remain in this neighborhood you will be captured. If that event does occur, you undoubtedly have it in mind to drag me into the affair. Therefore, how much? "

" How much to leave you out of it? "

" Exactly! "

He considered the proposal for a little.

" How much 'll you give? " he inquired cautiously.

Rosalind was nonplused. She was not versed in

the payment of hush-money. She had no idea whatever concerning the usual rates of compensation.

" I haven't more than about fifty dollars with me,"
she said.

" Fifty, eh? Um! Well, now, suppose I say I
don't want anything, ma'am ? "

" You mean —"

" I mean if I took it, why, it would seem like cutting loose from a pal. And I don't —"

" You beast ! "

" Another new one," he commented blandly.

" I have a mind —"

She paused midway in the sentence. She did not
know what she had a mind to do, to tell the truth.
Rosalind was completely dismayed. He meant to
hold this thing over her; to terrorize her; perhaps
— she turned cold at the thought — to attempt to
employ her in some new lawless raid!

" Don't worry, ma'am," he said as if reading her
thoughts. " I won't say a word to anybody. Lord!
I wouldn't tell on you; I just *can't*, you see. That
being the case, what's the use of my taking your
money in that fashion and only creating bad feeling
between us? "

The boldness of the fellow's assumption sickened
her.

" Please allow me to pay," she said coldly.

He shook his head.

" We'll let it stand the way it is. I never squealed
on a pal yet," he replied.

" I cannot remain under an obligation, no matter
how unjust it may be," she declared in a firm voice.
" I insist upon paying."

" There's no obligation, ma'am —not the least.

The account's all square. I did the job; you made the getaway. It's a fifty-fifty proposition. I'm not doing you any favor."

Rosalind was in a white fury. Her fingers curled around the stock of the little automatic in her pocket, although she knew quite well she would not employ the weapon. This creature called her his — pal! Called her — a Chalmers — by a vulgar name from his underworld! And she was helpless!

" You may take me back," she commanded suddenly.

" Right! "

He started the engine, swung the boat in a wide circle, and laid a course for Witherbee's Island. They had covered half of the return journey before she spoke again. Then:

" I may as well warn you that they are preparing to make a thorough hunt for the thief, and that the residents are about to organize, and probably to employ detectives."

" Thank you, ma'am."

" You may act accordingly or not, as you choose."

" It's very kind of you," he said humbly. " I'm sure you show the right spirit, ma'am. That's the way it ought to be between —"

Rosalind turned upon him.

" Don't you ever dare to employ that word to me again! "

" Oh, all right," he sighed. " I just meant to be neighborly."

It was some minutes later when she observed:

" I might add that one of the gentlemen staying with Mr. Witherbee is already on the watch for you."

The boatman looked surprised.

"He uses a pair of glasses to keep track of you."

"What's his name?"

"Mr. Morton."

An exclamation from the steersman.

"Morton — the Englishman?"

"Evidently you know him."

"N-no; I don't exactly know him. But I know who you mean. Tall man, yellow mustache?"

Rosalind nodded.

"Hum!" said Sam reflectively. "How long has he been at Witherbee's?"

"I haven't the least idea."

"He's spoken of me, has he?"

"Yes."

"What did he say?"

"Why, nothing really; except that he asked some questions in order to identify you and said he had seen you. I told him you had brought me down."

"Did you tell him when I brought you?" inquired the boatman.

"Well, I said — or perhaps I let him infer — that you brought me down this morning."

Sam laughed quietly.

"That's an alibi that might do nicely for both of us," he commented. "Much obliged. Did he mention my name?"

"He knows that you are called Sam," said Rosalind shortly.

"I see. Quite a chap, isn't he, don't you know?"

The voice of the boatman was rather satirical.

"And I'll tell you something else," she continued. "Mr. Davidson is convinced there is some queer work going on here, and he mentioned a boat hailing him last night while he was out in his yacht."

"So you've found out it was Davidson's yacht, then?"

"I have."

Sam seemed to find cause for gentle mirth.

"I think I can now understand," she added, "why you refused to let him help us. Even a burglar may have a certain delicacy about accepting a favor from his intended victim."

"That might be true," he admitted.

They were approaching Witherbee's Island when Rosalind's glance fell upon a book that lay open on the floor of the cock-pit. Idly she picked it up and glanced at the cover. It was a copy of Hamersly's "Social Register."

For an instant she stared at the title with astonished eyes. Not that the volume was strange to her; far from that. Rosalind Chalmers was thoroughly acquainted with this most exclusive of all publications that list the names of the families who are really and truly entitled to enter the social holy of holies. What amazed her was the presence of the volume in such an uncouth environment. She turned to the fly-leaf. Thereon was written in a bold hand:

HENRY DAVIDSON

She looked at the boatman. He was intent upon a course that would land them at the point where Rosalind had embarked upon her baffling voyage.

Davidson! This, then, was the explanation of the rummaged library! This — a Social Register — constituted the booty of a thief!

Again she ventured a glance at Sam. He did not appear to notice that she had picked up the book.

Her fingers marked the spot at which the volume lay open. Now she turned to the page. Rosalind gasped softly when she found herself among the C's — yes, and at that very page among the C's that listed the habitat, the personnel, and the lineage of the Chalmers family of New York!

The book dropped from her hands and thudded gently upon the flooring. A sensation of vague alarm succeeded her initial amazement.

What was the creature planning now?

As the boat touched the island she leaped ashore quickly, and started in the direction of the house.

" Wait, please ! " called the boatman.

She halted.

" I guess you forgot something, didn't you? " he said.

" Forgot? Oh — you mean I am to pay you? "

" Yes, ma'am. "

" How much? "

Her purse was in her hand.

" Only five this time. "

She handed him the money without a word.

" Any other time you want a boat," he observed, " you can find me 'most anywhere. "

" I suppose," she said frigidly, " that that is part of the price — of silence? "

" I didn't put it that way," he answered good-naturedly. " But I certainly do like to have a handy passenger on board. "

She was moving away when he halted her again.

" By the way, Miss Chalmers, you might tell me something. Once in a while this old bunch of junk they call an engine seems to get all heated up over nothing at all, even when she's not running fast. Now, when she does that, ought I —"

" Hire a mechanic! " she said sharply.

" That's what I thought," he drawled. " I'll be looking you up real soon at that rate."

Rosalind was gone.

CHAPTER VII

NEW SLANTS

THE boatman, after swinging well clear of Witherbee's Island, hesitated as to his course. "There might be an answer to-night," he muttered. "Still, it's pretty quick, seeing I only wired this morning. I guess I'll wait until to-morrow. I'll be sure to hear then."

Without further ado he headed the launch into the channel that runs between Wellesley and Hill islands, following a course so nearly midway between them that the wake of his craft would have served as a visible boundary-line between the United States and Canada. Several motor-boats passed him; one hailed sharply, warning him to show lights. He paid no attention, but steadily held his way.

Half an hour of running brought him opposite a small, dark spot on the water, around which he described a half-circle while he kept his eyes intently upon it. Then, apparently satisfied, he headed in toward what proved to be a rocky, wooded island.

There was a natural landing-place at the point he touched — a cove protected on three sides by bulwarks of the gneiss rock that rises stalwart, here as elsewhere, out of the great St. Lawrence.

Making fast his craft, he stepped ashore, and followed a narrow path that struggled over the stony surface, beset on either side by underbrush and small trees.

The path ended at a cabin. He pushed open a door, entered, searched about in the darkness for a moment, then struck a match and lighted the wick of a lantern that stood on a table in the center of the single room.

The cabin was clean, plain, and cheerless. There was a cot in one corner, a small iron stove, a shelf with a few cooking-utensils, and one chair.

"No place like home," he commented with a grin. "And I suppose I'll be kicked out of here if anybody gets wise."

He helped himself to a few crackers from a tin box on the shelf, sat down, and began munching them in an absent-minded manner. Presently his wandering glance fixed itself upon a broken mirror that hung from a nail driven into one of the walls. He picked up the lantern, advanced across the cabin, and held the light so that he could survey himself in the glass.

"You're a nice-looking object," he assured his reflection as one hand stroked his beard. "I've got a mind —"

A lidless cigar-box nailed against the wall contained a razor, a lather-brush, and half a cake of soap. He picked up the razor and once more studied himself in the mirror.

"No," he said, shaking his head slowly as he returned the razor to its place. "Don't get foolish. You can't be useful and beautiful at the same time."

He replaced the lantern on the table and went to the cot, where he stretched himself on the gray blankets and lay staring up at the roof-boards for many minutes. The boatman's thoughts were apparently amusing, for once he laughed aloud, while many times he chuckled.

"That was a close go last night," he remarked, addressing himself to a knot-hole, through which, by a little maneuvering of his head, he could focus a brilliant star. "Just a little closer and they'd have had me. It was the master mechanic who did the trick.

"Some mechanic, too! A pal worth having, that lady— a sort of lucky strike, it looks to me. She's not gentle exactly, with that tongue of hers; but she's all there when it comes to getting action. Had a gun in her pocket, too."

He laughed again.

"A gun — for poor Sam!" he added. "Guess I'll have to be careful. And yet —

"No, sir! I'm not going to lose sight of this proposition. It looks too good to me. And right on the same island, by Jiminy! Couldn't be planted better — for me. Why, she's just got to be a pal!"

Presently he closed his eyes and made an effort to sleep, a task which he abandoned with suddenness after five minutes.

"No use; I'm too curious," he muttered, rising. "I'm going up to Clayton. It might happen to have come in."

He blew out the light and walked from the cabin, making his way back to where the launch was moored. A moment later he was backing out of the cove. Then he headed northward, through the narrowing waterway that led him past Swiftwater Point, and then along the channel that sweeps the shore of Wellesley Island.

Abreast of the lights of Grand View, he swung almost due south and laid a course for Clayton, making the briefest possible détours to avoid the islands that lay in his path.

At Clayton he sought a small, obscure wharf, to which he made fast the launch. His excursion into town carried him upon none of the principal thoroughfares, but wound an irregular course through back streets, until he found himself at a small, poorly lighted frame building that served the double purpose of hotel and saloon.

He entered by a side door, took a seat at a table in a dingy corner of a back room and rapped smartly with his knuckles on the pine top. There was a shuffling of feet in the bar-room and a man appeared through a swinging-door, wiping his hands on a dirty apron as he came.

" Hello, Sam! " he said.

" Anything come? " asked the boatman abruptly.

For answer the man in the apron began a search of his pockets, finally producing a folded yellow envelope. The boatman reached for it quickly and ran his finger under the flap of the envelope.

" Ginger ale," he said briefly without looking up.

The bearer of the message went back to the bar-room to fill the order.

As Sam's eyes read the telegram they widened perceptibly. He smiled faintly, then nodded, carefully placed the telegram and its envelope in the pocket of his shirt, and looked up at the returning bearer of his drink.

" Everything O. K., I hope," observed the man in the apron, as he stood a glass and a bottle on the table.

" O. K.," confirmed Sam. " I might have to have another message sent here. Will it be all right? "

" Sure; as many as you like. It ain't costing me anything."

The boatman drank his ginger ale hastily, threw a quarter on the table, and went out.

Now, whistling softly and complacently, he strolled through a more pretentious part of the town, halting occasionally to examine store windows. He entered one place, made some trivial purchases, and offered in payment therefor a five-dollar bill that had until recently reposed in the purse of the master mechanic.

" Yep; a mighty useful pal," he murmured as he gathered up his change.

" How's that? " asked the storekeeper.

" I was just telling myself that money is a man's best friend," said the boatman as he strolled out.

The storekeeper watched the departing customer, then turned to the cash-drawer and made a second examination of the five-dollar note.

Sam made his way directly to the wharf where he had moored his launch, stepped aboard and made ready to cast off. Then he bethought himself of his engine.

" Needs oil, I guess. The master mechanic would give me the dickens if she knew how long I've run without filling the cups," he chuckled.

Forward under the half-deck he kept a gallon can. Now he got upon his hands and knees and crawled part way into the dark hole, groping ahead of him as he went.

There was nothing tidy or methodical in the arrangement of his ship's stores, so he spent a full minute, feeling about, before his hand came in contact with the oil-can. Then as he was backing from his cramped quarters a scraping sound attracted his attention. Another launch had touched the wharf.

Something impelled the boatman to remain quietly where he lay in the bottom of his craft. Perhaps it was the guarded note in the voice of a man who was talking.

" I knew it wouldn't do any good to go out tonight," said the voice.

" Well, it helped us to get the lay of the place a bit at any rate," answered a second voice.

" But I don't believe the stuff is coming out through Gananoque at all. And I'm not satisfied that it's coming in here, either."

" Where do you think it's coming from? "

" Kingston."

" That wasn't the tip from Washington."

" I know that. But Kingston's a lot more likely. It's bigger, and that's some advantage when you don't want folks to notice you too much."

" And where do you think it's coming in? "

" Oh, blazes! How can we tell yet? There's a dozen places anywhere along here for twenty or thirty miles. And you can bet it doesn't come across in the same place twice."

The boatman breathed softly and lay clasping his oil-can. The men in the other launch were making their boat fast now.

" You're dead sure Washington's not just guessing about this? " observed the second speaker, a note of doubt in his voice. " Not that I mind sticking around a nice place like this for a while, but I'd like to show something for my time."

" They've got to do a certain amount of guessing, of course," said the other. " But it's not all guess. They're getting the thing fairly well located, and it's ciphering down to this part of the river. We know mighty well that Canada isn't beginning to use, not by half, the diamonds that have been shipped in from Antwerp. They're getting across the line to a certainty. There was a bunch of stuff got into New York last week, and the man who brought it had a railroad ticket that read from Clayton. We're still holding the stuff, but we can't prove anything yet."

" Maybe there's a half-way joint out here? "

" You mean on one of the islands? I've had that in mind. That's one reason I hired the boat. We'll do a little sightseeing to-morrow and get some new bearings."

The talkers were on the little wharf now. Sam pressed his body close against the flooring of the cock-pit.

" Well, I'm tired," said one. " Let's go on up to bed. It's all right to leave the boat here, is it? "

" That's what the man said. It's his dock."

Footsteps passed close to the boatman's craft.

" There's a boat come in since we were here," commented a voice. " He didn't mind hogging the best part of the dock either, did he? "

The second man laughed as the pair went on up the sloping gangway that led to the shore.

Sam lay motionless until they were gone from his hearing, then cautiously rose to his knees and made an observation. The men were out of sight.

He crawled aft, put down the oil-can and sat for several minutes, motionless, considering carefully the fruits of his eavesdropping.

"So they've got their eye on the islands, have they?" he thought. "Interesting, that. I wonder —"

He laughed softly.

"Why not?" he asked himself after another period of thought. "It may not be a bit of use to Uncle Sam, but it just might happen to make his humble namesake real happy."

He stepped out on the wharf and went up the gangway, at the head of which he stood listening and watching for a moment until he was assured that the arrivals in the second launch were safely out of the way. Then he returned to his craft, lighted the lantern, and squatted beside it on the floor.

From a small locker at his hand he took Hamersly's "Social Register" and tore out a fly-leaf. A stub of lead-pencil appeared from one of his pockets. Using the book as a desk, the boatman began to write.

He paused occasionally in this occupation, squinting his eyes and frowning as if puzzled over a thought or a phrase. When he had come nearly to the end of his sheet of paper he stopped writing, read his composition carefully by the dim light, and nodded an approval.

Now he climbed back to the float again and crossed to where the second launch lay. It was a trim, well-kept little craft, a fact that he noted with an involuntary sigh when he thought of his own. There was a canvas cover that fitted neatly over the engine; this had been put in place carefully. He stepped into the cock-pit, lifted one side of the canvas and thrust his note underneath it.

" They can't miss that," he remarked, as he retreated to his own craft.

Immediately following, he loosed his mooring, started his engine, and backed out into the river.

It was late when the dingy launch rested once more in the rock-bound cove and the boatman walked up to his cabin. He was whistling gently and cheerfully, a lantern swinging in his hand. Entering the cabin and closing the door behind him, he drew the chair up to the table, fished the Social Register out of his pocket, and began another absorbed study of the C's.

" That's some family, believe me," he commented. " Strong on the Mayflower stuff, I notice. Been here ever since there was a New York. Pipe the old man's club-list! Not so big, maybe, but class — whew! And the missus — oh, yes; she's a Daughter, all right — three or four kinds of a Daughter. Fifth Avenue, Newport, Narragansett — uh-huh. That's the stuff!

" Mentions the yacht, too. I wonder how many limousines. I suppose the master mechanic takes care of those.

" And — well, well, look who's here! Brother C. Alfred. Fell down a bit on brother's name, it strikes me. ' Alfred ' doesn't quite class up. Ought to be either very flossy or very plain; that's the way most of 'em seem to run. But I notice Alfred is there with the Harvard thing. And all of papa's clubs, too.

" And here's grandfather, and great-grandfather, and the rest of 'em back of that. And mother — she's a Van Arsdale. That's nice; that's bully!

She kicks in with some considerable ancient lineage herself."

He grinned at the Chalmers page.

"Ah! And now the Lady Rosalind! They don't tell ages in this book, do they? Don't put the price-tags on, either. Rosalind — well, she just can't help it when you come to study the dope-sheet. On form, I'd back the Lady Rosalind to be a front runner in any company. Ow! Nothing like class — and nothing to it but class!"

The boatman bethought himself of the telegram stowed away in his pocket. Now he examined it again. He sat back in his chair and laughed until that article of furniture creaked.

"Time to go to bed," he said, rising abruptly. "To-morrow may be a right busy day. Who knows?"

He was crawling under his blankets when another thought came to him. Returning to the table, he tore from the Social Register the sacred page devoted to the house of Chalmers. It was closely printed, with marginal notes and annotations.

"I'm going to start a picture-gallery, just to brighten up the shack," he told himself.

After a careful study of the four walls of his cabin, he selected a spot directly opposite the door, and there he securely fastened the printed page into place with pins. Beneath it he affixed the telegram, which had come to him from New York, addressed only to "Sam," and in care of the obscure little hotel where he had found it awaiting him. The telegram said:

Five million. Unattached. Bidding brisk.

There was no signature.

The boatman stepped back, surveyed his work, and grinned. Then he darted to a corner shelf, devoted to a motley collection of odds and ends, and returned with a piece of chalk. Underneath the page from Hamersly's and its appended telegram he printed in bold letters:

PORTRAIT OF A LADY.

CHAPTER VIII

WHO COPPED THE BUZZ-STUFF?

MR. WITHERBEE dashed out on the porch, mopping his brow, although the morning was yet cool. The company paused at breakfast.

"Again, by Judas!" he shouted, glaring at his wife.

Mrs. Witherbee half rose from her chair and looked apprehensive.

"Again?" she echoed.

"Yes, again! Burglars!"

"Stephen!"

Mrs. Witherbee sat down abruptly and began fanning herself with a napkin.

"That's what I said — burglars!"

The master of the house rolled his eyes and breathed heavily.

"Is — is anything stolen?" asked Polly Dawson faintly.

"Stolen? Yes!" cried Mr. Witherbee so fiercely that his smallest guest shrank from him.

The company sat silent, wide-eyed.

"They've stolen the burglar-alarm!"

"Stephen!"

"Don't Stephen me! I tell you they've stolen it!"

"Upon my soul!" said Mr. Morton, putting down his tea.

" But who — how — when? "

The questions descended upon Mr. Witherbee in a volley.

" Who? How the blazes do I know? How? Why, just took it, of course. How does anybody steal anything? When? When nobody was looking, madam. That's my conclusion."

Mr. Witherbee glared truculently at his spouse.

" But why didn't the thing go off? " asked Gertrude in a mystified voice.

" It did! It's gone! " shouted her father.

" All the wires, father? And the gong? Why, I noticed the gong myself as I came down-stairs."

" I didn't say the wires and the gong! " stormed Mr. Witherbee. " You don't have to steal them to steal a burglar-alarm. I mean, they copped the works — the buzz-stuff — the juice! "

" Stephen! " protested his wife, still fanning herself, " that kind of speech doesn't —"

" What's speech got to do with this, madam? This is no time for speech; this is a time for talk! Do you understand that? Talk! I say they've stolen the works! "

" Dad means the batteries, mother," explained Tom Witherbee, rising. " Let's go and see."

The breakfast party followed him into the house, Mr. Witherbee storming noisily at the rear.

" There! Look for yourselves, if you don't believe me! " he cried.

Each member of the party, in turn, looked into the coat-closet under the front stairway. A small shelf in a corner had been built to hold six dry cells. It was bare of anything save dust now. Two wire connections projected uselessly from the wall.

Mr. Witherbee's guests looked at each other in silence.

" Now, who the deuce would do a thing like that? " said Tom Witherbee tentatively, when the pause had become prolonged.

" Who, indeed? " murmured Rosalind.

She was staring at the empty shelf as if it had a peculiar fascination for her.

" What I can't understand," said Mrs. Witherbee, " is why a burglar would want to steal the batteries out of a burglar-alarm."

" Why, madam? " exploded her husband, whirling upon her. " Why? Anybody knows why! Why does a burglar poison a watch-dog? To keep it from barking. Why does a burglar chloroform a family? To keep 'em from waking up! Why does he steal the works out of an alarm? To keep the bell from ringing, madam. Lord Harry, it's plain enough! "

" That does sound rather reasonable," assented Rosalind, still fascinated by the empty shelf.

" They're getting ready for a raid, I tell you — a raid on the house! " declaimed Mr. Witherbee furiously. " They're just paving the way. And when they come — by George — there'll be nothing to wake us up! "

Mrs. Witherbee shivered.

" But, Stephen," she said, wrinkling her forehead in puzzlement, " if they could get into the house to steal the batteries so as to make ready for a raid, why didn't they raid the house, instead of stealing the batteries? "

" That's a problem, too," commented Rosalind. " How do you account for it, Mr. Witherbee? "

"Account for it?" His flashing glance went from his wife to Rosalind, then back again. "Why should I account for it? I'm not a burglar. It takes a thief to know why! The point is, it's been done — that's all."

"It's cursedly odd," said Mr. Morton, as he stroked his yellow mustache.

Mr. Witherbee glared at his guest, opened his mouth to say something, then made a helpless gesture and remained silent.

"You just noticed this, dad?" asked Tom.

"When I went to get a hat."

"Did you ask any of the servants about it?"

"No! What would a servant want with an electric battery? If you're going to ask me if I suspect my servants, I'll tell you no — right now, sir."

"Father's right, Tom," said his mother. "The servants are perfectly trustworthy."

"Of course they're trustworthy!" snapped Mr. Witherbee. "They're also deaf, dumb, and blind — *non compos mentis* and plain dotty. But they're honest. Anybody might walk in here and steal the plaster off the walls without getting caught. Yes, and for all your servants might know, steal you out of bed, madam!"

"Mercy, Stephen!" exclaimed his wife faintly. "Don't suggest such a thing!"

"We can get more batteries, father," said Gertrude soothingly.

"Batteries! Of course we can get batteries. And what's to prevent anybody from stealing the new ones?

"I tell you, the whole neighborhood's overrun with thieves. First it's us, rung out of our sleep in the middle of the night; then it's Davidson; then it's us again. Now it's his turn. After that they'll probably steal the island."

Rosalind, abandoning her study of the empty shelf, went back to the deserted breakfast-table and resumed her grapefruit.

" I had no idea," she murmured softly, " that they worked the burglar-alarm. I thought they worked the door-bell. But — I'm glad! "

Rosalind was the only person who did not finish breakfast in desultory fashion. She ate deliberately and contentedly. There were no disturbing symptoms in her conscience. She was revenged — revenged for the shock of the midnight alarm, for the flight in the darkness, for the knee that bumped itself on the chair, for the night in the boat-house, for a gown that would never be worn again; yes, for everything save the bracelet. That was adorning the arm of Gertrude this morning.

But she would be revenged for that, too, she told herself. And when Rosalind Chalmers promised herself anything, she was a patient and persistent performer.

" What in the world are you laughing at, Rosalind? " asked Mrs. Witherbee.

" Was I laughing? It was rather rude of me. But a burglar-alarm seems such a funny thing to steal. Think of stealing a noise! "

" To tell you the truth, my dear," said Mrs. Witherbee, after making sure that her husband was not within hearing, " I'm glad the old batteries are gone. They frightened me nearly to death night before last. Of course, I don't like to have thieves about; but if they must come, I'd much prefer they'd let me sleep."

Tom and his sister, Polly Dawson and Mr. Morton were playing tennis; Fortescue Jones and the Perkins young man were smoking cigarettes, and the two Winter girls were knitting for the Belgians, when Mr. Witherbee hove in sight, leading a reluctant dog. There was a general suspension of industry.

" Where'd you get that, dad? " asked Tom.

" Been over to Davidson's in the launch," said Mr. Witherbee. "Here! Buck up — Rover, Prince, Fido — what the deuce did he say your name was, anyhow? Hold your head up; get that tail out. Some dog — eh? "

" What's he for? "

" Burglars."

Rosalind checked a smile and stroked the ears of the cringing animal.

" Is he well recommended? " she asked.

" Well, I wouldn't exactly say that," answered Mr. Witherbee, as he regarded the beast frowningly. " Davidson says he isn't worth a hoot. But he thought maybe if he was kept on a strange place where he doesn't feel at home, he might get fierce again. So I don't want any of you to make friends with him. I'm going to put him on short rations until he gets a mean opinion of everybody."

" He doesn't seem as if he ever had been fierce," observed Rosalind, as the dog thrust his muzzle into her palm.

" He's got a pedigree," declared Mr. Witherbee

as he dragged the animal away from the friendly hand. "His father bit a man once, so Davidson says. And one of his brothers got killed in a fight. He's got the stuff in him, if there's any way to bring it out."

"You mean to say, Stephen," remarked Mrs. Witherbee severely, "that you propose to train that animal to bite us?"

"Not us, madam; certainly not! I mean to train him to bite burglars."

"Of course," said Tom Witherbee, as he walked back to the tennis-court, "he'll need a practise bite now and then. Wait and see if dad doesn't call for volunteers."

"All right, young man!" snorted his father. "The amount of interest you show in protecting your mother, your sister, and myself is no credit to you. But let me tell you, sir, that other persons hereabouts are realizing the seriousness of this situation. We are organizing. Davidson has called a meeting at his island to-night. There will probably be a dozen owners there. We're going to do something about this thing, you can gamble on that. We'll probably establish a patrol. I expect some of the Canadian owners will come in on it, too."

"The international navy at last!"

"Shut up, Tom! Here, you beast — come on!"

Mr. Witherbee disappeared around the corner of the house, dragging the dog behind him.

Rosalind, having succeeded in discouraging the attempts of Fortescue Jones to explain just why the fox trot represented more foot-tons of energy per mile than the one-step, managed to escape alone for a stroll about the island.

She was not particularly interested either in her hosts or their guests. But she endured that patiently. What really annoyed her was the persistence with which her mind reverted to Sam, the boatman.

The uproar over the batteries had merely served to rekindle the matter. She was by no means at peace when she thought of the uncouth navigator and his slatternly boat. He not only puzzled, but vaguely disturbed her.

Of course, for his own safety, she felt well assured he would attempt to cause her no annoyance; and yet the foundation for possible embarrassments and unwelcome explanations was there. She was not a law-breaker, to be sure; but the boatman emphatically was. And in some measure it seemed that she had been an accomplice.

The rack and thumb-screw could not have extorted confession from Rosalind concerning some of the things that had happened. But the difficulty lay in the fact that the boatman, if he chose, could render her own confession superfluous. And what might he not do, if caught, to save his own neck?

She was particularly annoyed when she remembered the interview that had been of her own seeking. The result, so far as she was concerned, had been rather inglorious. He had even laughed at her! He had refused the bribe she offered; he would put no price on his silence.

And he had called her pal! Her cheeks went hot when she remembered that.

Down at the Witherbee wharf, Rosalind sat and idly watched a small power-boat that stood a mile off the island, evidently irresolute as to destination.

It was not until it finally laid an unmistakable course for the Witherbee place that her interest was awakened.

When the boat reached the landing, one of the two men who occupied it lifted his cap and inquired if it was Mr. Witherbee's Island. Being assured that it was, the men fastened their craft, stepped out, and went up the path toward the house, the direction of which Rosalind had indicated with a gesture.

Half an hour or so later they returned, Mr. Witherbee with them. All three were talking volubly. One of the strangers held a paper in his hand.

Rosalind, whose eyes were keen, deciphered two words that were written in a bold hand on one side of the sheet. Her pulse quickened, but that was the only manifestation of the excitement which the paper produced in her.

After a moment of talk on the wharf, the two men embarked, thanked Mr. Witherbee, and went on their way.

"That's a funny go," said her host, turning to her.

Rosalind raised her eyebrows in polite curiosity.

"American customs agents," explained Mr. Witherbee. "Looking for diamond-smugglers. It seems there's been a good deal of it going on. Last night somebody left an anonymous letter in their boat. That's what brought them down here."

"Here?"

"They didn't show me the whole thing, but it contained some sort of a hint about Mr. Morton."

"Mr. Morton?"

"Uh-huh! Ridiculous, of course; I told them so.

I think I satisfied 'em on that score. They said, of course, they were compelled to look up every possible clue.

"They didn't think of accusing Morton of anything. Just wanted to know something about him; that was all. I introduced him. They didn't seem to take much stock in whatever the letter said."

"Of course not," agreed Rosalind.

"But here's the queerest part. On the back of the paper was the name of Mr. Davidson. They went over to his island before they came here and showed it to him. And Davidson said that it was his own handwriting!"

"How curious! Of course he didn't know anything about the note?"

"Not a thing in the world. The note was written in lead-pencil in an entirely different hand. But there was his name on the back of it. It looks like a half-sheet of paper torn off from the other part. Davidson acknowledges the signature, and that's every blessed thing he knows about it. Now, wouldn't that get you?"

"It would," admitted Rosalind, forgetting her abhorrence of slang.

"I tell you I'm glad I got the dog," declared Mr. Witherbee as he went off muttering.

Rosalind was content to be alone again for a little. She knew where she had seen the piece of paper before; she remembered very distinctly the boatman's copy of Hamersly's "Social Register."

But smuggling! That was something brand-new to consider.

What did he know about smuggling unless he smuggled himself? In Rosalind's mind he began to appear as something more than a common thief. A little seemed to have been added to his stature.

What perplexed her most of all, however, was the reference to Morton, the Englishman.

Why Morton? Why had the boatman furnished Morton's name to a pair of customs officers? Perhaps a crude ruse to divert suspicion from himself, thought Rosalind; yet that theory did not satisfy her.

She was not quite sure that the boatman was crude in his methods, no matter how hopelessly ignorant he might be concerning gasoline engines. Now she remembered Morton's survey of the river, watching for Sam's boat; also, she recollected the questioning of Sam as to the Witherbees' guest.

What did these two know about each other?

Rosalind sensed a suddenly awakened interest in the Englishman, who had occupied a very minor place in her thoughts up to the present. She resolved to satisfy her curiosity, so, rising from her seat on the wharf, she went briskly up to the house.

Mrs. Witherbee, also a Belgian knitter, was in a corner of the porch. Rosalind dropped into a seat beside her. For a few minutes she watched the tennis-players, then remarked indifferently:

" Mr. Morton plays a rather strong game, don't you think? "

" Well, I don't understand tennis," said Mrs. Witherbee; "but they tell me he does. He's a rather interesting man."

" Is he? "

" Don't you find him so, my dear? "

" I hadn't thought about it," answered Rosalind. " You've known him for some time? "

" No, we haven't," said Mrs. Witherbee. " He's

been here most of the summer, but he's only been with us a few weeks. He was Mr. Davidson's guest at first. He's an old friend of Mr. Davidson, it seems. That's how we came to meet him.

" Stephen took a fancy to him and invited him over here. I imagine he was glad of the chance, because things were rather slow over at Davidson's without any young people, particularly after Billy Kellogg went away."

" Billy Kellogg? "

" Mr. Davidson's nephew. A nice boy, but an idler. You probably heard his uncle mention the fact that he was working in New York. Mr. Davidson forced him to. The straw that broke the camel's back, it seems, was when Billy lost a big sum of money playing bridge with Mr. Morton. That disgusted his uncle."

" But didn't Mr. Davidson feel any resentment against Mr. Morton for having won his nephew's money? " asked Rosalind.

" Apparently not," said Mrs. Witherbee, knitting busily. " You see, men are funny about those things. Mr. Davidson said if it hadn't been Morton it would have been somebody else, and that it was all a fair gamble. But he was furious at his nephew for losing.

" And now he gets reports from the banking-firm every day, telling him how finely the boy is getting on. And that's how, in a roundabout sort of way, we got Mr. Morton. Rather distinguished-looking, isn't he, dear? "

Rosalind shrugged her shoulders and watched the tennis-player.

" Of course he's dreadfully English," added Mrs.

Witherbee; "but he can't help that. And his name —it's Evelyn! Stephen thinks it's the funniest thing he ever heard — H. Evelyn Morton.

"But he likes him, just the same. Everybody does. You will, my dear. Why, Rosalind, you can't tell but he just might be the one who —"

"I think I'll go up-stairs and take a nap," said Rosalind hastily. "I have a slight headache."

CHAPTER IX

THE ASCENDING SCALE

ROSALIND did not have a headache, and she did not take a nap. Instead, when she had closed the door of her room she faced herself in the mirror.

"You are becoming a great liar," she said bluntly.

With the fidelity of a movie, the image in the mirror returned the compliment.

"On second thought," said Rosalind, "I withdraw that. You are not becoming a great liar — you *are* a great liar."

The lips of the animated image assured her that the amendment was accepted.

"You have lied about little things, big things, foolish things, serious things — everything. I detest lying. It is cowardly, vulgar, and demoralizing. Worse than that, it's troublesome. But "— she sighed softly — " occasionally it is necessary."

She turned abruptly away from the image, went to a writing-desk, and spent several minutes with a pen and a sheet of paper. When she had reviewed her composition with care, she folded it into small compass, slipped it into a vanity-box, and snapped the lid smartly.

"That's just to make sure," she murmured. "I suppose there will be more later."

After that she sat passively by the window for fifteen minutes, appearing to watch the tennis-players, yet devoting her complete attention to her thoughts.

Smuggling, of course, was not so bad as burglary, she reflected. Lots of excellent people smuggled — not in a really vicious way, and not with the least hint of sinister intent; it was just a sort of sporting proposition. They did not smuggle for a living, or even for incidental profit; they were not professionals.

She knew a lot of perfectly amiable, well-bred, and charming smugglers, who smuggled a trifle now and then for the excitement of beating the game. There was herself, for instance.

But professional smuggling was different, she told herself severely. And when it was coupled with burglary, it assumed a serious aspect. She would not permit herself to be lenient in this. Yet she was intensely curious.

If Sam was a smuggler as well as a burglar, who was H. Evelyn Morton? What did Sam know about Morton, and what did the Englishman know about Sam?

Of course, it was natural for Sam to attempt to divert suspicion from himself. But why throw it upon Morton?

"If it wasn't for the smuggling part I think I could understand," mused Rosalind. "If Mr. Morton won all this money from Mr. Davidson's nephew, I suppose it has been a matter of some talk. Probably this boatman has learned of the fact, and is merely waiting for an opportunity to rob Mr. Morton. And Mr. Morton probably has his suspicions, and is keeping a watch upon Sam for his own protection. That's perfectly reasonable.

" But, then, why should Sam try to get Mr. Morton into trouble, and probably thereby spoil his own chance of robbing him?   I can't understand that, unless he is incredibly stupid.   And — he isn't stupid."

At the end of her fifteen-minute study Rosalind made a resolution and went down-stairs to see about executing it.   She contrived, with no great expenditure of effort, to detach Mr. Morton from his tennis.

" Don't you think," said Rosalind, " that it would be great fun to go fishing? "

" Upon my word, I never gave it a thought," said Mr. Morton.   " But I believe you're right, you know, Miss Chalmers."

" Then let's."

" From the wharf? "

" No!   That's a stupid place."

" We'll try the point, then."

" No! "

Mr. Morton looked puzzled.

" We must get a boat," explained Rosalind.

" Oh! "

" A boat and a boatman who knows where there is good fishing to be found."

He considered the idea for a moment.

" I — er — believe Mr. Witherbee is using his own launch this afternoon," Mr. Morton observed. " But — well, you know, we might be able to get —"

He paused in doubt.   During an instant's silence their eyes met steadily.

" Yes, I think we might," said Rosalind.   " Will you see if he's anywhere in sight? "

With a bow, Morton strode in the direction of the shore.

"I am rather curious to see those two persons together," murmured Rosalind, as she watched him go upon his errand.

It was nearly an hour before he put in an appearance.

"Awfully sorry to have kept you waiting," he said. "But I had to take a boat and row about a bit to find him. It's all right, however; he's at the wharf."

"That's very lovely of you," declared Rosalind graciously. "We might bring some of the others, too, if you like. Suppose you hunt them up. I'll go down to the boat."

She found the boatman wiping the seats and otherwise engaged in the discouraging task of trying to make his craft tidy. He greeted her with a brief nod.

"Fishing?" he asked.

"Yes."

"Muskies?"

"Why — yes."

"Well, that's good sport," he commented.

"You can take us to the proper place, of course?"

"Who — me?"

The boatman shook his head.

"Then why in the world do you pretend to hire out —"

Sam interrupted her.

"You don't want to go fishing," he said.

Rosalind's cheeks assumed a pink tint.

"Not for muskies, anyhow," added Sam.

In his eyes was a hint of amusement that angered her.

"It is my intention to go fishing," she declared

coldly. "It is not my intention to have my word questioned."

He shrugged indifferently.

"Oh, very well, Miss Chalmers! How many in the party? Space is limited, you know."

"Myself — Mr. Morton — perhaps half a dozen others."

"Miss Dawson?" he asked.

Rosalind looked at him in quick astonishment.

"Because I can't take Miss Dawson," he added.

"You mean to say —"

"What I really meant to say was ' won't ' instead of ' can't.' I won't take Miss Dawson."

For an instant Rosalind was quite too surprised for speech, a condition easily apparent to Sam, who volunteered further:

"No use to ask questions, Miss Chalmers. I'll give no reasons."

"This is the most unheard-of thing yet!" she exclaimed. "You mean to say that you presume to select my own guests for me?"

"No, ma'am; not exactly. But in this case — Here they come now. I guess it's all right; I don't see her.'"

Morton appeared on the wharf, followed by the Winter girls and Fortescue Jones.

"This will be all, I think," he said.

Rosalind did not meet the boatman's eye as the party embarked. She had a feeling that there would be an insulting gleam of satisfaction in it.

For fully half an hour after they left the wharf she was a silent member of the party, engrossed in wonderment over this new development. It seemed to possess no meaning whatever; at least, none that she could even speculate upon. He would not take Polly Dawson in his boat.

Sam sat stolidly in the stern, smoking and watching the river. Occasionally his glance wandered to Morton, yet incuriously. This passenger seemed to possess no more interest for him than the Winter girls or the young man who toiled unskilfully over a jointed rod. As for Morton, the existence of the steersman did not appear to be within his ken.

Suddenly Rosalind remembered. She had come to study, not to fish. She had contrived a meeting so that she might observe a result. It was an experiment in human alchemy; put her Englishman and her boatman together and she felt that a reaction was inevitable. So now she began to observe.

Disappointment did not improve her temper. There was no reaction — no smoke, no fire, no explosion. They did not speak, neither did they exchange furtive glances. They were maddeningly at ease. Rosalind was soon disgusted with her experiment. She was quite willing to abandon it.

But the Jones young man was fishing by this time. The two strikes and two misses had rewarded his efforts, and he was brought to a pitch of absorbed excitement. Rosalind felt she was doomed to a dull afternoon. It had now degenerated into a common fishing-party, even though there was but one fisherman, and it did not lie in her mouth to explain that it was never meant to be an angling affair at all.

She attempted to put her mind into a state of resignation, the most difficult mental feat she ever attempted, and one at which she usually met failure. Morton was dull when he talked at all. He was three per cent. conversation and ninety-seven per

cent. silence.   The Winter girls knitted as if it were
a penance.   There was momentary hope when Fortescue Jones broke the tip of his rod, but that took
wings when he produced another.

Only the boatman truly enjoyed himself.   Hatless, he reveled in the sun that bathed his head and
bared neck.   His pipe was drawing smoothly and
steadily.   But, most wonderful of all, his engine
pulsated as rhythmically and surely as the power-
plant of a six-thousand-dollar limousine.   It was
fairly uncanny in its perfection.

The launch ranged past the eastern tip of Grena-
dier Island, then across toward the Canadian shore,
thence up-river, Fortescue Jones fishing desperately
and bringing nothing within fifty feet of a gaff.

" We're going too fast," complained the fisherman.

Sam turned a glance of inquiry at Rosalind.   She
shook her head.   The launch held its pace.

Another half-hour passed with scarce a word
spoken aboard.   Rosalind was bored to desperation.
Her experiment in alchemy was the flattest kind of
failure.   She turned upon young Jones with sudden and undeserved severity.

" I should think it would be exceedingly tiresome
to catch nothing," she said.

" It is," he assented hastily.

" Then why do you fish? "

" Why — why, I thought it was a fishing-party! "

" Without fish? "

" I've had half a dozen strikes."

She sighed and flashed a savage look at the boatman.   He grinned.

" Shall we turn back? " she asked Morton, who
was stroking his mustache in a preoccupied manner.

For answer he pointed toward a power-boat almost astern and following at a rapid rate.

" Seems, by Jove, as if they wished to speak with us," he said. " A chap just waved."

Rosalind studied the oncoming craft. It carried a small British ensign at the stern. Four men were standing in the cock-pit, staring intently. As she watched one of them signaled.

" Stop the boat! " she commanded.

Sam obeyed, then turned for the first time to observe the pursuing vessel, now close aboard.

As the launch slackened to a slow drift the smart-looking power-boat with the British flag ranged alongside. A man who appeared to be in authority touched his cap formally.

" Who's the owner of this vessel? " he asked.

" Me," answered Sam without removing his pipe from his mouth.

" Name of vessel? " demanded the stranger briskly.

" *Fifty-Fifty.*"

" What? "

" I said *Fifty-Fifty.*"

" Registered? "

The boatman shrugged his shoulders.

" Let's see your license."

" Oh, this is an American boat," said the owner indifferently.

" Well, you're in Canadian waters. I'm a Canadian officer. I am entitled to inspect your papers. Let's see them."

" Didn't bring 'em."

The man turned and held a whispered conversation with two of his colleagues. One of them nodded.

"We'll probably have to take you ashore for that," he remarked very sternly.

Sam displayed no evidence of interest. He merely looked at Rosalind. That lady had been suddenly aroused from boredom. She was very much interested.

"I am responsible for the boat being here," she said. "I am hiring it. What is the trouble?"

"The trouble is, madam, that this man is navigating Canadian waters without being able to produce proper papers."

"But that does not seem like a very serious offense," remarked Rosalind. "I imagine it is being done every day."

"It's been done a number of times by this vessel, madam. We've watched it."

"Still, I do not see that it is a matter of much importance. I am sure no damage has been done."

"We're not so sure, madam."

A second man twitched the sleeve of the speaker, and they conferred in low tones.

"What is your name, madam?" demanded the spokesman, turning again to Rosalind.

She told him.

"And the names of the members of your party, please?"

She gave him those, while he made a careful memorandum of each.

"And this man?" with a nod at the boatman.

"Sam."

"Sam what?"

" Merely Sam, so far as I know."

He looked at the boatman for further enlightenment.

" Sam merely," echoed that person.

Again there was a whispered conference aboard the second craft.

" Do you know a man named Schmidt? " asked the one in authority, speaking to the boatman.

Sam indicated that he did.

" Heinrich Schmidt? "

" I believe that's his name. They fit together, anyhow."

" Who is he? "

" One of my best customers."

" Where's he from? "

" Chicago, so he told me. What's the game? "

" You took him to Rockport three days ago, didn't you? "

" That's right."

" And to Gananoque? "

" Right again."

" And he's been to Kingston twice with you? "

" Three times," corrected Sam.

" What was he doing at those places? "

" Doing? How do I know? I didn't follow him."

The four men in the strange boat withdrew to the farther end of their craft and put their heads together. Rosalind watched them impatiently. Even Morton displayed a mild interest, while the Winter girls stopped knitting and looked worried.

" Where does this man Schmidt stop? " demanded the spokesman when he emerged once more from the conference.

" Oh, he's been drifting around at two or three places on the American side."

" Who does he meet? "

" Give it up," answered Sam.   " I'm not in charge of him.   I'm just his boatman."

" If you are looking for smugglers," interrupted Rosalind, " why —"

" We're not, madam," snapped the stranger.

He turned again to Sam.

" Did this man Schmidt ever discuss military subjects with you? "

" Yes, indeed.   That is, once."

The men exchanged significant glances.

" When — and what? "

" The last time I had him out," said Sam.   " He wanted to know if I didn't think Grant gave General Sigel a raw deal when he put somebody else on the job in the Shenandoah Valley."

The spokesman in the trim power-boat frowned heavily.

" That all? "

" All I remember.   Except he said his father fought with Sigel and always claimed that Halleck framed him.   I don't know whether he did or not, but I said I'd speak about it some time and see if I could find out.   You wouldn't happen to know yourself, would you? "

The man glared suspiciously.   Rosalind turned her face away and began dabbling one hand in the water, over the side of the boat.

" Well, I guess we'll take you up to Kingston," said the spokesman after a minute of deliberation. " There are a few things that need looking into."

Sam glanced about him casually.

"Not now you won't," he observed as he proceeded to refill his pipe. "We've crossed the line."

The man made a swift survey of the river and the islands and uttered an angry exclamation.

"You see, you talked too much," added the boatman deferentially. "You talked so long that we drifted over into American water. If you try to take me now they'll send a battleship after me, or an ultimatum, or something else just as bad."

There was a hurried consultation among the four strangers, with evidences of disagreement. It ended when the man in command turned upon Sam with a stern visage.

"Hereafter," he said, "you enter Canadian waters or ports at your own risk. In the name of the English government I warn you. I also authorize you to extend the same warning to the man Heinrich Schmidt. If he is found north of the international boundary-line let him look out for himself. That applies to you, your boat, and any passengers you may have aboard."

Marjorie Winter turned pale.

"But really," she ventured timidly, "I'm very sure that none of us is against you, sir. See — these are for Belgians."

She held up a half-finished sock.

The man who sounded the warning did not look at it. He gave a sharp command and the boat with the British ensign snorted off across the river.

"I think we will go home now," observed Rosalind.

Without a word Sam started his engine.

It was a silent party that returned to Witherbee's Island. Rosalind was glad it was so. The affair was at once too big with possibilities and too nebulous as to facts for idle gossip.

To the best of her knowledge she had never seen a spy. She wondered if she were really looking at one now. He did not look like one.

Nor, for that matter, did Morton, who might well be expected to display interest at the very least if it were true that Sam and the Schmidt man were making voyages into Canadian ports that might end in nooses.

First a common thief, next a smuggler — now a spy! Rosalind found pleasurable excitement in her thoughts. Gertrude Witherbee was on the wharf when the launch came in. She was waving a yellow envelope at Rosalind.

" Telegram for you! " she called.

Rosalind took the message and read as follows:

" Will arrive some time this evening.
        " WILLIAMS."

Reginald Williams, the persistent one, was coming! Rosalind gasped. Not that she minded Williams or his persistence. He was well enough in his way, and he could always be properly discouraged. She had no fears on that point.

But Reginald was the bracelet man! And the bracelet was now upon the smoothly tanned arm of Gertrude. And Reginald would see it — and recognize it. And he would wonder and ask questions and blurt something. There would be explanations and revelations and —

Rosalind shuddered, and pondered the matter deeply.

" It simply cannot be! " she exclaimed aloud.

"What can't be, dear?" asked Gertrude.

"Why — oh, nothing. I was just doing some oral thinking."

Gertrude smiled wisely. She knew about Reginald. And she knew — or thought she knew — that Reginald would ask again, and that, as Rosalind said, it simply could not be.

CHAPTER X

MRS. WITHERBEE, driven into a corner by an angry Rosalind, confessed that somewhere in the back of her mind there may have been a lurking purpose when she invited Reggy Williams to become a member of her summer household. Not being subtle in the least, Mrs. Witherbee interpreted the wrath of Rosalind at its face value. Hence, she sustained a shock within an incredibly short space of time.

"It was a most thoughtless thing," said Rosalind sternly.

"But, my dear, I didn't for a moment dream that his attentions would really —"

"Attentions? Bosh!"

Mrs. Witherbee opened her eyes wide.

"I'm not interested in his attentions — not in the slightest degree," said Rosalind. "They do not disturb me one way or the other. I am, however, purely from the standpoint of humanity, interested in the preservation of his life."

"His life!"

"Certainly. I thought you knew."

"But Rosalind, dear —"

"Why in the world you didn't ask me I don't know," said Rosalind, making a hopeless gesture with both arms. "Everybody else knows it."

Mrs. Witherbee's faced had attained a greenish pallor.

"Knows what?" she asked tremblingly.

"Knows that Reginald Williams has a heart that is liable to drop him in his tracks any time."

Mrs. Witherbee raised both hands and opened her mouth.

"Certainly," added Rosalind sharply. "He's been suffering from it for some time. He's not allowed to take violent exercise, or to undergo any excitement or sudden shock. He has to be kept perfectly quiet. And above all he must not be given the slightest hint of his trouble. You see, he doesn't know it himself."

"Doesn't know it!"

"Indeed not. The physicians are afraid that it would make matters worse to tell him. So they told only his family, and his family has informed his friends. And Reggy is really in the hands of his friends without knowing it."

"But he'll be with friends, here," said Mrs. Witherbee, brightening.

"Friends — yes!" exclaimed Rosalind. "But how about the excitement? Think of what's been going on here — of what may happen at any time. Why, it might kill him!"

Mrs. Witherbee sat down suddenly and limply.

"What shall we do?" she moaned.

"There is only one thing to do, of course; that is to make the best of it. He must be kept absolutely quiet, but he must not know that he is being kept quiet.

"Under no circumstances must he be told any-thing about burglars or smugglers or spies or anything of that sort. He must not know about the burglar-alarm, or the raids at this place and Mr. Davidson's — or anything! It may be a matter of life or death with him. Nobody must even suggest such a thing!

"Why, Gertrude mustn't even wear that bracelet, because it's so odd it will start him asking questions, and then the whole thing is likely to come out!

"Everybody must be told to say nothing whatever about anything that might give him a shock. Not only that; they mustn't even *do* anything exciting."

"I'm so sorry! I'm so sorry!" faltered Mrs. Witherbee as she rocked in her chair.

"It's too late to stop him, of course," continued Rosalind. "I suppose he's at Clayton by this time. So the only thing we can do is to take the utmost precautions. And we must be particularly careful that he does not even suspect!"

"Oh, we will; we will, my dear."

"And you'll tell everybody?" said Rosalind anxiously.

"Every soul! I'll tell Stephen immediately. We'll all help — we'll be *so* careful!"

Rosalind watched Mrs. Witherbee hurry in search of her husband and smiled grimly.

"Something had to be done about it," she murmured. "I couldn't think of anything else offhand."

It was dusk and the Witherbee household was sitting on the porch unnaturally quiet when a voice from the path that led to the wharf rent the air with a bellow.

"Ho there, somebody! Wonder you wouldn't welcome a guest!"

Simultaneously a tall, bulky figure appeared at the

edge of the lawn and crossed at a rapid walk. It stopped at the foot of the steps. Two grips that were carried in one hand were tossed upon the porch with a flirt of the wrist. Then followed a trunk, which had been balanced jauntily on one shoulder. And then Reggy Williams cleared five steps in one leap and began shaking hands with everybody.

"Nice folks!" he shouted. "Not a soul to meet a fellow! Hello, Rosalind; you're looking fine and fit. Hello, Gertrude! Hello, Tom, you lazy mucker! Why didn't you give me a hand? Didn't know I'd be here so soon, eh? I've a good mind to carry you down to the river and chuck you in."

He charged about the porch like a nervous rhinoceros, bawling salutations and leaving in his wake an array of painfully throbbing fingers.

Reginald Williams stood six feet three. He was wide and thick and boisterous, and there was a deep red tan on his face that actually served to exaggerate his bulk.

Mrs. Witherbee, her hands clasped to her bosom, regarded him with horror.

"Won't you — please — take a chair?" she whispered timidly.

"Chair? Why, thanks — if you'll stick it in front of a table. I haven't had a mouthful since noon, and I don't mind saying I can eat anything and everything you've got in the house. Here, Tom! Don't fuss with that trunk; I'll take care of that later."

Mr. Witherbee cautiously pushed a porch rocker against Reginald's legs.

"We'll get you some grub," he said anxiously. "Only sit down first. Rest yourself, old man."

"Rest! That's all I've done all day in a train that didn't have ambition enough to keep within two hours of her schedule. I could have pushed the blamed thing faster than it went."

"Yes, yes," said Mr. Witherbee, his brow furrowed in anxiety. "But just sit down a bit. Enjoy the air — it's great up here. See that view — isn't it amazing? Everything so quiet, so peaceful! Oh, it just puts ten years on a man's life to spend a little while up here! No worry, no cares, no excitement."

Reginald sat reluctantly.

"No excitement!" he exclaimed. "Then, by George, we'll make some! How do you live without it? I can't. I'm going to start something, sure as you live. But I'd like to eat first."

The Witherbee family ventured inquiring glances at Rosalind. That lady's face bore a curious expression of doubt and dismay. But she did not lose her self-control. Stepping behind Reginald's chair, she raised a finger to her lips and shook her head warningly.

"I'll get you some toast directly," said Mrs. Witherbee. "And how do you like your tea?"

Reginald guffawed, then apologized.

"Excuse me; didn't mean to be rude. But if you've got any cold ham in the house, and some bread and butter, and a scuttle of hot coffee you needn't bother about the toast and tea. And you needn't fetch it out here; lead me to it."

The Winter girls exchanged apprehensive glances. Mr. Witherbee made a sign to his wife, who disappeared into the house. Rosalind followed her. The two ladies met in the pantry.

"I — I'm frightened to death," whispered Mrs. Witherbee. "Is he always that way?"

"Nearly always," sighed Rosalind. "That's what makes it so sad."

"I hadn't thought of it as being sad, my dear. It — it just seems sort of terrible. Doesn't he know?"

"Ssh! Of course not. He doesn't even suspect."

"The poor man!" said Mrs. Witherbee softly. "Then it is sad, isn't it? Isn't there any way to — control him?"

"It's very difficult," admitted Rosalind. "He's headstrong. And of course, not knowing, you can't expect him to restrain himself. He's always been accustomed to leading an active life."

"Active, my dear! Why, he's violent. My knuckles are still aching. Do you really think we ought to let him have ham — and coffee?"

"We might as well," said Rosalind in a hopeless voice. "He'd probably make a scene over toast and tea."

"And he seems so healthy, poor fellow! And so strong!"

"He's deceptive," Rosalind observed hastily.

There was a heavy tramping of feet overhead, then a crash that rattled the dishes in the pantry. Mrs. Witherbee rushed into the hall, stifling a scream. Rosalind bit her lip.

When the mistress of the island returned her eyes were wide with terror.

"He — he carried his trunk up-stairs!" she gasped. "He wouldn't let Stephen or Tom touch it."

"He does those things," said Rosalind unhappily. "He doesn't realize, you know. We can't restrain him by force, but we must do all we can."

"Does he have — attacks?"

"Oh, often. Terrible ones."

Mrs. Witherbee clasped her hands.

"And it's a two-mile sail to the nearest doctor!" she moaned.

"Never suggest a doctor to him," warned Rosalind. "He wouldn't understand and you can't tell what he might do. Don't think of such a thing!"

"But if anything should happen —"

"We must run the risk. We must make the best of it somehow. I'd cut more ham than that, I think; he'll only be out after more if you don't. I'll get the bread; no need to call the servants. I imagine we'd better bring it to him on the porch."

An awed household watched Reginald Williams eat. It was a rapid and extensive proceeding.

"Sorry to have put you out," he roared genially as he emptied the coffee-pot. "But a man has to have a bite now and then to keep his body and soul in close relation."

"Of course," assented Mrs. Witherbee gently. "Good food, rest, and plenty of sleep."

"Oh, I'm not sleepy! I'm good for all night if there's anything doing."

"We live very quietly here, Mr. Williams."

"Oh, well, we'll manage to start something. Won't we, Tom?"

Tom Witherbee mumbled an unintelligible reply and glanced at Rosalind. She shook her head severely.

Suddenly Reginald missed the master of the house.

" Where's Mr. Witherbee? " he demanded.

" He — he went out in the launch," faltered Mrs. Witherbee.

" Why the dickens didn't he invite somebody? Nothing I'd like better on a night like this."

" He just went over to Mr. Davidson's island," explained Gertrude in a soothing tone. " He didn't think anybody would want to go."

At this point Fortescue Jones, who had been regarding Reginald with amazed eyes, entered the conversation. Said he:

" He went over to see about bur —"

The elbow of Tom Witherbee put an abrupt end to the sentence.

" To see about what? " demanded Reginald.

Mrs. Witherbee rolled her eyes helplessly. Her husband had gone to the burglar meeting.

" To see about burlap," said Rosalind hastily.

" Burlap? "

" Certainly — burlap. He wants it to wrap things in."

" Must want it pretty badly," commented Reginald, " if he has to make a special voyage to get it. Oh, well, if we can't go sailing let's start something. Let's dance! "

Rosalind leaned weakly against a pillar of the porch.

" We — we don't dance," said Gertrude.

" Don't dance! "

The eyes of Reginald Williams successively met those of the two Winter girls, Polly Dawson, Gertrude, and Rosalind.

" You haven't all sprained your ankles, have you? " he asked.

"I mean we haven't been doing any dancing here," explained Gertrude desperately. "We — Mother doesn't like it."

This statement astonished Mrs. Witherbee to such an extent that she opened her mouth and held it that way for several seconds. Then she nodded.

The next half-hour on the Witherbee porch was crowded with the efforts of ten persons to curb the restless spirit of a young man who wanted to do something.

They spoke softly and upon soft topics, such as gardening and clothes and fresh air. They argued nothing, but agreed upon everything. They urged Reginald to sit down. They tried to make him wear Mr. Witherbee's top coat. They watched with sickening dread as he smoked. They scarcely breathed when he proposed to take a moonlight swim.

Then one by one they went off to bed, yawning prodigiously and declaring that it was getting very late. Reginald and Rosalind found themselves alone.

He waited to make sure that the last of the company had disappeared, then turned to her with a bewildered look.

"What on earth is the matter with this crowd?" he demanded.

"What seems to be the matter?" asked Rosalind.

"Matter! They all act as if they were afraid to make a noise or turn around. They even whisper. Nothing's gone wrong here, has it?"

"No, indeed!" hastily.

"Well, it's about as cheerful as a shipwreck. Has it been going on like this very long? I don't see how you and the rest of the younger folk stand it."

"It's rather pleasant to be quiet for a change, Reggie."

"Quiet! I don't call that being quiet — it's sepulchral. I came up here to have a good time. I'm going to shake this crowd up to-morrow."

"You mustn't!"

Rosalind's voice was anxious. Something more would have to be done, she was certain. Reginald was capable of executing his threat.

"I'll tell you," she said in a low tone. "But you must not mention the fact to any person that I did tell you. It's on account of Mr. Morton."

"The Englishman? What's the matter with him?"

Rosalind hesitated. What was the matter with Mr. Morton? She felt that she was rapidly becoming mired.

"Well, you see, Mr. Morton is just recovering from a breakdown," she ventured.

"What kind of a breakdown?"

"Mental."

"Loose in the bean, eh?"

"Reginald! You know I hate slang. No; he's not — that. Not nearly so bad. But he had a breakdown — mostly nervous, I think. It came from overwork, I believe. He must have absolute quiet — no excitement, nothing to irritate him.

"But you must not mention it to a soul, Reggie; and particularly you must not let him see that you notice anything peculiar. He's very sensitive."

Reginald grumbled.

"So that's why we all have to keep very quiet," said Rosalind with finality.

"He ought to be shipped off to a nut college," declared Reginald. "Anybody like that is liable to break loose at any time. I didn't come up here to be a keeper."

"Well, you are not compelled to remain."

Rosalind's voice was cool.

"Oh, but I am! You know very well I couldn't stay away. Why, I practically invited myself."

He tried to capture one of Rosalind's hands, but she, alert, easily evaded his clumsy caress.

"Please don't begin that again," she said in annoyance. "If you do I'll go home to-morrow."

"But, Rosalind, you know very well —"

"Will you stop?"

"Oh, very well! But I give you fair warning that I haven't stopped for good."

She sighed and frowned.

"I thought I'd struck the limit of unsociability on the way down here," observed Reginald. "The fellow that brought me was deaf and dumb."

"Really?"

"Couldn't speak a word. Couldn't hear, either. I had to write on a piece of paper where I wanted to go."

"A boatman, was he?"

"Yes. And the worst of it was, his boat broke down a couple of times on the way, and he didn't seem to know much about fixing it. I couldn't help him, and he didn't even have the satisfaction of being able to swear."

Rosalind found herself listening with breathless attention.

"What sort of a boat was it?" she asked.

"Not much to look at. Rather dirty, too."

She had more than a suspicion.

"What did the man look like?" carelessly.

"A chap with a beard. Long, thin person. Why?"

"Oh, nothing! I think I've seen him around. You say he is a deaf-mute?"

"Absolutely. I met him on the wharf up at Clayton, and when I asked him a question about the boats he made signs at me. Then I felt sort of sorry for him, and thought I'd give him a job."

Rosalind's brain was in a whirl. Sam, the boatman, playing the deaf-mute! She could not even begin to guess a reason.

"He knew where the place was, all right; I'll say that for him," added Reginald. "But it's not particularly entertaining to be cooped up with a dummy in a bum boat for a couple of hours."

"I should imagine not," she murmured.

"But I did the swearing for him, anyhow. And — funny about that, too — he must have understood what I was doing, for he grinned from ear to ear and nodded his head. It must be tough not to be able to do your own cussing."

"I don't suppose it does afford much relief to do it with your fingers," Rosalind agreed. "That is," she supplemented righteously, "if it ever does give one any relief. It's a miserable habit."

"It's not a habit," said Reginald. "It's a vocation, if you do it right. Who's this coming?"

Heavy, deliberate footfalls announced the return of Mr. Witherbee from the meeting of the vigilants.

"Get your burlap?" inquired Reginald pleasantly.

" Burlap? " echoed Mr. Witherbee.

Rosalind interposed hastily.

" You must have forgotten your errand," she said, laughing. " You know perfectly well you started out to get some burlap."

" Burlap? "

Mr. Witherbee repeated the word with a rising inflection.

Rosalind had slipped behind Reginald and was making a frantic pantomime. The master of the island stared at her for a few seconds, wrinkling his forehead.

" Why, certainly," she said. " Don't you remember saying you were going to see if Mr. Davidson had some? "

" Oh, yes," answered Mr. Witherbee slowly. " Come to think of it, I did start out to get some. And just as you say, I forgot all about it. By the way, sit down, Williams. Take it easy. You must be tired after a long day's journey."

" Everybody seems to think I'm tired," sighed Reginald. " I guess in order not to disappoint them I'd better go to bed. Good night."

He stamped noisily inside and up the staircase.

" Is — is he all right? " asked Mr. Witherbee in a hoarse whisper.

" Oh, perfectly. We've kept him just as quiet as possible."

" That's right; that's right. Poor chap. And he's so healthy to look at, too! By the way, what's this burlap game? "

Rosalind laughed.

" It's all on account of that stupid Jones boy," she explained. " He started to blurt something about why you had gone to Mr. Davidson's, and he had half of 'burglar' out when Tom bumped him with his elbow. Then I had to finish it somehow, and all I could think of was burlap. You see, it had to be something that couldn't possibly excite Reggy."

" I get you," grinned Mr. Witherbee. " Burlap, eh? I'll have to remember to get some now."

Suddenly his expression changed and he became grave.

" We've organized," he said in guarded tones. " There were seven islands represented. We're going to hire a patrol. Some of them are going to get watchmen, too. And it's high time, Rosalind."

He stepped closer and looked about him cautiously.

" Somebody's been on the island again," he whispered. " But don't say anything yet! "

" Again! "

" To-night, I think. Somebody's stolen the dog! "

" You are sure? "

" Positive. I tied the beast up near the dock when I went out in the boat. And he's gone! "

Rosalind could only blink at this intelligence.

" But I don't want to worry Mrs. Witherbee about it," added that lady's husband. " And of course we've got to keep it from Williams. So don't say anything. Good night. Grand watch-dog, that; I guess he needed stealing."

CHAPTER XI

TREED!

IT was early afternoon when Sam nursed the *Fifty-Fifty* into the rock-bound cove that formed his island harbor, made her fast, and stepped ashore. He advanced up the winding path to his cabin. Midway in its length he paused and listened.

A dog barked.

The boatman resumed his advance at a quicker pace. He caught sight of the cabin, then of an agitated red setter that ran to and fro beneath a tree whose branches brushed the roof of the dwelling. The animal was yelping nervously.

Next the boatman saw a pair of feet, shod in snowy white and outlined sharp and clear against the dark-green foliage. The feet were attached to a pair of ankles, also in white — ankles that were slim, aristocratic, even haughty.

Then as he stepped forward the rim of a white skirt came into view. A second later his advance brought him to a point from which he obtained a full view of Rosalind Chalmers, sitting on the branch of a tree.

" Call off your dog! " she commanded.

Sam removed his gaze from the vision in the tree and studied the animal thoughtfully. The setter, having sighted the boatman, ceased baying and sat down with an alert eye upon the quarry.

"The dog, I said!" said Rosalind harshly. "Call him off!"

Sam's glance returned to the lady on the branch.

"Good afternoon," he said pleasantly.

Rosalind returned the inspection through angry eyes.

"Are you going to call off the dog?" she demanded.

"Why, I was just thinking about it," drawled Sam. "I don't know that I ought to discourage him."

The lady in the tree uttered an exclamation.

"You see," added the boatman, "the dog is only doing his duty. His job is to protect my property. He looks out for it when I'm away."

She observed that the boatman was staring intently, not at her eyes — where it is customary to look at a person — but at her ankles, where it is not always polite to stare. She knew they were conspicuous, but she also realized the futility of flinching. Sitting on a limb, there was absolutely no way to make her skirt cover them.

"This — this is an outrage!" she stormed.

"Why, perhaps — ma'am. But whose fault?"

"The beast — he — chased me!"

"I told him to."

"You told him to?"

"That is, I told him to chase anybody. I hardly expected he'd tree you. Did I, old sport?"

The dog relaxed his vigil long enough to turn his head, wag his tail furiously, and give throat to a joyous bark.

"You see, this is where I live," added Sam with a nod at the cabin. "He's in charge when I'm not here."

"In charge since —"

"Yesterday."

"You stole him!"

The boatman seemed indifferent to the charge.

"That dog belongs to Mr. Witherbee," declared Rosalind. "You know perfectly well you stole him. And — will you call him off?"

"Perhaps — by and by," answered the boatman.

He seated himself on the ground ten feet below her and began fumbling for tobacco. Rosalind was pink with rage.

"I'm coming down!" she declared.

Sam did not appear to hear the announcement.

She slid cautiously along the limb for a few inches, steadying herself by a tight grip on another branch. The dog sprang to his feet and yelped furiously. Rosalind became rigid again.

"Will you call him off?"

Sam studied her ankles, then resumed the methodical filling of his pipe.

"What brought you here?" he asked after a pause.

"I came in a rowboat."

"Alone?"

"Certainly."

"I didn't see the boat."

"It drifted away — I wouldn't be here except for that."

"What did you come for?"

Rosalind gritted her teeth and wondered if the dog would really bite.

"I was merely rowing," she said, trying to calm her voice. "I — I thought the island was unoccupied."

"You didn't happen to be looking for a smugglers' cave, did you?"

"No!"

"Or a burglars' den?"

"*No!*"

"Or an international spy?"

She remained furious and silent.

"It's rather important for me to know," he explained as he scratched a match. "There's so much hunting going on that it isn't safe to ignore it. You don't happen to be a member of a posse, do you?"

"Will you let me down?"

"That's his affair," answered the boatman, nodding in the direction of the dog. "He seems to like you where you are. I don't know that I ought to interfere. It might discourage him and make him careless in the future. Did you visit my cabin?"

Rosalind remained silent.

The boatman whispered something to the dog, then arose lazily and walked over to the shack. Rosalind saw him disappear within the door. She made a second tentative move toward descent. The dog, which lay watching her with his nose between his paws, sprang up and snarled.

A moment afterward Sam emerged from the cabin, staring ruefully at the sheet of paper that was in his hand.

"You tore down my picture-gallery," he said reproachfully. "Why did you do that?"

Rosalind flushed and compressed her lips.

"I thought quite a lot of that picture," he mused,

seating himself again. " It seemed like such a good likeness."

" You beast! "

" That's not the way to make friends with him," cautioned the boatman.

" I mean you! "

" Oh! Well, that's not the way to make friends with me, either. Didn't you like my portrait of a lady? "

" I'm coming down! " she warned desperately.

" I wouldn't — yet. He can really bite, ma'am. Have you been there long? "

" An hour."

" Is it comfortable up there? "

She remained grimly silent. It was *not* comfortable. The limb was very hard and its diameter was meager. Her feet were asleep.

The boatman returned to a study of the " portrait." He even began to read aloud from it, when Rosalind stopped him with an imploring exclamation.

" Please — please! " she cried.

" But it's such a good portrait," he protested, looking up at her mildly. " It's a new kind of art. It's got the cubists beaten a mile. Statist, I suppose you'd call it. It gives all the dope — just draws a picture in facts and figures. I'm strong for it.

" Listen. Here's where it says you —"

" Stop! "

" You are the daugher of —"

" Oh, *will* you stop? "

He paused in his reading and observed her attentively. What he saw appeared to please him. Rosalind was never more charming. She was a god-

dess, all in white save for the fiery tint in her cheeks
and the dangerous glint in her blue eyes.

" Say," he said with sudden interest, " how'd you
get up there, anyhow?   It's some climb."

" I — I had to climb."

" Meaning he pushed you pretty hard," nodding
at the dog.

" Of course ! "

" I'd have given a lot to have seen you make it,"
he mused.   " If I call him off will you do it again? "

She flushed hotly and shot him a look of stinging
contempt.   He never winced.

" You see," he explained, " there's no branch below the one you're sitting on.   And that's a good ten
feet up.   You must have jumped for it and swung
yourself up, or else you shinned the tree.   In either
case it was a stunt that's a credit to you.   I'm certainly sorry I missed it — ma'am."

He drawled the last word with maddening emphasis.

Rosalind was in despair.   It was not fear of the
dog — now.   She knew that Sam would not dare to
let the animal attack, even if she descended from her
refuge.   It was fear of the boatman's mocking eyes.
He was smiling.   What would he do when she,
Rosalind, the dignified, began the scramble that must
precede her arrival at *terra firma?*

Dignity scarcely sat with her on the limb, even
now; it would be a thousand miles away when she
made the first decisive move.   It was a sense of dignity wholly that restrained Rosalind.   She did not
care particularly about her ankles; she was not
ashamed of them and had no reason to be.   But she
was bitterly resolved that she would cling to the

very end to whatever shred of haughty poise remained to her.

Temper loosed her tongue again.

"Thief! Smuggler!" she exclaimed. "They'll
make short work of you when I'm free from this."

"Well, we're all little pals together," he observed
serenely.

"Spy!"

"Say, that was a funny one, wasn't it?" he said,
brightening. "Me *und* Schmidt — spies! That
was one you never even thought of, ma'am."

"Will you stop calling me ' ma'am ' ?"

"Excuse me. I was only trying to be respectful.
What do you want me to call you — Rosie?"

Rosalind almost lost her balance. She recovered
herself with a desperate grab at a branch and made
a choking noise in her throat. It shamed her to
know that tears were in her eyes, but she could not
force them back.

"About that spy business," he went on. "Did
you believe that?"

"I see no reason to doubt it."

He mused over that for a while.

"It's hanging if it's true," he remarked presently.

"I hope so!"

"Hanging for me *und* Schmidt. I hate to think
about it."

Rosalind could contemplate it with pleasure.

"Poor old Schmidt! Fat old Schmidt — who
never did anything worse than buy and sell wheat on
the Chicago Board of Trade! Think of hanging
Schmidt as a spy!"

Rosalind paid little attention to the uttered
thoughts of the boatman. She was trying to concen-

trate on her own case.   Thus far conversation had
been futile while the dog and the man remained inexorable.

She blamed herself bitterly for the panic that had
driven her to an arboreal refuge.   If only she had
stopped and faced the beast all might have been
saved!   As she looked down upon him now she did
not believe he would bite.   But he had come upon
her so suddenly, so clamorously, that self-possession
fled from her in a flash.

And now, even though she lacked faith in his
ferocity and remembered how insinuatingly he had
nosed his muzzle into her hand back on the Witherbee place, there were other reasons.   Chief of
course was the sardonic boatman.

Yet she was frantically anxious to descend from
her tree.   To gain that she was almost willing to
sacrifice everything save dignity.   She was even content to sue for peace — to make terms, if need be to
humiliate herself before this common creature who
calmly smoked and watched her discomfiture.

" May I come down now? " she asked so sweetly
that the alteration in her voice startled him.

He stared at her and whistled.

" Please! "

Rosalind's tone was liquid in its smoothness.   And
— she smiled!   The boatman dropped his pipe.

" Do it again," he said incredulously.

" What? "

" Smile! "

She did it again, this time with less obvious effort.
His complete astonishment helped to lighten the
task.

" Great heavens, you *can* do it! "

" And now may I come down? "

She suited a movement to the question, but the dog growled again. The boatman recovered his composure.

" Well, I don't know about that," he said. " It depends. You see, you've invaded my island and you've been prospecting around my cabin, and maybe you're fixing to get me into trouble."

" I promise! " she exclaimed hastily.

" But you've got me for a thief, a smuggler, and a spy, and that's a whole lot to have on anybody."

" I'm willing to ignore the matter, then. It's none of my business."

" Hum! That's sounds fair enough, of course. But how can I tell they won't wheedle it out of you? "

" Do you think I'm a child? "

" I should say not! "

She did not relish the emphasis nor see the need for it.

" Well, am I to be released? " she asked after a pause.

" I'm thinking about it. Why did you tear down my picture-gallery? "

" It was an insult! "

" Not a bit, ma'am. It was just a portrait — a bully one. Anyhow, why shouldn't I have one? Thousands of 'em have been printed."

Rosalind bit her lip.

" They're in common circulation, all over. Anybody with three dollars can buy one."

" You stole it."

" That's a compliment to you, ma'am. See the risk I ran — for a picture."

" They — they are not for common people," she said frigidly.

Sam surveyed her leisurely.

" I suppose that means me," he remarked.

She answered with a gesture.

" And of course you're something better than common clay," he mused.

She did not stoop to answer him.

" Say ! " he broke out suddenly. " Far be it from me to be impolite to a lady, particularly a lady with her portrait written in a three-dollar society book. But do you know that you make me good and tired? "

The lady in the tree gasped.

" Yes; dead weary. I've heard about you. I read the papers sometimes. You're one of the exclusive bunch; you're in the ' it ' class. Everybody outside of it is plain common dirt — to you. You've got the coin and the pedigree, which is supposed to make you something extra special. You're supposed to be a shade higher up than human. They tell me you're a heart-breaker, too."

Rosalind turned white.

" Just why you should be such a heart-breaker," he continued, examining her with a critical eye, " is something I don't quite get. You're a good-enough looker, so far as that goes, but — shucks! There are lots of those. Never saw a man yet that was fit to marry you, I understand. A sort of a man-hater, maybe.

" Yet you never try to head a man off if you see he's in a fair way to get his heart cracked. That's your favorite sport, according to the dope I get. You just take it as something that is naturally coming to you.   If it didn't happen you'd feel insulted.   Oh, yes! I've heard about you."

She was rigid as marble and almost as breathless.

" Let me tell you something — Rosie. You can't put that stuff over on me.   You can swing it across on some society guy, but it doesn't go here. Why, I can tell things about your doings in the last forty-eight hours that'll knock you clean out of the Blue Book.

" As I said before, I don't want to be rude to a lady, ma'am, and I don't intend to say anything that would hurt her feelings — not for anything.   But you make me plain and plumb tired."

Rosalind was crying in sheer helpless rage.   The boatman watched the tears stonily.   After a short pause he arose from his seat on the ground and whistled to the dog.

" You can come down if you like," he informed her.

Torn with a storm of sobs and mortification, Rosalind made no move to descend.   He watched her for a minute, then went into the cabin and returned, dragging the table.   This he placed beneath the limb where she still clung, quivering.

Mounting the table, he reached up and in a most impersonal way grasped her about the waist and swung her clear of the tree.   For an instant Rosalind found herself poised in the air.   Then she was deposited on the ground.   She walked a few steps and leaned weakly against the tree.   The dog barked in delight.

" Well, you've got to get home, I suppose," said Sam.   " And your boat's gone.   It's up to me to take you.   I don't mind earning a little money.

"You may as well quit crying, too. You're not hurt and you're not down-hearted. You're just good and mad; that's all."

He turned to lead the way down the path, then stopped and stared through an opening in the trees.

"Another visitor," he observed with a grin.

Rosalind followed the direction of his glance. Reginald Williams in a motor-launch was just making the shore of the island. He glimpsed her white-clad figure and waved his hand.

"Oh!" she gasped.

"Trouble?" inquired Sam.

"You mustn't tell him! How shall I explain? What shall I do? I can't ever, ever —"

Her tears began to flow afresh.

"Needn't worry about me telling him anything, ma'am. I'm deaf and dumb — to him."

"But — but —"

Rosalind Chalmers was deserted by her cloak of calm disdain. She was in a panic.

A sudden change came over the boatman.

"Come on, buck up!" he said, cheerfully. "I'm sorry I made you cry. I take it all back — honest. Just forget it. We'll get out of this easy. Get your nerve now — quick! He'll be here in a couple of minutes. Be a sport, Miss Chalmers! Be a pal; just make believe you're the master mechanic again. Think hard now. We've got to hand him something."

"But he'll think that I —"

"No, he won't," declared Sam soothingly. "He won't have time to think anything. That's it; brace hard, now. I knew you were game."

He actually patted her on the shoulder. Some-

how Rosalind neglected to resent the vulgar familiar-
ity.

"Here! I've got the scheme!" he exclaimed.
"Only *you'll* have to spiel it at him because I'm a
dummy. Now, listen!"

CHAPTER XII

SAM talked rapidly and with many gestures, the latter for the benefit of Reggy Williams in case Reggy might be looking up from the landing-place, where he was now making fast his boat.

" You went out rowing," explained Sam hurriedly. " You rowed up close to my island."

" By why did I go rowing? I've got to know that. I told Mr. Williams I was going up-stairs to take a nap."

" Oh, you changed your mind about napping, or you went rowing in your sleep. Anything will do; what's the difference about why you went? The point is, you went rowing. You're old enough. While you were close to my island you were upset in a sudden squall."

" There hasn't been a breath of wind to-day! "

" Well, cut out the squall, then. You rocked the boat, or did something silly, and fell overboard. You screamed and I —"

" You're deaf and dumb? How could you hear me scream? "

" That's right. Cut out the scream. I saw you; that'll do. I'm not supposed to be blind. I rushed down, got into my boat, went out and rescued you. Then I brought you to the island to recover. How's that? "

Rosalind looked doubtful.

" He'll be here in a minute," warned Sam. " Either take that or invent a better one."

" But it makes me sound so foolish — so helpless! " she protested.   " And he knows I can swim."

" Tell him you forgot how — your skirts tangled you up — anything! "

Rosalind nodded her head reluctantly.

" All — right."

Reggy Williams was now hidden from view at a bend in the path, which he was already ascending. Rosalind gasped abruptly.

" My clothes! " she exclaimed.   " I fell overboard and — and I'm not even wet! "

" Ouch! " cried the boatman.   " I forgot.   But wait! "

He dashed into the cabin, then reappeared carrying a large galvanized-iron pail.   It seemed to be heavy.

A second later and the contents of it — cold, pure water from the great St. Lawrence — descended upon Rosalind like a cloud-burst.

" Now you're O. K. for the part," grinned the boatman as he tossed the pail aside.

" You — you —"

" S-sh!   It's a grand make-up.   Had to be done, you know."

Rosalind, a beautiful, dripping statue of white, shot him a glance of fury and hate.   Her drenched costume clung clammily.   Wet strands of hair plastered her cheeks, while her eyes blinked painfully from the effects of the deluge.

" Here he is," whispered the boatman as Williams entered the scene.   " Remember — I'm a dummy! Talk up now like a rescued lady."

Reginald Williams, momentarily halted by the spectacle of a moist and miserable lady, sprang forward with an anxious cry.

"Rosalind!"

She waved him back and made a wild effort to smooth her hair.

"You're hurt!" cried Reginald. "What's happened?"

"I'm — I'm not hurt," she answered. "Don't be silly. I'm merely wet."

"Wet! You're saturated, child!"

"I'm not a child. Please don't get hysterical, Reggy."

"But how — why —"

"Naturally I've got to explain," she sighed.

The boatman, standing behind Reginald, winked enthusiastically and waved his hand.

"You see, I didn't take a nap," said Rosalind. "I changed my mind about that. I went out for a row. Why didn't I tell you? Why should I, Reggy?"

"But you nearly drowned yourself!" blurted Reginald in a dismayed tone.

"On the contrary I did nothing of the kind. This — this fellow here is the cause of everything."

Reginald whirled swiftly upon the boatman, who stood open-mouthed, staring at Rosalind.

"What have you done?" roared Reginald, his great figure advancing threateningly.

With a swift look of pained surprise at the dripping one, Sam made a gesture of incomprehension and backed away a step.

"He is deaf and dumb, remember," interposed Rosalind. "Don't hurt him, Reggy. Of course he

didn't do it intentionally.   But he is such a clumsy
fool!"

The boatman's mouth was still open.   He seemed
to be holding his breath.

"I don't care if he is deaf and dumb," declared
Reginald savagely.   "If he's done anything to
you, I'll break his neck.   Tell me, Rosalind —
hurry!"

She smiled very faintly, and bestowed a sweeping
and deliberate look of malice upon Sam.   As Reginald removed his glance from the object of his threat
the boatman shook a fist at Rosalind and went
through a frantic pantomime.   It had no effect upon
her.

"Why, you see, Reggy, as I said before, I went
rowing.   After a while I came to this island.   I was
tired of rowing and I came ashore for a rest."

Sam was glaring and shaking his head.   He even
pointed at the tree, then at the dog.   Reginald, who
caught the gesture, was puzzled.

"What's the matter with him?" he demanded.

"Don't pay any attention to him," advised Rosalind.   "He's a little unbalanced, I think."

"I'll tie him up if you say."

"No, indeed; he's quite harmless."

The boatman, making sure again that Reginald
was not looking, shook his fist and pointed to the
pail that had so recently played its part.   Rosalind
ignored the implied exposure.

"Where was I?" she mused.   "Oh, yes; I came
ashore.   While I was sitting on the rocks, resting,
I saw this man approaching in his launch.   He had
the engine stopped and was leaning over the side of
the boat, which was drifting along slowly.   He

seemed to be engaged with something that was in the water. It — it was a fish-net, I think."

"Against the law," observed Reginald, nodding.

"Of course. And then, while I watched him he fell overboard."

Sam, who had been listening with steadily widening eyes, broke into a furious pantomime. He shook his head violently and pointed at his clothing. Rosalind bit her lip and remembered. The boatman's clothes were dry.

For an instant she paused, dismayed. The web of her fiction was becoming tangled. From sheer stubbornness, hardened with a desire for revenge, she had embarked upon a tale of her own. If there was lying to be done Rosalind was resolved to be the architect of her own falsehoods. She would *not* become a parrot for the lies of another.

Nor had she a mind to play the weak and conventional part of a maiden in distress, rescued by masculine courage and brawn. Even though wet and undignified she proposed to preserve some shred of superiority to the sex that scattered hearts at her feet.

"As I said," she resumed suddenly with a swift flash of her eyes in the direction of Sam, "the creature fell overboard. He began floundering about in the water quite helplessly, and it was evident he could scarcely swim a stroke. I couldn't see him drown, so I had to go to the rescue."

"And you rowed out —"

"That was the trouble," continued Rosalind. "My boat had drifted loose and had disappeared. So there was nothing else to do but swim — unless I wanted to see him drown."

" Rosalind! "

Reginald's eyes were blazing with admiration.

" Oh, it wasn't much of a swim," she said care-lessly.   " Not over a hundred yards, I should say."

" But you risked your life, child! "

" Not at all.   I can really swim, Reggy; you know that.   Well, I got to him after a while, at any rate, and I found him in such a panic of fear that it was difficult to do anything for him."

She paused long enough to allow her glance to wander again toward the boatman.   His symptoms were those of hysteria.

" Finally I managed to get him by the collar from behind," continued Rosalind calmly.   " I had to choke him a little, I think.   It wasn't very easy to get him to the launch, which had begun to drift, but we made it after a while.   Then —"

Another inspection of Sam seemed to afford her satisfaction, for she smiled.

" Then it was a question of getting him aboard. He was in a complete funk; did nothing but cling to the boat and roll his eyes.   I had to climb in myself and then drag him after me.   And then — think of it, Reggy — he began to weep.   That great, grown man shed tears like a child! "

Reginald surveyed the great, grown man with pity and contempt.

" That's all of it," added Rosalind.   " It was just a question of running the boat to the island."

The suitor from the city gazed upon Rosalind Chalmers in adoration.

" You wonder! " he exclaimed.

She made a careless gesture and turned a pair of triumphant eyes in the direction of the boatman.

He had ceased his pantomime and was regarding her with an expression even more rapt than that of Reginald.

"Wait till they hear of this at the Witherbees'!" exclaimed Reginald.

"They mustn't!" she said hastily. "Not for anything!"

"But my dear girl, it's so —"

"Remember Mr. Morton!"

Reginald frowned. The boatman's manner became suddenly alert. The name of Morton had a galvanizing effect. Then he remembered his rôle and relapsed into vacant passivity.

"Hang Morton!" blurted Reginald. "If the man's insane, as you say he is, I don't see why he isn't sent away. He's got everybody walking around on tiptoe and whispering. They've got the habit so bad that they even do it to me."

Sam's brow was furrowed, and the look he devoted to Rosalind contained a perplexed inquiry. She did not meet his eyes for long.

"At any rate I don't care to have you mention the matter," she said firmly. "It's nothing."

"Well, I think when a girl does a fine, brave thing like that she's entitled to all the credit for it," Reginald grumbled. "And to think of it being wasted on that boob, too!"

Once more he inspected the boatman. Then, as he studied the loose-jointed figure, surprise came into Reginald's eyes. He looked back to Rosalind.

"That's funny."

"What?"

"Why, his clothes are dry!"

The boatman was having a convulsion of some kind. His body twitched violently and bent almost double.

"Oh, yes," said Rosalind. "You see, he was chattering so with cold or fright, probably both, that I told him he'd better put on some dry clothes. He had some in the cabin."

Sam managed to straighten himself.

"You told him?" repeated Reginald wonderingly.

"Yes; he seems to have no initiative whatever."

"You don't mean to say he heard you?"

Again the boatman had a seizure.

"Of course not," answered Rosalind easily. "I had to write it on a piece of paper."

Sam turned abruptly and walked to the cabin. His shoulders were shaking.

"He isn't over it yet," commented Reginald.

"I don't imagine he will be over it for a good while," said Rosalind a little savagely. "I think you may take me home now, Reggy."

The boatman stood in the doorway of his cabin, watching them descend the path. He was grinning broadly.

Rosalind felt that she had in some measure achieved revenge for the indignity of her bath. It was no more of a falsehood than the story Sam had attempted to put into her mouth; certainly it was better to be a heroine than a clinging creature.

And by all odds it was an improvement on the preposterous and humiliating truth!

She and Reginald heard a clatter of footsteps behind them as they stepped into the Witherbee launch and turned to see the boatman running down the path. He was making gestures that were clearly intended to delay their departure, so they waited.

As he reached the rock from which they embarked he dropped to his knees, stretched his arms wide and looked up at Rosalind with eyes that conveyed to her an expression of doglike devotion. If there was a hint of something else in them, it was not Sam's fault. As an actor he was but an amateur.

Before the lady in the wet gown could divine his purpose he seized her hands in his own, bent his head over them and began kissing them. Rosalind uttered a cry of disgust. His beard tickled! Also she detested sentimentality.

" The poor fellow is trying to tell you how grateful he is," said Reginald.

Rosalind struggled to release her hands, but the boatman clung to them.

" Reggy! Make him let go! " she called sharply.

Reginald laid a rough hand on the boatman's shoulder and shook him. The man lifted his head and stared reproachfully. Then he dropped Rosalind's hands and sighed deeply.

She found as she drew back with a little shudder of annoyance that in the palm of one hand there was a folded bit of paper. Instinctively, her fingers closed over it; there was no need of explaining more things to Reginald.

Not until some time later, when the launch was far on the way to Witherbee's Island, did Rosalind find an opportunity to examine it. Then, her back turned to Reginald, she unfolded the crumpled sheet, and read:

" PAL ROSIE:

" You put one over on me that time — but just wait."

CHAPTER XIII

WHY the fat Mr. Schmidt from Chicago wanted to go to a dance was a problem that Sam made no serious effort to solve, for in a modern day when neither fat nor age nor bodily infirmity checks the universal human impulse it was of little avail to seek the motive in a given case. You simply go and dance — or think you do — and that's an end of it, with no questions asked.

The dancing-desires of the fat grain-broker from Chicago had taken him from the American mainland to Wellesley Island, a passage safely accomplished aboard the *Fifty-Fifty*. And when Schimdt had been set ashore at the wharf-entrance to a hotel-property that blazed with light Sam backed a little way into the river and made fast to a handy mooring.

Boats by the dozen, churning in from all directions, passed close to the dingy launch. They were freighted with people, much dressed and wholly abandoned to laughter and chatter.

The boatman watched the procession with close attention. It had a cheering effect upon his loneliness.

" No sense to it — but why should there be? " he reflected. " If it's not dancing it's something else just as crazy. I don't blame 'em. I say, go to it; yes, even Schmidt.

"Doll up and walk like a duck while the band plays. It's easy and foolish, and if you do it wrong everybody tries to imitate the new step. Far be it from me to complain. On with the dance!"

Besides, Schmidt paid in cash and paid well — and Sam was not a boatman for his health.

A sharp, incisive voice, clear as a bell across the water, reached his quick ears. He turned in the direction of the sound. Out of the gloom came the shape of a large, white launch, passing close, and inbound for the festivities.

"Of course," said the voice in a tone of bored protest, "it will not be necessary to meet — persons in general."

"Not unless you wish to," the voice was answered by another. "We have our own crowd."

"That's something, of course. I hope we shall be able to keep together; I hate a mixture."

Sam smiled and wrinkled his nose.

"Same old master mechanic," he murmured. "Royalty going to watch the peasants frolic."

He watched the Witherbee yacht make the landing, and saw, by the glow of the colored lanterns that bespangled the wharf, a tall, slender figure in white that was not unfamiliar. An instant later it was lost in the crowd.

From the shore came the sounds of a band. The lips of the boatman pursed; he whistled softly. Presently his feet were tapping on the floor of the cock-pit. His shoulders swayed rhythmically to the beat of the music.

"And Reggy — she calls him Reggy — is there," he murmured as the tune faded away. "And the English gink, too. And the child with the fishing-rod. And they'll all be dancing with the master mechanic. Huh! Maybe even Schmidt will horn in, too."

By the feeble light of the lantern that stood on a seat he surveyed his costume and frowned.

" Who said clothes don't make the man? " he demanded aloud. " They make him dance at any rate. It's against the rules of the game to do it in rags."

Through the trees he had brilliantly lighted vistas of a broad hotel-porch, whereon a crowd surged ceaselessly in all directions with but one common impulse — to keep in step with the band. Again Sam's feet rattled on the flooring, and again his body rocked from side to side.

Then, abruptly, without waiting for the end of the music, he became rigid.

" Why not? " he demanded.

There was nobody to explain.

" Once more, why not? Now is the time for any grain of sense that may happen to be in my nut to speak up, or forever after do the oyster act. I wait — I still wait. I hear no answer. Therefore I have no sense. Therefore — why not? "

He went forward quickly, cast loose from the mooring-buoy, scrambled aft to the engine, cranked it with a nervous jerk at the fly-wheel, and headed out into the river.

For half an hour the launch ran down-stream, passing numerous craft that were obviously bound for the place of the whirling feet.

Sam maintained a close watch upon the procession. He was looking for a particular vessel, and eventually he believed he sighted it, for with a nod of satisfaction he altered his course and bore in toward the cluster of islands that included those of Mr. Witherbee, Mr. Davidson, and their neighbor vigilantes.

Now he extinguished his lantern — he never bothered with port and starboard lamps — and proceeded cautiously into the little archipelago that stood aloof from the other islands in its exclusiveness. Somewhere, probably in a dark shadow near a shore, lurked a patrol-boat.

It was nearly an hour later when the dimly marked hull of the boatman's launch, still devoid of any light, made its reappearance in midstream and laid a return course for the blaze of lights that beckoned hospitably to the islanders of the St. Lawrence. Opposite the hotel, Sam chose a new anchorage, farther from the shore and comfortably remote from that occupied by any other craft.

He relighted his lantern and chuckled as his glance fell upon a roughly wrapped bundle in the bottom of the boat. Seating himself beside it, he ripped off the paper and brought to view a series of articles that caused him fresh mirth.

First came a tiny mirror not much larger than a pocket-glass. This he propped beside the lantern. Then came a brush and comb, and after them a collar and a soft-bosomed, spotless white shirt. He handled the linen gently with grimy fingers.

Next he produced those three unmistakable garments so persistently demanded in the lower left-hand corner of certain cards of invitation —" evening dress." And then a pair of shining pumps.

For a minute he studied his bearded visage in the mirror, a scrutiny that ended in a grimace.

" If I took these chinchillas up to the hotel the bouncer would toss me out on my neck," he muttered. " But I guess I can trim 'em up some.   What did I do with the scissors ? "

Fumbling among the remnants of the paper wrapper, however, failed to produce the weapon he sought.   An exclamation of dismay escaped him as he again inspected his beard.

" Some of it's simply got to come off," he told himself sternly.   " We'll try a knife."

The knife was dull and rusty, while the beard was tough and tenacious.   He groaned at the first stroke and barely suppressed a howl at the second.   It was a two-handed proceeding, one set of fingers being employed in grasping a tuft of hair, while the other set, grimly gripping the knife, essayed the function of severing the tuft at a point half-way between the tip and the roots.

For several minutes he toiled in agony.   Then nature weakly yielded to the pangs of pain and he tossed the knife overboard with an anathema.

" And still people go to beauty-doctors ! " he growled, as he surveyed with disgust the meager results of his work.

" I'd singe it down a bit if I was sure it wasn't inflammable," he added.   " But I'd hate to turn myself into a torch.   Besides, I might lose it all, and that won't do — yet."

Then came to the boatman, as often to other persons, an idea.   He turned to his tool-box and extracted therefrom an instrument which he regarded for an instant with doubtful eyes.   Gritting his teeth, he faced the mirror once more.

You can bale out an ocean with a thimble if you

have sufficient time and persistence. A task relatively similar is that of trimming a beard with a pair of wire-cutters. Sam set himself to it.

Compared with the operations of the discarded knife, it was happily free from serious pain. But it was mournfully slow. A wire-cutter is designed to sever one wire at a time, so its jaw, though powerful, is short. To the boatman it seemed an almost impossible feat to make the instrument cut more than one hair at a time.

He toiled doggedly, bending close to the little glass and twisting his head into such positions as promised the most favorable opportunity for attack. Patience was finally rewarded with a certain degree of expertness. The beard slowly diminished in length to an extent visible to the naked eye. Whether he was really achieving a Van Dyke he did not dare to guess, but he was at least bringing it to a point at the chin, and was cropping away some of its shagginess on the cheeks.

The mustache was a distinct problem. Twice he caught his upper lip between the jaws of the cutter and — swore.

" There! " he exclaimed at last. " If anybody objects to the effect let him say so at his own risk. Before I'll trim any more hair with a wire-cutter I'll let the blamed thing grow until — yes, even until Carrie Catt is President! "

Stripping himself of a gray flannel shirt, he next performed ablutions in a tin water-bucket, alternating soap with sand as he tried to reduce the grime that clung to his hands.

Again the wire-cutter came into play as he manicured his nails. Then there was a new period of torture when he drove the comb through locks that had not been raked for weeks.

To dress was the simplest part of all. He arrayed himself briskly in broadcloth and linen, even submitting patiently to the iron grip of the collar that encircled his neck. His quarters were so cramped that he sat most of the time in order to avail himself of the services of the mirror; but this was an inconvenience that gave him little concern. The worst was over, he reflected, until —

" For the love of Mike! "

That remark was in celebration of the discovery that he possessed every garment of a gentleman save a tie.

He viewed his image with a look of despair. His raiment fitted him astonishingly well, as nearly as he could judge. He had managed to button his collar into place without soiling it. The shirt-front was still immaculate. But no tie!

" You need a nurse," he told himself glumly. " What are you going to do now? "

Yet even at this catastrophe he would not acknowledge himself beaten.

" I suppose it's possible," he muttered, " to go ashore as I am and sandbag a waiter, or even a guest if I can catch one alone. But that has risks, and I don't feel like taking too many to-night. Any kind of a tie would do; I wouldn't be particular. Come! Get clever now and invent something. Remember the wire-cutters! "

Twice he made a search of the pockets of his clothes, faintly hoping that one of them might conceal the article he lacked, but his quest was unrewarded.

" Why does a man have to wear a necktie? " he raged. " And if he feels that he positively must wear one is he really a man? Talk about your slaves to fashion! You never see a necktie on a lady — and you never see a gentleman without one!

" Yes, I said ' gentleman.' Just a while back I was a man, now I'm a gentleman! Being one of those things, I have to have a necktie. I can't see that a man's clothes make anything out of him except a confounded coward."

Speech ceased suddenly as he spied a white object lying under a seat directly in front of him. He reached for it and held it up to the light.

It was a tiny and very thin square of linen, embroidered at the edges. As he brought it close to his eyes he became aware that it exhaled the faintest possible perfume.

" Bless the ladies! " he exclaimed. " One of 'em — I don't know which — has left me a handkerchief. We'll see what can be done."

With careful yet ruthless hands he tore the linen square into four strips of equal width. These he folded once lengthwise. Next he knotted them together, end upon end. The result was, at least in the semidarkness, something that resembled the necktie of a gentleman.

He grinned at himself triumphantly as he fashioned a bow out of the ends, after passing the strip of linen about his neck. There were frayed edges here and there, but they did not count against the general effect. It was a tie!

The boatman rose to his feet and glanced shoreward. Faintly there came across the water the quick, inspiring notes of a fox-trot.

"Time to hurry, I guess," he observed as he slipped forward and set the boat loose from her mooring.

As the *Fifty-Fifty* edged her way gently to the float he stepped out briskly and made the painter fast to a ring. Not until he reached the head of the gangway did he give a thought to a possible difficulty. Then it was forced upon him suddenly.

"Your ticket, sir," said an attendant deferentially, holding out his hand.

"Ticket?"

"Admission is by card, sir."

"Oh — of course." The boatman smiled graciously and waved his hand toward the float. "One of the other gentlemen in my party has the cards. He will be up directly."

The attendant bowed and Sam passed onward. He did not stop to note that the man at the gangway, after a period of reasonable waiting, peered down at the float and discovered it to be quite empty of persons; nor that the same functionary immediately took a few futile steps in the direction whither the lone guest had gone and strained his eyes in an endeavor to locate the man without a card.

Sam had anticipated these things. He had mingled with the trees and was approaching the hotel, not by the broad path, but by a circuitous route across the lawns.

He paused as he neared the broad veranda and studied the throng. It was an interval between dances; some of the guests were descending the steps to the lawn, which was overhung with paper lanterns. He saw no familiar face.

" We'll wait till the band plays," he murmured, " and then we'll give it a try-out."

Furtively his fingers groped their way to the tie and found it bravely in place. He shook out his cuffs, smoothed his shirt-bosom, and examined his glistening pumps. Thoughtfully, even a little anxiously, he stroked his beard. Then —

The band again. The boatman strode forward jauntily and made his way to the crowded porch.

CHAPTER XIV

WHAT THE PAUL JONES DID

ROSALIND had been sitting most of them
out, instead of dancing them. There was
not the least doubt the crowd was "mixed."
Besides, after one experiment with Morton, one with
the Jones boy, and a mere recollection of other dances
with Reggie Williams, Rosalind found that sitting
out was the nearest approach to having a good time.

Incidentally it furnished odd minutes for reflection, for it was possible to despatch her squires upon
errands and thus obtain solitude. Her fertility of
invention, when it came to errands, was quite astonishing; at the fact that all of the errands were
useless, her conscience was pricked not at all.

She was a woman with a problem that challenged
her. Back at the Witherbees' they gave her no
time for cogitation; there seemed to be a universal
obsession that somebody had to entertain her.

And Rosalind was a difficult person to entertain.
She chose her own amusements and she resented
having diversion thrust upon her.

It was not at all a matter of hardship — save to
others — for Rosalind to be exceedingly untractable
and unpleasant, both in manner and speech and the
general loftiness and disdain of her bearing. If
ever there lived a lady who needed, for the good of
her soul and her conduct, to be clubbed briskly on

the head by some conscientious caveman, dragged by the hair to his domicile, and set to pounding corn between two stones, that lady was Rosalind Chalmers.

And she was beginning to wonder if some such proceeding was not actually under way. The caveman, of course, was Sam. She knew he was not a real caveman, even, perhaps, of the kind that possess a veneer of civilization; yet he behaved like one.

His manner toward her was shocking and uncouth, as well as without explanation. He had contrived to involve her — she did not admit any of the contriving to be of her own — in a series of vulgar and embarrassing events; and she felt with a keen degree of uneasiness that he proposed to capitalize her misfortunes or misadventures in a manner as yet undisclosed and therefore peculiarly to be dreaded. Who he was, what he was, even why he was, Rosalind did not know.

Had she been free to ask questions and to conduct a systematic investigation perhaps something might be learned. But necessity, by which she really meant the veiled threats of the boatman himself, bade her be cautious.

In truth, Rosalind for once in her life was timid, although she would have perished rather than acknowledge it, even to herself. It was no physical fear, awakened by a dread of something that might happen to herself. Rather it was a more or less abstract apprehension, yet none the less poignant because of that fact.

It shaped itself into the idea that in some manner, and perhaps at some remote time, something would be done or said or even whispered that would bring into ridicule the Rosalind Chalmers who was known

and recognized only by the fixed and inexorable
standard of Hamersley's " Social Register." Not
for all her wealth and her distinction would she be
unmasked before her fellow denizens of the book!

The hotel-dance, therefore, while it forced her
elbows to touch common clay, had a measure of con-
solation in giving her moments of solitude. She
wanted to grapple with her problem. She did. It
proved elusive and slippery and tireless. Worse, it
grinned at her.

Yet Rosalind was game. Only once had fortitude
failed her, and she blushed with hot shame when she
thought of that unhappy time — the time during
which she sat ten feet above the ground and yielded
to the humiliating weakness of begging for release
from a captivity that resulted directly from her own
curiosity. That was an affair of bitter and venge-
ful memory; she had not even begun to pay off the
smallest fraction of the score.

Tom Witherbee came to claim her. She had the
bad grace to sigh as she rose. She hoped he would
not step on her feet, but she was not optimistic; for
the Jones boy, who would not have been picked by
the casual observer as an awkward person, had displayed the appalling accomplishment of stepping on
both her feet at the same time, and doing it with no
apparent physical effort or acceleration of breath.

They were hurrying swiftly across the floor, Rosalind trying to decide whether Tom Witherbee danced
like a frog or a rabbit, when somebody blew a shrill
whistle. With an abrupt apology she found herself
released by her partner.

Then something horrible happened. She was a
link in an endless chain of persons who had joined

hands and were boisterously whirling in an undulating circle, like children playing "London Bridge."

Rosalind had heard of such things. In some places they called it the Paul Jones; in others it had equally undescriptive names. But by whatever term it was always the same; it meant changing partners every time a fiend blew a whistle — taking pot-luck with the crowd.

Another shrill toot sounded. The men began weaving in and out to the right, the women to the left. Rosalind was driven onward remorselessly by the necessity of saving her heels from being stepped on. She did not look like a lady who enjoyed being among the peasants and humble villagers. Her jaw was set at too grim an angle.

The whistle blew again at an instant when Rosalind's left hand was grasped firmly by one knight of the white shirt-front, while her right had just been seized by another. The signal, she knew, meant another partner. She wavered; it seemed like a chance to escape.

The captor of her left hand whirled about and stretched forth his arms. It was a fatal and short-sighted maneuver, for in doing so he released her fingers. Then with compelling force Rosalind found herself drawn into a firm grip by the person who still retained her right hand. She was dancing again.

It happened so swiftly that her half-formed intention to flee from the dance was never carried into execution. She was angry at herself, at Tom Witherbee, at the whole undignified affair.

And yet — this man could dance! She knew he was a stranger, although she had not even glanced above the second button on his shirt. Beyond doubt he was a vulgarian — one of the countless herd. But he could dance!

For the moment her irritation gave way to surprise. She had not expected this — after Morton and the Jones boy and Tom Witherbee. Here was a man who did not step on her feet, who did not employ her as a ram to batter his way through the swinging crowd, who did not crush her in a bearlike embrace, and who did not persistently fall out of time with the music.

He danced; he was neither a laggard nor a racehorse. He respected the functions of the band. To Rosalind it was like being rescued from a trampling mob and expertly piloted into a path of ease and safety and perpetual rhythm.

A common villager, perhaps; yet she yielded to the temptation. She also danced. And when Rosalind Chalmers really wanted to dance she was capable of attracting the eye and the envy of a Pavlowa. She was even conscious of a pang of regret that it would be so brief, for the fiend with the whistle would soon be playing his killjoy tune. But it was an oasis at least; one tiny, bright spot in a desert of clumsiness.

Rosalind half-closed her eyes and abandoned herself to the sway of the music. She was almost enjoying herself. He was not in her set, of course; yet there was a distinction about his dancing that seemed for the moment to lift him to that exalted plane.

She dreaded the whistle; it meant unknown terrors — perhaps even the Jones boy, who was circling near her with his arms full of a large lady in pink.

The ominous blast sounded.

" Please, if you don't mind —"

Rosalind marveled to find herself speaking, then checked her tongue and flushed.

A second later and she was marveling again, for her partner had understood. They were opposite one of the big French windows that led to the porch. As easily as if the maneuver had been rehearsed they swung through the opening and whirled away from the crowded room.

She glanced back and glimpsed another merry-go-round of couples, fated to be presently resolved into hopelessly mismated pairs. But Rosalind and the man who could truly dance went on and on, down the porch, still in the thrall of the rhythm that was so spirited and compelling.

" Thank you," she said.

He made no answer, save a quick pressure of her fingers. It was this silent acknowledgment of his gratitude that awakened Rosalind. Her fingers had, it is true, been pressed before, when she was taken unaware; but never by a stranger. She now remembered the pedestal she occupied in the world. She glanced upward.

For several seconds her vision remained fixed upon the most extraordinary necktie she had ever seen.

It was filmy and semitransparent. Also, it was ragged, frayed and rumpled. But — and this was its really amazing feature — it was marked with her own exquisitely embroidered monogram!

Her feet halted abruptly. She flung herself backward out of the arms of Sam, the boatman. He was smiling benignly.

" This — this —"

" Has been a great pleasure," he supplied, but the

bow that accompanied the words was slightly satirical.

Rosalind stood gasping and angry.

" You dared! "

" Yes, ma'am."

" You deliberately planned —"

" Sure I planned it. A man's got to do some figur-
ing in this world if he wants to get anything."

She stared at the outraged handkerchief that
graced a neck about which at that moment she would
willingly have passed a rope. This creature had
danced with her. She had been in his arms! And
she had been seen there!

" I had to break into that dance without a partner," he explained lightly. " It was the only way
to get you; to horn in and take a chance. I knew
there wasn't any use asking you for a dance."

Her eyes blazed. Her spirit was raging, yet her
wits had not deserted her. Perhaps they had not
been noticed after all. The room was crowded and
most of the dancers were heavily engrossed with
their own woes. Chance might have been kind; she
would soon know.

Meantime it was an atrocious risk to stand there
talking to him. Yet if she fled she knew not what
the man might do. Probably he would follow.

" I wish to talk with you," she said with sudden
resolution.

" That'll be another pleasure."

" But not here! "

" Well, there's a lot of good talking-places down
on the lawn," he suggested.

She nodded grimly.

" Come along," he said cheerfully. And the

creature offered her his arm. She affected not to notice the insult.

" Better take my arm — ma'am. It's customary."

She walked beside him, but did not touch him.

" We'll look more like a regular couple if you do, ma'am."

Still she paid no heed to his advice. He halted at the top of the steps.

" If you don't take my arm," he announced, " I'll grab you and shoot you right back into that dance, ma'am."

Trembling with anger, she took it.

He led her down the veranda-steps and out among the lantern-lit trees. They walked slowly and in silence for a minute, until Rosalind felt she was safe from possible observers at the hotel.

Then she whipped her hand from his sleeve and drew a pace away from him. Carefully she measured him with a glance which rested longest upon the monogramed tie.

" Now I wish to know exactly what this means," she said sharply.

" It means just what happened," he answered, smiling.

She shook her head. She knew better than that, and she feared even more.

" Is this what you meant — in that note? "

" You mean where I said, ' Just wait '? "

" Yes."

" No, indeed; this is just a sort of extra, thrown in. When I said, ' Just wait ' I meant it. Time's not up yet — just wait."

He grinned.

" Then I demand that you explain what it *does* mean."

" Why, I told you what it meant, ma'am. It meant that I wanted to dance — with you."

" Never! "

" But you're unjust to yourself. Honest, that's exactly what I came for, and it's exactly what I've done. And if you'll only let me have one more dance — a hesitation — I'll do almost anything in the world for you. Yes, I'll give you a free ride in my launch."

Rosalind shuddered.

" You came here for another purpose," she said.

" I see it's no use trying to make you believe," sighed Sam.

" You will be thrown out if the servants find you."

" That's a risk, of course. But it's worth it — for a dance, ma'am."

" You may even be arrested."

" That's possible, too — but I've had one dance anyway."

" I shall not permit you," she went on, ignoring him, " to do what you came here to do."

" Which is —"

" To rob people! "

The boatman stared at her, then broke into a laugh.

" You are here disguised — made up as a guest."

" Wrong, ma'am," he assured her. " I'm a man — made up as a gentleman."

" You came here to steal. You know it! "

" Raffles, eh? That's not a bad idea now. I

hadn't thought of it; honest I hadn't.   But now you
propose it —"

"I didn't!"

"But you certainly did, ma'am. You've put the
idea into my head when I hadn't the least notion of
it.   That makes you a sort of —"

"Stop!"

He shrugged resignedly.

"You're always snapping me up with that word,"
he complained.   "You go and hand me an idea and
then when I get ready to do something with it you
tell me to stop."

"Will you tell me why you persist — in annoy-
ing me?"

"Do I?   Why, I didn't think you were annoyed
at all, back there while we were dancing.   You even
asked me not to turn you back into the scramble
again, but to keep on as your partner."

"I never!   You —"

"That's what you started to ask anyhow, ma'am.
Because you remember you thanked me for doing
it."

She flushed crimson.

"But I intended to do it anyway," he added complacently.   "I wasn't going to lose a chance like
that.   They don't come often.   I knew the minute
I laid eyes on you that you could dance."

She hastily changed the subject.

"My handkerchief — where did you get it?"
she demanded.

"Found it in my boat; lucky of me, too.   I'd forgotten a tie.   How does it look?"

Rosalind was beginning to sense the futility of
the interview.   She was rapidly losing control of

it. Yet she was anxious to prevent the man from carrying out his very obvious purpose. Robberies among the guests might entail risks — for her. It was scarcely possible that nobody had seen her in the company of the boatman.

As she studied him, however, she admitted to herself that he might not have been recognized. He was very different in appearance now. But aside from the possibility that none save herself had paid attention to him was his evident and persistent purpose to link her misfortunes with his misdeeds. She had the sensation of a captive held for ransom, yet kept in ignorance of what the ransom might be.

" You *must* go away," she told him firmly.

" Can't, ma'am. I've got a passenger to ferry."

" You must leave the grounds; go back to your boat."

" And I was just beginning to have a good time," he said ruefully, surveying his costume.

" I will pay you if you will go away."

" I haven't asked you to. I — Here comes Reggy! "

Rosalind uttered a little cry and turned swiftly. The bulky figure of Reginald Williams was moving toward them.

" I'll hide," said the boatman cheerfully. " Try and save another dance, will you? Don't forget."

He slipped away from her and disappeared behind a thick clump of shrubbery. A moment later Reginald arrived.

" I've been looking all over for you, Rosalind," he exclaimed. " What are you doing out here? "

" I wanted some air."

" And you came alone? "

" Yes — alone."

" Tom Witherbee was looking all over for you at the end of that last dance," said Reggy petulantly. " You're not treating any of us decently to-night, Rosalind. First you won't dance, then you run away."

" I didn't wish to come in the first place."

" But you always used to dance. You used to dance with me, too. I know I'm not much good at it, but — oh, hang it, Rosalind! I'm having a rotten time. There isn't a girl in the whole crowd that'll dance with me. They all ask me to please sit down and talk to them, and they look at me as if there was something the matter with me."

" Perhaps you're not popular, Reggy," suggested Rosalind a little viciously.

" That worries me a lot so far as the rest of the crowd are concerned. But if I could only seem to be a little more popular with you —"

" Please don't start that again."

" I'm never going to stop it! Look here, Rosalind, it's not fair! Why, you won't even wear that bracelet, although you said you were crazy over it."

Rosalind bit her lip and remained silent.

" I haven't said anything about it before," continued Reggy grumblingly. " It seemed sort of kiddish to get sore. But you wore it once and I don't see why you can't wear it now. You don't have to be engaged to me to do that; it's not like wearing a ring. Why won't you wear it? "

" Why, I —"

Rosalind faltered in speech, then made a little gesture of annoyance.

" There's not another bracelet like it in the world,"
he went on.   " It was just made for you."

" It was made for a mummy," corrected Rosalind.

" She wasn't a mummy — then.   She was a live
wire.   I'll bet she wore it every day she took a walk
around the pyramids.   And don't forget — she was
a princess, Rosalind."

" I haven't forgotten it; you won't let me.   Besides, it was second hand."

That was a brutal thing for Rosalind Chalmers to
say, but she was in a savage and exasperated mood.
She was far more disturbed over the absence of the
bracelet than Reggy himself, but she could neither
betray nor explain that fact.   She would have given
a small slice of her ample fortune if it were only
upon her arm at that moment.

" Second hand! " snorted Reggy.   " Second hand
because a princess wore it?   That's the first time you
ever pulled that stuff on me."

" Reggy! "

" Oh, well, those are my sentiments at any rate.
Perhaps they're not very elegantly expressed.   But
honestly, Rosalind, I'm sore.   I think you might
wear it once in a while.   Will you wear something
else for me, if I get it for you?   A ring? "

" Oh, don't begin again, Reggy."

" I'm just picking up where I left off.   Rosalind,
why won't you marry me? "

" Because I do not choose to."

" But you know I love you."

Rosalind nodded her head wearily.

" So why not? " he persisted.

" Reggy, you are positively dense," she said hopelessly. " Am I to marry a man just because he loves me ? Suppose I do not love him."

" Well, you can come as near to loving me as you can anybody, I guess.   I wouldn't expect you to love me a great deal.   I don't think you're that kind."

" You mean, I suppose," she said coldly, " that I am incapable of affection."

" Oh, come; not like that, you know," broke in Reggy stumblingly.   " But — well —   Oh, I can't put it the way it ought to be put, Rosalind.   Of course you *could* love anybody, if you wanted to. But what I mean is, that — you're not apt to."

" Thank you for making it so clear, Reggy."

" And I'd be willing to get along with just — just —"

" Just toleration, I imagine."

" Yes, toleration ! " he blurted.   " So long as it was from you."

" Well, I'm not in a tolerant mood at present," said Rosalind.   " Will you take me back to the hotel ? "

" Will you dance with me ? "

" I think not."

" Will you wear the bracelet then ? "

" Well — perhaps."

As they moved away the boatman stepped from his hiding-place.

" Bracelet," he muttered.   " That's funny now. I wonder if it could be the one."

CHAPTER XV

HE waited until Rosalind and her gloomy suitor passed from view, then made for the hotel by another entrance. The door by which he obtained access to the building led into a broad lobby, where superior clerks yawned behind a counter that resembled a bar, and where there was a news-stand, also other details of hotel-equipment arranged with a view to reducing the amount of Federal reserve in individual depositaries.

Sam walked through the lobby at a casual pace. He was at ease with a cigarette between his lips. The make-up had been tested and had not yet buckled under the strain. None save Rosalind had paid the least attention to the tie, which argued powerfully for its propriety.

At the farther end of the lobby was a great glass case, supported upon a table. Within the case were many things. The boatman viewed them deliberately.

The variety was rather extraordinary. There were things made of leather, of linen, of silk, of worsted, of metal and of stone; things that were old, others that were middle-aged, still others that were palpably new; things that were ugly, arrayed beside things that were pretty; big things, little things, nondescript things. Some of them bore labels; others presented themselves to the eye without explanation or excuse.

He lingered at one end of the case for a full minute, but his vision did not penetrate the transparency of the glass. It was concerned wholly with the case itself — its joints, its locks, its sliding doors.

Then his glance roved about the lobby. He counted the number of persons that crossed it within a given interval and the directions in which they went, as well as those from which they came. He noted the varying degrees of occupation among the clerks, the news-stand girl, the flower-stand girl, the porters and the bell-boys. He studied the lights, the doorways, and the windows. He made a mental note of distances and directions.

After that he strolled lazily back to the porch, where he made a topographical inspection that involved the smoking of an entire cigarette.

"Now for the master mechanic," he said as he moved along the veranda in the direction of the dancing-room.

But the master mechanic was busy, quite beyond his reach. She was one of a group gathered about the portly figure of Mr. Davidson and she was listening to his words.

"It's been done again!" affirmed Mr. Davidson with gestures. "And the patrol is supposed to be on the job! Right under the noses of James and Eliza, too! And here I am, going away to-night! I'll not stand for it."

Rosalind signaled to Polly Dawson, and Polly invented a reason for leading Reggy Williams beyond ear-shot. For Reggy's heart must be subjected to no stresses other than those that might incidentally be imposed by the charms of Polly herself.

"Anything gone this time?" asked Tom Witherbee.

"Clothes!" exploded Mr. Davidson. "My room ransacked, Billy's room turned topsyturvy, bureau drawers dumped out on the floor and all that sort of thing."

"But when?"

"Since we came up here, of course! I had to send the boat back for my grips. I'm going away to-night and I forgot 'em. And then they saw what happened. A fine mess! I'd like to know what good it did to organize. He slipped right in under their noses and slipped out again."

"And no clue?"

"Clue —"

Mr. Davidson checked the word that was intended to follow immediately thereafter and glared at the Jones boy, who was the questioner.

"Clue!" he said, beginning afresh. "I've quit looking for clues. I'm looking for results. And I can get bunches of one and none of the other. And here I am, headed for Denver to-night, and nobody but a pack of fool servants to look after the place. I suppose the island'll be gone when I get back."

"It's appalling," said Marjorie Winter.

"You're right, ma'am," declared Mr. Davidson truculently. "It's worse than appalling. It's hell! Excuse me. But that's what it is."

"Couldn't you get detectives?"

"Detectives my eye! I never knew one yet that could detect anything except an expense-account. No, sir! I've sent for Billy."

"His nephew, Billy Kellogg," explained Mrs. Witherbee in a whisper to Rosalind. "The one that was sent away."

"Hated to do it, too," said Mr. Davidson. "But something had to be done. Wired down to Hastings & Hatch a little while ago to ship him up here the first thing to-morrow. Somebody's got to sit on the lid while I'm gone.

"He's learned some sense, I hear. Got a report only this morning. Sticking to his job like a nailer; that's why I hate to pull him off it. But I'll ship him back — the young rascal! I'll not spoil him again. Just as soon as I can get back from Denver, off he goes to the bank again."

"You think he'll be able to manage?" ventured Mrs. Witherbee.

She had never met Billy Kellogg in the flesh, but had heard reports.

"He'll manage or I'll break his neck," said Mr. Davidson savagely. "And I guess I won't have to do that either. Why, ma'am, he's a changed person, so Hastings & Hatch tell me. On the job at eight-thirty every morning, half an hour for lunch, sticking to it till five and six o'clock every night. A regular horse for work, ma'am! Hang it if I don't think he's earned a vacation — the scoundrel!"

Rosalind strolled away from the group as Mr. Davidson prepared to make his departure for Clayton. She wondered if the boatman would have the hardihood to show himself again in his stolen raiment.

Slow but persistent footfalls behind her warned her that she was being followed. Finally she turned and beheld Mr. Morton.

"Strolling?" he asked in vacuous tones.

She answered with a nod that was not meant to encourage.

"I might go along?" he suggested.

"You might, I suppose."

Rosalind once more sought the cool softness of the grass underfoot, with the tall and evidently preoccupied Englishman at her elbow.

"Oh, I say, Miss Chalmers," he exclaimed abruptly after they had walked in silence for several minutes.

"Yes?"

"Would you — er — do you think you could — er — marry me?"

Rosalind eyed him with frank astonishment. A smile trembled on her lips, but she did not allow it to blossom.

"I — er — love you tremendously, you know, Miss Chalmers."

"Really?"

"Oh, as sure as you live. Do you think you could, you know?"

"I'm afraid I neither would nor could, Mr. Morton," she said placidly.

"Hum! Ha! By Jove, but that's beastly hard luck, Miss Chalmers!"

Rosalind hovered between offense and amusement. She did not know whether the eighteenth or the nineteenth offer was a compliment or otherwise. She compromised by admitting to herself that she was bored.

"Rotten luck," he repeated musingly, stroking his yellow mustache.

"You speak as if it were a game of chance."

"I — er — Oh, I beg your pardon. No offense whatever intended — really. Only you see these things go awfully hard with a fellow, Miss Chalmers."

"After less than a week's acquaintance?"

"Ah, but you know I'm an impetuous chap. That's the worst of it."

Rosalind laughed in spite of her efforts to check the outburst. He did not appear to notice it, so wholly was he engrossed with his own misfortune — and his mustache.

"Then I suppose there's no hope?"

"Oh, none whatever!"

"Thanks awfully, you know. It's downright good of you to take it in such a sporting way."

"I'm — I'm trying to bear it," she said, choking.

With a deep bow Mr. Morton excused himself and stalked silently away. Rosalind looked after him, shaking with mirth.

"That makes the score two to-night," remarked a voice from behind her.

She turned quickly. The boatman had appeared as if by magic.

"Eavesdropper!" she said contemptuously.

"Couldn't help it the first time," he explained. "Had to hide from Reggy. Do you always turn him down that way?"

She ignored the question.

"As for the second case," added Sam, jerking his finger in the direction of the departing Englishman, "I'll admit I followed you. But it wasn't for the purpose of overhearing a man get his death-sentence. I wanted to see you about something."

"I don't propose to be annoyed by you any further."

"It's something important, ma'am."

As she started to walk toward the hotel he whispered a single word:

"*Bracelet!*"

Rosalind halted in her tracks.

"I thought that would stop you," he nodded.

"What do you know about a bracelet?" she demanded.

"I've seen one."

"Where?"

He looked mysterious and answered her with a question:

"Do you want me to show it to you?"

"You mean — *my* bracelet?"

"A sort of hand-me-down bracelet," he grinned.

"A gold bracelet, carved —"

"One that they burglared a tomb for, perhaps, ma'am."

Rosalind was afire with excitement.

"Where did you see this thing? What do you mean? Have you — stolen it?"

"No, indeed. I haven't laid a finger on it, ma'am. But I wouldn't be surprised if I'd laid eyes on it — the one that Reggy was sore about."

Rosalind thought swiftly. Neither Gertrude nor Polly was wearing it that evening, she remembered. Where was it? She had a numbing sense of misgiving.

"Show it to me," she commanded.

"Of course it's possible I've made a mistake, ma'am, but —"

"Where is it?"

"Perhaps it's in the hotel."

"Who is wearing it?"

" Nobody."

" Is it in your pocket? " suspiciously.

The boatman laughed.

" I told you I hadn't touched it," he said.

Rosalind was losing control of her little trifle of patience.

" Take me to it! " she said peremptorily.

He led the way toward the veranda. She followed as far as the steps, then halted. Sam divined the cause of her hesitation. He laughed once more good-naturedly.

" I see you don't want to take another chance with me in there," he remarked, pointing. " In a way I don't blame you. That's a mighty catchy little thing the band's playing. I've almost a mind to take a dance in payment. But we'll postpone that, ma'am.

" Now, do you see that second doorway? No; the second to the right. It's the office entrance. Go through it and walk straight back until you reach the rear of the lobby. You'll see a glass case there. Take a look at some of the things in it."

She started swiftly up the steps.

" I'll be out here among the trees," he called after her. " I've got an idea you'll want to see me again."

Rosalind hurried along the porch and entered the second doorway to the right. Just beyond the threshold she paused and her glance swept the lobby. Yes, there was a glass case at the farther end. She stepped forward without further hesitation.

There, its aristocratic beauty undimmed by the cheap, gaudy gew-gaws that hedged it about, lay her bracelet!

She was too bewildered even to gasp, but stood

rigid as a statue, staring. Her bracelet — lying in the midst of a tawdry collection of jewelry, silver-ware, and brass ornaments!

What did it mean? How did it get there?

As she stood in awful fascination, a bell-boy approached.

"The sale is to-morrow afternoon, ma'am," he said.

"The sale!"

Rosalind spoke so explosively that the boy was startled.

"Yes, ma'am; at three o'clock. There's the sign."

He pointed to a placard that rested on the top of the case. She read:

"These beautiful articles in this case, donated through a spirit of humanity by residents and summer visitors at the islands, will be sold at three o'clock to-morrow afternoon for the benefit of the war sufferers in Europe.

"If you cannot add your mite to the collection, you are cordially invited to attend the sale and become a purchaser, and incidentally a helper in a noble cause.

"Mr. Heinrich Schmidt of Chicago has kindly consented to act as auctioneer."

Rosalind clutched at something to steady herself and found that she was grasping the sleeve of the bell-boy.

"Ouch, ma'am!" he exclaimed as her fingers bit sharply into his arm. "Would you like a glass of water, ma'am?"

She released her victim and shook her head. The boy saluted and went back to his bench.

Horror of horrors! And the Witherbees had done this thing! Her bracelet — that dull circlet of gold that once girdled the arm of a princess of Egypt — that strange and beautiful bauble that had not its match in the whole world — was to be vulgarly hawked to a rabble by a grain-broker named Schmidt who came from Chicago!

The picture that flashed into her mind made her shudder with disgust. There would be a bargain-counter rush, a noisy clamor of voices shouting offers — putting a price on *her* bracelet! And it would be held aloft in the fat, ruthless hand of Schmidt, dangled before the eyes of a mob, while he goaded them to bid higher and higher!

" Never! " she muttered through clenched teeth.

Valiant resolution! Yet in the same instant she realized her impotence to carry it into effect. The case was securely locked. Besides, there were other persons in the lobby. She felt sure at the very least that the bell-boy was watching her.

She could summon the Witherbees, of course — they who had done this awful thing — but that meant confessions and complications — and ridicule!

She might come to-morrow and buy her own bracelet, rub elbows with a scrambling and motley crowd, and match her lungs and her purse against the hardiest of them. But her very soul shrank from that; she knew that she could not do it. Better never see the bracelet again.

Yet Rosalind would not for an instant yield weakly to what seemed the inevitable and permanent loss of her dearly prized property. She was brimming with fight, even though she did not know how to fight, or whom."

"I'll get it!" she whispered grimly.   "I'll get it if I have to burn down the hotel."

As she glanced helplessly about her, her eyes met those of Reggy Williams, approaching from the doorway that led to the ballroom.

Here was fresh dismay. Reggy could not — must not — look into that fateful showcase! He was coming to her swiftly, and Rosalind, pulling herself together sharply, advanced to meet him.

"What's the attraction?" he asked, looking over her shoulder.

"Oh, nothing.   Let's go out on the porch."

"But what's the stuff in the glass case?" he persisted, trying to dodge past her.

She grasped him firmly by the arm.

"Please take me outside, Reggy," she said.   "I want some air. Nothing there but some things they're going to sell for the Belgians. They're — not interesting."

It was Rosalind who took Reggy outside, rather than Reggy who assisted Rosalind. She did it with an expedition and a determination that puzzled him, particularly when, having walked him to the farther end of the porch, she turned him over to Polly Dawson with a severe injunction — whispered — to make him sit down and keep quiet for half an hour.

Then with a swift seizure of opportunity Rosalind escaped to the lawn and walked out among the trees, stern purpose in her heart and a whirl of desperate ideas in her brain. She was looking for Sam!

CHAPTER XVI

ROUGH STUFF

"YOU'RE quite sure it belongs to you?" asked Sam, his scrutiny of Rosalind's face pointed to the verge of annoyance.

"I have said so," she answered with finality.

A fifteen-minute conversation had preceded.

"It's not the kind of a job I'd pick of my own choosing," he remarked reflectively.

"I tell you, it *must* be done!"

"Why not give me a handful of money and let me go in to-morrow and buy it?"

"No! It's mine!"

"Why not claim it, then?"

"I cannot. I —"

He waited patiently for the remainder of the sentence.

"Oh, what is the use of explaining?" she exclaimed irritably. "The point is, it belongs to me. I must have it. I *will* have it! Why should you haggle over the question as to the real owner — after what you have done?"

"Which is to say —"

"Come," said Rosalind. "You and I have no need to beat about the bush in this matter. You are perfectly well aware that I know what you are. I'm not blind, or even dense."

"No, ma'am," he said meekly enough.

"The point is, you know how to do it."

194

" I suppose that's a compliment."

" Judge it as you please. It may be a compliment or a reproach. I'm not talking about the ethics of the matter, I'm talking about results."

" Well, what is there in it for me ? " he demanded bluntly.

" I'll pay you ! "

" How much ? "

" Why — almost anything you ask."

" You don't drive a very sharp bargain, ma'am," he commented.

" I am not accustomed to dealing with —"

" Thieves ? "

Rosalind nodded.

" Well, it might be done," he admitted slowly. " But it has risks. And it can't be done alone."

" It will be necessary for you to have help ? "

" Yes ! that's certain. I'll need you, in fact."

Rosalind evinced no hesitation. She was thinking only of her bracelet, in the winning of which she was willing to burn all bridges.

" Very well; what do you want me to do ? "

The boatman eyed her curiously.

" It depends," he answered, " on just what we figure to do. Of course, we could crack the case and make a run for it. But that's too simple to get away with. No chance.

" We could get a crowd into the lobby perhaps, and then try it. That's a little better. Or we might be able to manage to get everybody out of the lobby, even the clerks, and make a stab at it that way. I'm not very strong for that, either."

" Couldn't you wait until the hotel was closed? " asked Rosalind.

It did not occur to her for an instant that she was plotting against the criminal law.

He shook his head, after appearing to consider the suggestion.

"There's always a bell-hop on duty," he said. "I don't see how it could be done, unless we both hang around until after the crowd is gone. And I suppose you've got to go home with your people."

"That's true," she admitted.

"No," said the boatman. "If it's going to be done at all it must be pulled off while the crowd is still here. That's a cinch. I may be willing to take a chance after hours somewhere else, but not here. It seems to me if we're going to get that bracelet we've got to make a different sort of play. How about stealing the whole show-case?"

Rosalind stared.

"That is, stealing it for a while," he continued. "I don't mean carting all that truck away; we wouldn't know what to do with it. Besides, most of it isn't worth anything. You don't happen to be wearing a badge, do you?"

"A badge?"

"One of those red-and-gold affairs that say something about the Belgians."

"Of course not."

"We need a couple," he reflected. "Will you get them?"

"Where?"

"Well, a lot of the men are wearing them. I've seen a few on the women, too. You might go in and dance a couple of times."

"You mean —"

The boatman nodded.

" Impossible ! "

" Not a bit, ma'am, if you'll only dance the way you did with me. You can make a man forget everything else except his feet. It'll be dead easy. He'll be in a trance. All you do when you've got him under the influence is to cop his badge. And be sure to get two; that means two dances."

Rosalind was unconvinced.

" Tell me more," she commanded.

For another five minutes the boatman talked earnestly. She hesitated doubtfully and shook her head several times, yet she listened. When the wavering instants came upon her she thought of the bracelet. Whenever she remembered that fresh resolution reenforced her soul.

" It is despicable — hateful ! " she said.

" But it's reasonably sure," he supplemented.

" And then — if I get them ? "

" Meet me at the end of the porch."

She hesitated.

" Of course, it really belongs to me," she remarked parenthetically.

Sam chuckled.

" Now you're getting back to the morals of it. That won't get you anything, ma'am."

" But —"

" Take the bull outside and shoot it," he interrupted tersely. " What difference does it make whether you own it or not ? Maybe you do; perhaps you don't. I'm not asking you to produce any title-deeds. The point to aim at is — get the bracelet !

" It may belong to the Queen of England for all I know. I don't think you'd be particular if it did,

provided you wanted it. You asked me to go shares
on this job —"

"I didn't!"

"I guess that's right, too. You wanted me to do
it alone. That's worse because you were sticking all
the chances on me. But so far as stealing it goes,
you'll have to admit that I didn't suggest it. I only
told you where the thing was. Then you make a
proposition to hire me."

She flushed, but remained silent.

"So it becomes a fifty-fifty deal," he concluded.

Rosalind thought of the name of the boatman's
launch. It assumed a new significance.

"So it's up to you to get those two badges and get
'em quick," he declared bruskly. "I don't care how;
only I suggested a way. If you can think of a better
one, go to it."

Rosalind compressed her lips and started toward
the hotel.

"Any time you get cold feet," he advised, "just
remember the bracelet."

It was superfluous advice. There was no fear
she would forget it. It constituted her whole sus-
taining motive.

Three dances went by, and the boatman still
waited under the trees. The music had heralded a
fourth when he sighted a tall, slim figure in white
approaching with quick steps.

"Here they are," said Rosalind shortly.

She thrust two red-and-gold badges into his hand
so roughly that the pins pricked him.

"It took you three dances," he grumbled as he
sucked one of his fingers.

"Well, I got them!" she exclaimed fiercely. "Now let me see you do something."

For answer, he coolly pinned one of the badges against her snow-white gown and stepped back to study the result.

"Now we belong," he commented as he affixed the second badge to the lapel of his coat. "Of course, it makes us just like common folks, but we can't be particular, considering what we're after. Did your partners happen to notice that they'd been frisked?"

Rosalind forbore to answer; she was outraged and incensed.

"Remember, now!" he cautioned. "We're both on the committee. What we say goes. And if you try to run out on me, look out, ma'am."

Her figure stiffened perceptibly.

"Not afraid?" he asked.

"I'm rather inclined to believe that you are," said Rosalind coldly.

"Come on, then," said the boatman.

Together they walked into the lobby of the hotel. All of the dancers were elsewhere, but the clerks and the bell-boys were in their accustomed places. Across the lobby, their red badges proclaiming ostentatious sympathy with a war-stricken hemisphere, the boatman and Rosalind Chalmers made their way at a deliberate pace. There was a flush in her cheeks — not of guilt, but of shame. If any one should see!

"Loosen up a little," he cautioned in a whisper. "Act human. Remember you're just common folks now. Smile at me; you're not headed for a funeral. That's better; that's more natural."

They paused in front of the glass case. For a second time Rosalind's glance rested upon her bracelet. The sight filled her with new courage.

Sam turned and beckoned authoritatively toward a uniformed youth who lolled on a bench.

" Yes, sir," said the boy as he advanced and saluted.

" Get some of the other boys or some porters. We want this case moved," he said briskly.

The boy eyed him doubtfully.

" It's to be taken into the ballroom, isn't it? " inquired the boatman, turning to Rosalind.

" Of course," she answered.

" It's getting no display here at all," said Sam, turning to the boy. " The committee wants it where the guests can see it. Hurry up, now. Get some boys."

" I'll speak to the manager," said the bell-hop.

" Mr. Saunders? No need; I've already spoken to him. And he said to make you boys jump. Incidentally, there's half a dollar apiece in it for you. Step lively! "

The boy was galvanized. He made a swift gesture to a uniformed group on the other side of the lobby, and was joined by four other boys.

" Now, boys," explained the boatman, " this case is to be moved into the ballroom. We want it to get a little advertising. You must be very careful with it."

The five boys nodded and ranged themselves about the table.

" You'll see why you must be careful if you look inside," continued Sam. " There's a lot of valuable stuff in there, boys — stuff that can be broken if it's

handled roughly. Stuff that might be lost, too —
and couldn't be replaced.

"See that pair of earrings? They'll sell for fifty
dollars, easy. See those brass candlesticks?
They're worth twenty-five. And if there wasn't anything else in the case, that bracelet is enough to make
you careful. It's worth a hundred at the very least;
perhaps five hundred. Now, do you understand?"

The five boys were staring in fascination at the
magic bauble. The boatman made a swift scrutiny
of their faces.

To Rosalind his harangue was without meaning.
She tapped one foot restlessly upon the floor and
looked about her.

"Well, if you're sure you're not going to drop
it, grab hold," advised the boatman.

The captain boy and his four assistants laid hold
of the case and raised it gingerly from the table.

"Which way, sir?"

"By way of the porch," said Sam. "Careful,
now! I'm responsible for this stuff, and I'd hate to
have to replace some of it — especially that bracelet.
That's it; steady! Take it easy."

The five boys moved slowly across the lobby to the
main entrance, clinging grimly to the glazed box that
contained so many wonderful trinkets. Their eyes,
hitherto incurious concerning its contents, were now
fascinated.

"Nothing like a little judicious barking," whispered the boatman to Rosalind as they followed in
the rear of the procession.

The owner of the bracelet was mystified. Something, she knew, had not been confided to her. But
there was no time to demand an explanation.

Out upon the porch the burden-bearers, breathing rapidly, turned in the direction indicated by Sam, and began a laborious journey between tables and chairs.

"Take it slowly," cautioned the boatman. "There's no hurry."

"If we don't hurry, we'll have to set it down!" gasped the captain. "It's heavy!"

"Tired, eh? Well, take a rest. No use running a chance of dropping it. Here — not that way! Tilt the end of it up on the rail. There! Now ease up on it. That's it. Take a breathing-spell."

The show-case lay balanced across the railing of the veranda, while five boys recovered breath. One of them steadied it with a hand, while four mopped their brows. Sam bent over the gaudy display beneath the glass, and seemed to be talking to himself.

"Good stuff, some of that. It ought to sell high. I wouldn't mind bidding on that brooch myself. But the bracelet — whew! That's going high, I'll bet. Why, I know a dealer —"

The boatman's foot slipped and he lurched heavily against the case. There was a warning cry from the boy who balanced it upon its precarious perch, echoed by a sharp exclamation from Rosalind as the case upended and slid gently over the railing. An instant later it landed with a jingling crash on the gravel path, six feet below.

Sam swore fervently at his own carelessness.

"Quick!" he commanded. "Get down here, you, and pick up the stuff!"

Five boys scrambled over the railing and leaped to the ground. Rosalind, almost in a frenzy of solicitude for her precarious property, started to run toward the nearest steps. She was pulled back.

"S-sh! Stay here!" commanded the boatman. "Watch!"

He leaned over the railing and looked down upon the wreckage, amid which his uniformed helpers were already on their knees, heedless of broken glass and intent only upon retrieving the treasures that had come such a melancholy cropper.

Bit by bit they rescued the miscellaneous donations to the cause of Belgian relief. Bit by bit they tossed aside the broken glass and piled in a loose heap the gaudy gifts that had been so tenderly guarded.

"Watch!" repeated Sam in a whisper.

Rosalind watched, but she was still bewildered. A moment later her lips parted and her eyes widened with alarm.

"Keep still!" cautioned her companion. "I saw it, too. It's the black-haired one, isn't it?"

She nodded.

"That's the way I made it. I spotted him back in the lobby," said the boatman in a low tone. "Leave him to me."

"But another one — that one "— she pointed — "has a ring, and I think —"

"Hush! What do you care? It's the one with the black hair for us."

A minute later the captain looked up at the watchers.

"We've got it all picked up, sir," he said. "What'll we do with it?"

"Carry it back to the lobby," said the boatman. "It was my fault; I'll explain how it happened. We'll see if we can get another case."

"Go get an omnibus tray," ordered the head bell-
boy.

A uniformed youth with black hair detached himself from the group and hurried to obey. But he
did not move in the direction of the dining-room.
Instead, having ascended to the porch, he headed in
an opposite direction and made off at a brisk pace.

"I'll attend to him," said the boatman hurriedly
to Rosalind. "It's all right. Beat it, you! Take
off that badge and make yourself scarce. That's
what I'm going to do as soon as I interview our en-
terprising young friend. See you to-morrow, maybe.
Don't worry — pal."

He was gone down the porch. Rosalind looked
after him doubtfully. Then, with a swift movement, she tore the red badge from her dress, concealed it in her hand, and moved off in an opposite
direction.

There was nothing more to be done save escape.
The enterprise was on the knees of the gods. Only
one thing was certain — Mr. Schmidt, of Chicago,
would never desecrate the property of a princess.

In a dark angle of the porch a wriggling boy in
uniform was pinned against the wall by a sinewy
hand that grasped his shoulder none too gently.

"Fork it out!" hissed the boatman.

"I — I —"

"You little crook, I saw you! Come on! Kick
in with it!"

"But I didn't mean — honest!"

"Produce! I don't care what you meant. I saw
you pipe it, you young burglar! Ah — I thought
so!"

The boatman held a heavy yet flexible object close to his eyes to make sure. Then he slipped it into his pocket.

" If I catch you around this hotel again it'll be you for the lockup! " he growled as he swung the youth away from the wall and held him at arm's length.

Then the bell-boy was booted off into the gloom.

The boatman waited until the sound of terrified footsteps faded away. He laughed, a second later, as he vaulted the railing to the sod beneath and vanished among the trees on the darkest part of the lawn.

CHAPTER XVII

THICKENING MYSTERY

THE Witherbee yacht was nearing Clayton, with Rosalind as its only passenger. Principally, its errand was to meet William Kissam Kellogg, the nephew who had been summoned so peremptorily from his banking career in New York to take charge of the Davidson place.

Although the Witherbees were not acquainted with the young man, they had volunteered to take charge of his comfort and entertainment while his uncle was in the West. He was arriving on a midday train.

Rosalind was going shopping, she told Mrs. Witherbee. If she was also seeking temporary escape from a household where she found herself somewhat bored, her shopping errands were none the less *bona fide*. And if, further, she had a certain curiosity concerning Billy Kellogg, even a proper regard for the truth did not require her to say so, for she really had things to buy.

There had been less commotion over the exploit of the glass case than either she or the boatman expected. Thus far, it passed for a mishap. The fact that none of the bell-boys was able to point out the two badge-wearing conspirators, because of their disappearance, occasioned no unusual comment, for there were so many committee-members.

Nor did it appear that anybody possessed an inventory of what the glass case contained. As for the boy who did exactly what Sam expected him to do, there was nothing to be feared in that quarter. He was a frightened and chastened youth.

Rosalind had not yet recovered her bracelet, but, curiously perhaps, she found more comfort in the reflection that it was in the hands of a burglar than she would had it remained to be sold by the volunteer auctioneer from Chicago. To make sure that her conscience would not trouble her, she contributed a liberal cash donation to the Belgian fund.

Just when and how the boatman would deliver her property she had not been informed; but, although she was still undecided as to whether his major profession was that of spy, smuggler, or thief, or whether he skilfully combined all three vocations, she had a rather illogical yet firmly grounded belief that the time was not distant when her bracelet would again be clasped upon her arm.

Her shopping-tour in Clayton concerned itself mainly with the purchase of postage stamps. She maintained a furtive watch for Sam, but got no sight of him, nor did she see his boat at any of the wharfs. When she returned to the Witherbee yacht the new passenger was aboard.

He was sitting forward, under an awning, chewing an unlighted cigar and shifting his feet restlessly as he glanced about him. Rosalind was disappointed; he was not at all as she had imagined him. He was short and chunky, with a tendency to flesh lamentable in one so young. He did not look in the least devilish.

"He's as meek as the *White Knight*," thought

Rosalind as she studied him. " The reformation
must be very great."

He did not see her until she was close to him,
and then it was to greet her with a startled leap from
his chair and an embarrassed scrutiny.

" Mr. Kellogg, I believe ? "

" Why — eh ? "

" You are Mr. Kellogg, whom the Witherbees are
expecting ? "

" Certainly; of course. I beg your pardon."

Rosalind smiled. Evidently he was one of the
difficult kind.

" I am Miss Chalmers," extending her cool fingers
to him.

He shook hands nervously.

" You got Mr. Witherbee's telegram aboard the
train ? "

" Oh, yes; I got it. Very kind of him, too."

" They thought it would be rather lonely for you
over at your own island, while Mr. Davidson is
away, with none but the servants there."

" It would, it would," he assented quickly.

" So I am to bring you down to Mr. Witherbee's,
where he hopes you will become his guest for as long
a period as you find it agreeable. If it is necessary
for you to be over at your own island at night, it is
only a few minutes' run in the launch."

" I'm — I'm not sure it will be necessary at all,"
he broke in earnestly.

Rosalind was faintly puzzled. She could not understand Mr. Davidson's supreme confidence in this
nephew as a protector of his island home. He did
not seem in the smallest degree anxious for the
task.

"You have heard about all the trouble, of course?"

"Er — what?"

"About the burglars and the smuggling and so forth?"

"Oh, yes — yes! But my uncle didn't give any details. He's — he's gone, I suppose?"

There was anxiety in his voice that did not escape her. Rosalind concluded that Billy Kellogg was very much afraid of his uncle.

"He's well on his way to Denver by this time," she assured him. "He has been speaking very well of you, Mr. Kellogg."

"Yes?"

"Indeed, yes! He has told us frequently about your success in New York."

"Has he? Good of him, I'm sure."

"He was reluctant to take you from your work," she continued, determined, if it were possible, to put this young man at his ease. "He felt that, perhaps, you would not want to come."

"I didn't!" he answered explosively.

Rosalind studied him in silence.

"You find banking — interesting?"

"Tremendously!"

"That's odd!" she said before she thought.

"How's that? What?"

"I beg your pardon," said Rosalind. "I didn't mean it exactly that way. Only — Well, you know, we've heard about you, Mr. Kellogg, and we rather pictured a young man who wouldn't be particularly absorbed by anything· so serious and important as running a bank."

He blushed vividly.

"I hope I haven't been clumsy in alluding to anything unpleasant," she went on quickly. "I didn't intend —"

"Oh, not at all; it's all right, I assure you. I don't mind. Only — I've changed; that's all."

"Were you very wicked?"

She asked the question gravely; the mischief lay only in her eyes.

"Oh — I — hum! Why, I don't know that I was actually *wicked.*"

He was squirming most unaccountably for a young man with a Billy Kellogg past, and Rosalind was speedily becoming more mystified. She felt that she was looking upon a miracle — and was not entirely sure that she approved of it.

Wickedness, or what passed for it in the average youth of her world, was infinitely more entertaining than the goodness of a young man who patterned his life after the hero of the *Rollo* books.

"You were simply thoughtless, I presume," she remarked.

"Thoughtless? Indeed I was — very."

"Tell me about it."

Rosalind was not wholly averse to the practise of a woman's wiles. Here was a young man, she decided, who was vulnerable to the most ancient wile of all — flattery of feminine sympathy and curiosity.

Yet the curiosity on her own part was genuine enough. Billy Kellogg had been sent away because of an episode which included H. Evelyn Morton as one of its actors, and Rosalind was still unsatisfied in her quest for information about the Englishman.

"There isn't much to tell," he answered diffidently.

"You may light that cigar," she informed him. He was still chewing upon it abstractedly. He availed himself of the permission, but without any advance toward ease of manner.

"They said that you gambled — rather heavily," she suggested.

"Oh — that!" he exclaimed.

"But did you?"

"I suppose so. There — there wasn't much else to do."

"I'm sure there wasn't," she said sympathetically. "It must have been quite dull so early in the season."

"That was it — dull," he assented. "You see — er — I wasn't working then, and I had to have something to fill in my time."

"And you lost —"

"Ten thousand dollars."

She arched her eyebrows slightly. It was a sum that did not impress Rosalind as stupendous, but the tone in which he mentioned it was one of awe.

"You are a more desperate person than I imagined," she said chidingly.

He looked at her, startled; then flushed again.

"You see, it was a year's income — a whole year!"

"Was it? I hadn't heard. How interesting!"

"I don't know whether you are familiar with the circumstances, Miss Chalmers," he went on slowly.

"Not a single one — but I'd like to know awfully. That is, if you don't mind. One is so apt to get false impressions when one does not understand."

"Why — er — yes," he sighed. "You see, I have an income — ten thousand dollars a year. The estate itself is in the hands of a guardian — my uncle."

" Mr. Davidson? "

" Yes; Uncle Henry. He manages things until I'm thirty. All I get — or did get — was the income."

Rosalind nodded.

" Well, I used to play cards a good bit. I was always losing, somehow. I was always drawing in advance on Uncle Henry. I suppose you can understand how that was."

" Oh, thoroughly! "

" Of course, he didn't fancy that much. He said I was getting into disastrous habits, and — I guess he was right. He wanted me to stop playing cards for money."

" Was it bridge? "

" That was it — bridge."

" It's rather fascinating," she commented.

" I thought so — once," he said gloomily. " Well, Uncle Henry had some friends up from the city, and we had a pretty heavy game one night. There was a Mr. Morton there."

" I know. Go ahead; it's becoming exciting."

" Well, Morton cleaned me; that's all. Cleaned me for a year's income. Of course, I hadn't saved anything before that; in fact, I was overdrawn. So that settled it."

He stared disconsolately at the river.

" And Mr. Davidson? " she suggested.

" Uncle Henry? Well, he hit the ceiling, if you know what that means."

" I have a notion. He was very angry? "

" He said he wouldn't stand for any more of it.

He wouldn't advance me another cent until it was due. That meant a year, you see. I couldn't live on nothing for a year."

" I should say not! "

" So when I saw I had to go to work, he offered to get me a job. He — he wrote a letter to Hastings & Hatch, in New York, and they took me in. I've been there ever since."

" Wasn't it very hard — at first? "

" Why, it was luck — I mean, I liked it! "

" How fortunate! "

" Yes," he went on; "I got to like it right away. I really didn't want to come back at all, only Uncle Henry insisted. He telegraphed the firm. I tried to get out of it, but they made me come."

" I'm sure you've earned a rest," declared Rosalind, nodding positively. " Your uncle thinks you are doing so splendidly. I know that he will be very glad to see you."

" You don't mean to say — he's here! "

There was something very much like terror in his wide eyes.

" Oh, no; he's on his way West. What I meant was, he'll return before you go back to the city. You are to stay in charge until he gets here."

" I don't see how I can. Honestly, I don't see how. I've got to get back to work — soon."

" You are a very unaccountable person, Mr. Kellogg," commented Rosalind. " I never knew anybody who underwent such a change of heart in such a short time. Do you mean to tell me that it doesn't make you glad just to be here? "

He surveyed the river, the islands, and the passing craft. Then he shook his head.

" Perhaps I know the reason," she suggested.

He looked at her suspiciously.

" Perhaps it is that you are not anxious to meet Mr. Morton again."

" Is *he* here? "

" He is one of the guests at our island."

Kellogg lifted his ungraceful bulk abruptly from his chair and walked to the rail, where he stood for a moment gazing down at the water.

" I beg your pardon," he said, turning. " I — I didn't intend to be rude. But it was a sort of surprise, you know."

" I didn't know there had been a quarrel."

" Oh, no; not a quarrel exactly. But —"

" You are afraid it may be embarrassing."

" That's it — embarrassing."

" But your uncle seems to have no feeling against him, Mr. Kellogg."

" I know; I understand. But that's different. He didn't lose a year's income."

" Of course, we could have the yacht leave you at your own place," went on Rosalind, " if you positively insist on avoiding Mr. Morton. But, as I said, there are only the servants there."

" I wouldn't go there for the world! " he exclaimed hastily. " That is — not now."

" Then, of course, you will stay with us."

" I might go to a hotel; yes, I think I'd better."

" But there is none within several miles of your island. How could you look after things so far away? "

" That's so; I'd forgotten."

His old uneasiness had returned. Rosalind was

again in perplexity.   She considered Billy Kellogg as not only unaccountable, but colorless.

She was rather glad he had lost a year's income, if this was his spiritless type.   An hour before she had been anticipating a welcome accession to the Witherbee house-party — welcome because she felt quite sure that no young man could fail to be an improvement upon Mr. Morton, Reggy, Fortescue Jones, and the Perkins boy.   Now she was rapidly reaching the conclusion that Billy Kellogg was even worse than any of them, and it was peculiarly a shock because it so wholly reversed her anticipations.

"You won't be paired off with Mr. Morton, at any rate," she told him consolingly.   "There are lots of others.   Polly Dawson, for instance; she knows you, I understand."

"Er — she is there?"

"Yes, indeed," and then Rosalind enumerated the other guests.

He shook his head as she named each person, and then returned to Polly Dawson.

"That's another surprise," he confessed.

"Not unpleasant, I hope?"

"Oh, no; not at all.   I assure you I didn't mean that.   Only — well, it's a surprise."

"Polly is really a very nice girl.   And I've heard her speak of you so often."

"Er — have you?   That's good of her, I'm sure."

After this he fell into a period of silence, from which all the arts of Rosalind Chalmers were unable to extricate him, save for fitful and brief intervals. Ordinarily, she would not have wasted her time upon such a dull and diffident young man; she would have taken his manner as an affront to her natural claims upon masculine attention.

But in this instance Rosalind's curiosity was piqued. She could not reconcile him with his reputation. If ever a devil-may-care spirit lurked in this beefy youth, something supernatural had exorcised it.

"Your island," she said, pointing.

"Looks all right," he commented, after a moment of staring.

"You don't seem particularly glad to see it."

He merely shrugged.

"Your uncle's yacht went to Kingston, I believe, to obtain some supplies."

"That's good."

"That's why Mr. Witherbee sent his own boat."

"Mighty kind of him, I'm sure."

Rosalind sighed. By all odds, this was the most difficult young man of her experience. She was glad that the voyage would terminate speedily.

A knot of persons was standing on the Witherbee wharf, awaiting the arrival of the big power-launch.

"There are Mrs. Witherbee and Gertrude and some of the others," said Rosalind, her eyes busy. "I don't see Mr. Morton; I imagine you won't mind that, however. But — yes, Polly's there."

"I — I don't see her," declared Kellogg. "Where?"

"In blue, the third from the left."

"Oh, yes; now I see."

He studied the short, plump figure of Polly Dawson with absorbed interest as the boat neared the wharf. There was a hunted expression in his eyes; his fingers twitched.

Mrs. Witherbee welcomed the new guest effusively.

"We've heard so much about you, Mr. Kellogg,
that it really seems as if we knew you.   But you left
before we came up for the season.   We're going to
try to make up for it."

"That's awfully good of you," stammered the
prodigal.

"My daughter, Gertrude."

He shook hands and bowed.

"Miss Winter."

He repeated the same perfunctory ceremony, but
his glance was wandering restlessly.

"Mr. Jones, Mr. Perkins, and my son, Tom."

Kellogg responded mechanically to the greetings.
Rosalind, following the line of his glance, saw that it
encompassed the figure of Polly Dawson.   And in
Polly's eyes, which were staring at the new guest,
was an expression that completely baffled her.

"Oh, Polly, where are you?" called Mrs. Witherbee.   "I believe you've met Mr. Kellogg, haven't
you?"

Polly stepped forward and extended her hand.
Rosalind watched the meeting narrowly.   She sensed
a situation that she did not understand — but she
proposed to find out.

"Hello — Billy," said Polly in a queer voice.

"How do do — Polly?"

There was the same hesitation in Kellogg's tone.

"You're looking very well," she murmured.

"Feeling fine, thanks," he returned awkwardly.

Rosalind believed she was beginning to see a light.
Here were the surface indications of heart-trouble,
either on one side or the other, possibly on both.

Yet on the many occasions that Polly had spoken of Kellogg, never once, either in word or manner, had she betrayed the existence of an affair of sentiment.

"Polly is deeper than she seems," Rosalind told herself.

It was Mrs. Witherbee who broke the tension.

"You must come straight up to the house and meet the others," she commanded. "We've all been expecting you, and we're delighted to have you. I told your uncle that we'd probably keep you here most of the time, unless it's absolutely necessary for you to stay at your own place."

"It isn't," he said quickly.

"I knew it wasn't," declared the hostess with emphasis. "I told Mr. Davidson the servants could do without you. So you may as well have a good time with us. Come along."

She linked an arm within that of the stammering guest and led him toward the house. Some of the others followed.

Polly lingered on the wharf, watching. So did Rosalind. When the procession had passed from ear-shot, the two women looked at each other.

"I had no idea, of course," said Rosalind, "that there had been — well, that anything had happened between you two."

Polly stared and was silent for half a minute.

"Nothing ever did happen between Billy and me," she answered slowly.

"But —"

"Where did you find him?" demanded Polly.

"At Clayton, of course. He came aboard while I was shopping. One of the men met him at the train and brought down his grips."

Polly's brow was furrowed deeply.

"I cannot understand it," she muttered.   "It's — it's beyond belief."

"What?"

"His coming here."

Polly pointed at the retreating figures.

"Mr. Kellogg?"

"Kellogg?   That's not Billy Kellogg!"

"Not Billy Kellogg?" echoed Rosalind.   "Why, Polly!"

"That man is *not* Billy Kellogg," repeated Polly, shaking her head.

"Then — then who is he?"

"I haven't the slightest idea."

CHAPTER XVIII

WHO? WHAT? WHY? WHERE?

"BUT, Polly, it's inconceivable!"

Rosalind was preyed upon by confused emotions. She was mystified, shocked, startled, apprehensive, even angry. Dominant was the sensation that this chunky, colorless young man had played a hoax upon her.

"It's true," affirmed Polly stubbornly. "I surely know Billy Kellogg when I see him."

"Of course! But what does it mean?"

Polly made a helpless gesture.

"He came aboard as Mr. Kellogg," said Rosalind, talking as if in self-justification. "He pretended to be Mr. Kellogg. He knew all about having been sent for by his uncle. Of course, he did act strangely. But he knew Mr. Morton; he even knew you!"

"You're sure?"

"Well," admitted Rosalind, on reflecting, "now that I think of it, in your case, I had to point you out on the wharf. But he said he recognized you. And you called him Billy!"

"I didn't want to make a scene," said Polly. "I knew there was something wrong, of course. So I just pretended — thought I'd wait till I got my bearings."

"But who *can* he be?"

"I tell you, Rosalind, I don't know. I never saw the man before."

"But he's pretending to be Mr. Kellogg — if he isn't!"

"Evidently. Oh, dear! It's beyond me."

"It has something to do with these burglaries," declared Rosalind.

"I suppose so. It's awful!"

"He's probably a thief."

"Very likely."

"Yet you've recognized him — or pretended to! Do you realize what you've done, Polly Dawson?"

"He called me Polly," she answered defensively.

"And just because a stranger calls you Polly, is he to be turned loose upon your friends?"

"*I* didn't bring him here. I hope you're not blaming *me*, Rosalind!"

"No-o; of course I didn't mean that. But how was I to know he wasn't Billy Kellogg?"

"I don't suppose you could tell," admitted Polly. "Is — is he nice?"

"He is the stupidest and most hopeless creature I ever talked to!"

Polly sighed.

"You must go to him and demand an explanation," added Rosalind.

"I? Why, Rosalind, that's impossible! I don't even know the man!"

Rosalind regarded the plump, young person with severity.

"But *you* have given him the very last word in introductions!" she exclaimed. "You pretended you knew him. Mrs. Witherbee and everybody else have taken him at face value. You passed him

without even a challenge. Are you going to allow
this stranger to live here and call you Polly? Why
— why, it may make you *particeps criminis!* "

Polly's lower lip quivered.

" I — I couldn't think of anything else to do," she
faltered. " Oh, Rosalind, you must help me! "

" It looks as if we must help each other," declared
Rosalind. " We simply cannot allow this man to im-
pose upon the Witherbees."

Polly was on the brink of tears. She was thoroughly frightened. Not until Rosalind, in self-defense, had placed the burden upon her did she realize
the enormity involved in her recognition of the
stranger. It was a mere procrastination, of course,
due to bewilderment; but it had served as an authori-
tative introduction for the impostor.

" Mr. Morton! " exclaimed Polly suddenly.

" Well? "

" But they'll meet — don't you see? And they're
supposed to know each other! "

" True," murmured Rosalind. " I'd forgotten
that. Well, we've got to face it. Let's go and see
what has happened."

Polly shrank back.

" You go," she begged.

" We'll go together," said Rosalind firmly. " We
must see it through."

" But —"

" And listen! Not a word of explanation, unless
something has already happened. Understand?
No! Not a word! Go on calling him Billy. Keep
it up until we find out something."

" I — I can't," wailed Polly.

" Nonsense! " Rosalind was losing patience.

" Didn't I travel all the way down from Clayton with him, talking to him just as if he were really Mr. Kellogg? It's a pity if you can't help a little — after deliberately turning him loose on this island."

" Why not ex — expose him? "

" Not yet! We must find out some things first. We must know what it all means. Come, now! For Heaven's sake, brace up, Polly! Nobody has been murdered yet."

" I'm afraid! "

" Then let me take the responsibility," declared Rosalind in a disgusted tone. " Only you've simply got to play your part — now that you've started it."

She seized the trembling Polly by the arm and started her at a rapid pace toward the house. Rosalind was bewildered not less than her companion, but she betrayed the fact by no outward sign. Even in the face of possible disaster, resolution did not desert her. Besides, her anger was still hot at the deception practised by the pudgy young man who was now so inadvertently a guest of the island.

Polly's efforts to hang back were ineffectual. There was grim energy in Rosalind's grip, so that the unwilling young woman found herself propelled forward, despite her vanished courage.

The Kellogg impostor was the center of a group on the porch. As they joined it, Mr. Morton approached from the other direction. The stout visitor was mopping his brow assiduously and answering questions in monosyllables. He seemed unable to decide between his feet, for he stood first upon one, then upon the other, but never upon both at the same time.

As Rosalind and Polly appeared, he observed

them with an alarmed and imploring glance. Polly's eyes did not meet his, but the cool stare of her companion never winced.

"Here's Mr. Morton now!" exclaimed Mrs. Witherbee. "Of course, you know each other. Oh, Mr. Morton! Mr. Kellogg is here!"

Morton glanced casually over the head of the Perkins boy and studied the newcomer for a brief instant.

"By Jove, Kellogg, but I'm glad to see you!" he drawled.

The words were accompanied by the thrusting forth of a long arm, the hand attached to which seized the limp fingers of Kellogg. That young man permitted his jaw to drop an inch, where it hung, irresolute.

"Why — hello, Morton," he murmured.

"Glad you've joined us, I'm sure," said the Englishman unemotionally. "Awfully glad. How's New York?"

"F-fine!"

"And business?"

"Oh — er — excellent."

Rosalind was too deeply engrossed in the exchange of greetings to notice that Polly's hand was clasping her own with desperate energy. The haughty lady whom everybody wished to marry was dumfounded. Morton had accepted the stranger! Morton — who knew as well as Polly that this was not the Billy Kellogg from whom he had won a year's income!

What *did* it mean?

"Mr. Kellogg is up to take charge of his uncle's place while Mr. Davidson is away," explained Mrs.

Witherbee, breathing a soft sigh of gratification at the absence of animosity between these knights of the gaming-table.

Perspiration streamed down the cheeks of the stout young man. He stared at Morton with the fascination of a bird looking upon the mythically hypnotic serpent. His glance finally wavered and met that of Rosalind. She saw the muscles of his jaw tighten, and watched him while he breathed deeply.

"Oh, I say," he began. "Something's wrong. I —"

Rosalind's head was moving slowly from side to side, and her glare was truly ferocious. The young man stopped. Then all traces of resolution wilted.

"Wrong?" asked Mrs. Witherbee anxiously.

"Why — er — you see —"

He gulped and looked again at Rosalind. Her head was still moving, and her lips were grim.

"What I meant was, Uncle Henry said there was something wrong at the island, and — well, you see, he wanted me to look out for it."

"What's wrong?" demanded the voice of Reginald Williams.

Unanimous dismay overspread the faces of the group. They remembered Reggy's heart!

"Nothing at all," said Rosalind coolly, as she stabbed the stout young man with a warning glance. "What Mr. Kellogg meant was that his uncle is engaged in some agricultural experiments, and that when he was called away it was necessary to have somebody there to look after them. So Mr. Kellogg came up."

It was a shot in the air, but Rosalind felt that agriculture was safe and non-exciting. The members of the group breathed again and looked at her in admiration. The stranger was also staring at her without comprehension.

"Agricultural experiments!" snorted Reggy.

"Certainly," said Rosalind freezingly. "Exactly that. He is experimenting with a new kind of cauliflower. It's very delicate, and it has to be looked after whenever there is the least danger of frost. That's why he wanted — burlap. Isn't it, Mr. Kellogg?"

"Why — yes," the fat youth assented faintly.

Once more Rosalind received a tribute from grateful eyes, but this time they contained astonishment as well as gratitude. She accepted the homage complacently. The rôle for which she had cast Reggy Williams was still his.

"After tea," suggested Mrs. Witherbee, "if it's really necessary, you can have the launch and go over to look after the cauliflower."

"It's not necessary!" exclaimed Kellogg hastily. "It's not a bit chilly this afternoon — not a bit."

Rosalind gently detached Polly from the circle and led her along the porch.

"Get that man aside," she ordered, "and pump him."

Polly quailed.

"You must! We've simply got to find out something about him. And you're the only one to do it; you're supposed to know him."

"But — did you see Mr. Morton? He recognized him."

"He pretended to," declared Rosalind. "And that's one of the things I want to know something about. That makes two people who have pretended to know him. Are you quite sure, Polly, that you're not mistaken? "

" Rosalind! "

" Oh, well, I suppose you're not. At any rate, it's your business to do some investigating."

" But I don't know what to ask."

" Heavens, Polly! There are a lot of things to find out. Who is he? What is he here for? Why did he pretend to know you? Why did Mr. Morton pretend to know him? Where is Billy Kellogg? How did a telegram to Kellogg fall into his hands? Why, he may have murdered Kellogg! "

Polly shrieked faintly.

" Of course, I don't believe he did," added Rosalind contemptuously. " That man, whoever he is, wouldn't murder a rabbit. But there's something exceedingly strange about the whole affair, and it is our business to find out what it means. Go and get him! "

" But what shall I say? " wailed Polly.

Rosalind sighed hopelessly.

" Go and ask him anything," she said. " Take him down to the summer-house to see the river — anything, I tell you! And then pump — pump — *pump!* "

Polly Dawson shivered, but obeyed. When it amounted to a clash of wills, Rosalind was irresistible.

The latter lady watched the couple depart in the direction of the summer-house and smiled resignedly. Polly was so literal! Had it been her own task, Rosalind would have taken him to the first available place — anywhere that was beyond ear-shot of the

others.   But Polly needed a sailing-chart and a compass.

Rosalind managed a meeting with Mr. Morton,
but it resulted in no information, because she did
not choose to acquaint that gentleman with the fact
that she knew the Kellogg to be spurious.   And Morton volunteered nothing.   So far as the surface of
him went, the meeting had not occasioned even a
ripple.

It was half an hour later when Polly reappeared
and beckoned Rosalind to a corner of the porch.

"He's — he's not Billy Kellogg!" whispered
Polly triumphantly.

Rosalind regarded her with a minute of patience
and pity.

"Is *that* all you learned?" she asked.

"He admitted it!"

"Of course he did.   What of that?   You knew
it, anyhow, didn't you?"

"Ye-es — but he confessed."

"And what else did he confess?"

"Nothing."

An exasperated gasp was Rosalind's only comment.

"He — he said he couldn't explain," added Polly
in an agitated voice.   "And he seemed so nervous
about it that I felt sorry for him.   Truly I did, Rosalind."

"I haven't the least doubt," icily.   "Tell me exactly what you said."

"He said it first.   He said that he knew that I
knew that he wasn't Billy Kellogg, and I admitted
that I did know it, and that I thought that he knew
I knew it.   And then before I could say anything, he
said that he couldn't explain, and he hoped I would

not say anything — particularly to you. He — he seemed to be afraid of you, Rosalind. And, of course, after he said he couldn't explain, I couldn't very well ask him. Now, could I? "

"Of course not," said Rosalind in a withering voice.

"And he doesn't look like a murderer either, Rosalind; so I didn't ask him about that. He said he'd explain as soon as he could, and he wanted to know what Mr. Morton thought about him. I told him I thought Mr. Morton probably thought what you did. Was that right? "

"I am not accountable for Mr. Morton's thoughts."

"At any rate, I'm sure he won't do any harm, Rosalind — he seems so dreadfully embarrassed."

"And after talking to him for half an hour, you haven't the least idea who he is or why he came here? " Rosalind demanded.

"I — I'm afraid not."

Rosalind threw her hands wide in a gesture of hopelessness.

"What do you propose to do about this — impostor? " she demanded. "You are the person chiefly responsible. You permitted Mrs. Witherbee to receive him."

"Why don't *you* expose him? " asked Polly meekly.

Rosalind ignored the inquiry.

"Besides," added Polly, " he says he will go away to-morrow."

"He will *not!* " exclaimed Rosalind.

"You mean —"

"I mean that he will not leave this island until we

know something about him if I have to sit up by my-self and watch him."

Polly uttered an exclamation of awe.

"The man's an impostor — probably a thief," added Rosalind. "Do you suppose I shall permit him to go as he came? I think *not!*"

"You think we ought to tell the others?"

"Not yet. There is only one thing to do for the present — watch. That will be your business and mine. We must see to it that this man is not allowed to go away until everything is explained. Mean-while, we will send for the person who is evidently the principal one to be concerned — Mr. Davidson."

"And wait?"

"Certainly. It cannot be very long. I shall tele-graph to Mr. Davidson this evening; right away, in fact. It will not be difficult to reach him on the train. And we will keep this man here until Mr. Davidson returns."

"Suppose he will not stay, Rosalind?" ventured Polly timidly.

"Leave that to me. He'll stay!"

CHAPTER XIX

STUNG!

ROSALIND not only wired to Mr. Davidson but, as an afterthought, she sent a message to Hastings & Hatch. The answer to the latter came promptly the following forenoon.

It did not serve to restore her equanimity. It described William Kissam Kellogg minutely, as Rosalind had requested, and the description was a photographic likeness of the young man who had confessed to Polly that he was no such person.

"Nothing to do but wait for Mr. Davidson," said Rosalind.

She spent some of the time, when it was not devoted to standing watch upon the stranger, in writing. After the call of the customs agents at Witherbee's Island, Rosalind had begun the preparation of a memorandum. It had already reached a length of several pages; there were daily additions. Also, there were classifications, thus:

What I Really Did.
What They Think I Did.
What I Know about Certain Things and Persons.
What I Must Find Out About Them.
What Must Never Be Found Out About Me.
Things That I Have Said (for reference in con-

nection with other things I may have to say before
this is over).

Suspicions That I Have.

Under the last head there was much writing, for
Rosalind's mind was as crowded with suspicions as
that of a crowned head is thronged with troubles.
It was not strange, of course, that a large part of
the memorandum dealt with the boatman. At every
turn and corner of it his name and his deeds intruded.

But there were some things that Rosalind, even
in the privacy of her diary, would not suffer herself
to commit to plain English. These were represented
by a cipher code, the key to which lay only in her
memory.

For instance, a Maltese cross represented her experience in the tree; a star the shower-bath that came
from the boatman's bucket, an asterisk the dance at
the hotel where she found herself in the arms of
Sam. All this was by way of mitigating the disaster
that would befall if her memorandum chanced to
come to the eyes of another.

The task of keeping watch upon the strange young
man was more tedious than difficult. Most of the
time he sat on the porch, staring at the lawn with in-
consolable eyes. He made not the slightest attempt
to escape; rather, he appeared to be in a sort of
stupor. Polly felt sorry for him; Rosalind had only
contempt.

A day passed thus and a second began with the
young man still sitting and staring. Even Mrs.
Witherbee granted that he was an unhappy acqui-
sition, while everybody was unanimous in agreeing

that work had produced an appalling effect upon Kellogg.

It was mid-morning when Rosalind, unable longer to endure the sight — she classified him as a vegetable — left Polly on guard and betook herself to the river. One thing she wanted was her bracelet. Of the boatman she had seen nothing; he had made no effort to restore her property.

With an intent that was really subconscious, she rowed one of the light skiffs in the direction of his island. There was also something mechanical rather than deliberate in the act of her landing there, making fast her boat, and ascending the path that led to his shack. Only the sound of voices awakened her from a day-dream.

She halted and listened. One of the voices was unmistakably that of Sam. The other, subdued and indifferent in tone, she finally identified as that of Mr. Morton.

Now all of her senses were alert and tingling. Perhaps it was a chance meeting; perhaps a plot; perhaps —

But it might be any one of so many things that it was not worth while to speculate. It was entirely a matter for observation.

Rosalind advanced cautiously, taking care that no stick snapped or stone rolled underfoot, and keeping herself screened behind the small trees and bushes that sheltered the path. Presently she sighted them. The spectacle was one that surprised her.

Sam and the Englishman were seated on the ground, facing each other. Between them lay a folded blanket. The boatman was shuffling a pack of cards.

"What I can't make out," Sam was saying, " is the luck of it — you walking right into my parlor, just as the fly went calling on the spider, and without an invitation at that. I'd been trying to think up a scheme to get you here, and, by jingo! you save me the trouble."

"Um — ah — just rowing about a bit, you know. Exercise and that sort of thing. Saw your island, and came ashore to have a look."

"And you didn't know it was my hangout, eh?"

The boatman was watching the Englishman closely.

"'Pon my word, no! Awfully sorry I've intruded."

"Intruded! Man alive, you're as welcome as good news! Sit still; you positively mustn't be going yet. I insist. I hear you're something of a card-player. That's why — Confound that pack! My fingers are like thumbs lately."

The boatman gathered up the scattered pack and resumed his shuffling.

"You are about to make the acquaintance," he said, " of that certain branch of the great American sport known as freeze-out. You have ten chips; I have ten. Your chips are worth a thousand each; you'll have to take my word for it that mine are worth the same. The limit is anything you have in sight."

Morton yawned.

"Really," he drawled, " I'm not interested, you know."

"You will be," the boatman reassured him. "It's going to be highly interesting. Will you cut?"

"Rather, I think I'll say good day," and Morton made as if to rise.

Then Rosalind noticed that a pistol lay at the boatman's side and that his hand sought it. Morton observed the movement, too, for with a bored sigh he settled back on his crossed legs.

"I'll cut," he said.

The boatman dealt and picked up his hand. For a few seconds his antagonist seemed not to know the purpose of the five cards that lay, face downward, before him; then he lifted them languidly.

"I say," he yawned, "is a pair any good in this game?"

"Not too good," answered the boatman cheerfully. "How many?"

Morton took three, while Sam contented himself with one.

The Englishman tossed a chip into the center of the blanket, the boatman two.

"Er — what should I do now?" inquired the prisoner listlessly.

"Quit, call, or raise — anything you please."

"To call is — er — to equal the amount of your stake?"

"You've got the idea."

Morton added a chip to the pot and laid a pair of eights on the blanket. The boatman displayed tens up and nonchalantly raked four chips toward himself.

"Your deal," he said, tossing the cards across.

Rosalind frowned as she stared at the Englishman.

"I am afraid he is a fool, after all," she thought. "Why didn't he —"

The Englishman was dealing abstractedly. He had to be reminded to look at his own hand.

Sam drew three cards, Morton three. This time three of the Englishman's chips crossed the blanket to the other side. He showed not even a pair.

" It's plain robbery," whispered Rosalind to herself. " The man doesn't know the first thing about poker. Can they really be serious? "

A second look at the boatman's pistol reminded her that they probably were.

For five minutes the game progressed. Twice, by an accident of fate, the Englishman gathered the pot, but for the most part his own pile was receding chip by chip. Even in his winning moments he seemed bored almost to the point of somnolence. The boatman alternately grinned and whistled.

" I'll just tap you for what you've got," Sam said after examining his final draw. " Two checks, I believe."

" This is a deuced stupid game, you know," remarked Morton as he pushed the last of his stack to the center.

" Doesn't strike you quite so favorably as bridge, eh? "

" Rather — not."

" Do you happen to have anything as good as three of a kind? "

Morton looked down at his cards as if he had just discovered them.

" Er — what would you make of them? " he asked, displaying them.

Rosalind gasped. She could see the hand from where she stood. It contained not even a pair!

" I'd make a resolution to quit," advised the boatman as he took the last of the chips. "This freezes you."

"Can't say I think much of your American game," and Morton yawned again prodigiously. "Ah — how much?"

"You've lost ten thousand, my friend."

"Really, now?"

"Honest and truly."

The boatman's hand crept toward his revolver.

With a listless shrug Morton began feeling in an inner pocket. Presently he drew forth a wallet.

"The idiot!" fumed Rosalind. "He's been swindled!"

A moment's search within the folds of the leather resulted in the appearance of an oblong slip of paper. Glancing casually at it, Morton handed it to the boatman. The latter examined it closely, then looked up with a smile.

"I — er — think you'll find it good," drawled Morton.

"I'll take a chance," said Sam as he thrust the paper into the pocket of his shirt. "Mighty nice of you to carry this around with you. But let me give you a chunk of advice. Next time you trim a guy at bridge, either keep your mouth shut about it or don't carry the stuff around with you. You are liable to tempt some of us poker kings."

"Ah — thanks, by Jove! Not a bad idea, that. You'll not be wanting me now, I take it?"

"School's out."

The boatman rose to his feet.

The placidity of Morton was undisturbed as he stood and flecked a few patches of dust from his trousers.

" I'll be going, if you don't mind," he remarked. " My boat's at the other end of the island."

Although the affair was none of hers, Rosalind found herself angry. If there was one thing that annoyed her beyond endurance, it was sheer stupidity. She believed she had just witnessed the apotheosis of it.

Yet something struck her oddly as the Englishman turned and walked away. She was quite sure that she heard him chuckle. The boatman must have heard the same thing, for he stared after Morton curiously.

" A bad check, I'll wager," whispered Rosalind to herself. " But where was the sense in the whole affair, anyhow? Never mind; it's not my business. But I want my bracelet."

She stepped from her concealment, and an instant later the boatman turned at the sound of her footsteps.

" Hello! " he said cordially. " You just missed the performance."

" My bracelet, please," was Rosalind's only remark.

" Why, I'd clean forgotten it, ma'am."

" You haven't — lost it? "

" No fear; it's safe."

He turned and entered the cabin, appearing a moment later with the golden circlet lying in his palm. Rosalind seized it with more joy than dignity. The touch of it, as she snapped it about her arm, was exhilarating. Her eyes shone with the light of triumph.

The boatman watched the expressive pantomime with evident approval.

"You're rather lucky to get it, in a way," he said. "I've just been taking a chance at freeze-out, and if I'd lost I guess it would have been up to me to fork over the bracelet as part payment."

Rosalind made no pretense of being startled at the idea. She knew he was capable of no such infamy, no matter what he might be.

"I saw what happened," she remarked.

"Oh, did you?"

"I saw you steal ten thousand dollars."

The boatman studied her quizzically.

"And never made a move to stop me," he commented.

She winced, but decided to ignore the implication.

"I didn't steal it, ma'am," he added. "Poker's a perfectly fair game. I didn't stack the cards; I didn't shove a cold deck at him."

"Fair! When he didn't know the first principles of it?"

"He certainly didn't play as if he did," admitted Sam. "But if he didn't know poker, he had no business to sit in the game."

"Not with a gun at his head?"

"Hum! I'd forgotten the gun. I suppose that did have something to do with it. It wasn't loaded, though."

"It was no better than stealing. It *was* stealing."

"Funny thing about it," mused the boatman, as if he did not hear her, "but he didn't seem to care much, one way or the other. Why, he yawned in my face, ma'am."

The creature baffled her completely.

"Have you no compunctions whatever about the

manner in which you took his money?" she asked curiously.

"Compunctions — about him? I'm afraid not. He stole it in the first place, didn't he?"

"He won it — fairly!" exclaimed Rosalind. "You knew he had it, and you've been plotting and planning to get it for days and days."

"Maybe," he admitted.

"I hope the check he gave you is bad," she added viciously.

"That would be a horse on me; wouldn't it, ma'am? But that's a chance that folks like you and me have to run. Still, I heard he stole it, or what amounts to the same thing."

"I tell you he didn't!"

"You seem mighty sure about that. How do you know, ma'am?"

"Because Mr. Kellogg told me so."

"Kellogg?"

"Yes; he's here."

The boatman eyed her for several seconds.

"He is staying at Mr. Witherbee's," she added.

Of course, Rosalind knew that this was a fib; but somebody who called himself Kellogg was staying there, at any rate, and she saw no need of explaining to Sam.

"So Kellogg's here, is he?" he remarked. "I suppose he came back to have another try at the Englishman. That'll be hard luck for Kellogg, because I think his lordship is about cleaned, ma'am."

"He came for no such purpose," declared Rosalind, half wondering why she was hastening to the defense of an impostor. "Mr. Kellogg has — reformed."

"Reformed? Was he— Hum! Well—was he one of us?"

Rosalind's cheeks flamed.

"He was a good-for-nothing idle gambler!" she explained.

"Oh!" said the boatman in a relieved tone. "He's turned over a new leaf, eh?"

"He's very much engrossed in his new work."

"What's he doing here, then?"

"His uncle sent for him."

Again the boatman appeared to reflect.

"What for?" he asked.

"To look after his island while he is away. Mr. Davidson has gone to Denver. And Mr. Kellogg is going to try to put an end to all these burglaries. So there's a warning for you."

He pondered the warning and wrinkled his forehead.

"Customs officers still hanging around?" he asked.

"I am told they are."

"And that Canadian spy-chaser — is he still on the job?"

"I saw the launch again yesterday."

"Is Davidson's police patrol cruising, too?"

"Of course. And they've put on another boat."

Rosalind noted with satisfaction that he was showing traces of worriment.

"I expect that's going to make things pretty warm," he observed.

"Dangerous!" she supplemented.

"You'd advise flitting, then, ma'am?"

"Beyond all question. And — well, it's only because of the bracelet that I give you this warning."

" It's certainly kind of you — mighty kind."

Rosalind felt that the sword no longer dangled over her head by a single hair.

" You're a good, square pal to tip me off," he went on. " I guess you're dead right about it. The jig's up for us.

" Yes, ma'am. We'd better blow."

" *We!* "

" We'll be starting in a few minutes. It never pays to stick around after the last hand's played."

Rosalind was tongue-tied with astonishment.

CHAPTER XX

" GOOD WORK, PAL! "

"YOU see," Sam went on, seemingly unaware of her consternation, " it's foolish to take any more chances than are absolutely necessary. Now that we've got a fairly good stake, it would be silly to wait. We'll run over to the American side somewhere, and once we get ashore there's small chance of getting pinched."

" Are you utterly mad? " asked Rosalind, abruptly finding her voice.

" Mad? I should say not, ma'am. Just cautious — that's all. I'd be mad if I stayed."

" But you are saying that I —"

" That you are going with me. Certainly. Why not? "

Rosalind was not frightened, yet something in his tone chilled her. She examined his face with searching eyes. He seemed to be quite composed; there was no trace of wildness in his eyes, no betrayal of mental agitation in his speech. Were it not for his astounding words, she would have considered him entirely normal. She decided to laugh, but the attempt was poor. His was infinitely more successful.

" It may be a little sudden, ma'am," he admitted; "but it seems a case for quick action. I'm sorry we won't even be able to stop at Witherbee's for your trunks."

She decided to try a reasonable tone.

"Think what you are saying," she advised, controlling her voice. "It is quite impossible — this thing you propose. But, of course, you're not serious."

"Never more serious in my life."

The look in his eyes gave her a twinge of alarm.

"But don't you see — Sam —"

"That's the first time you've called me by name," he interrupted with a bow. "Thanks, partner."

"But don't you see there is no reason whatever for me to go."

Rosalind was trying to talk to him as if he were a petulant child to be placated, or a lunatic to be argued with until help arrived.

"There's every reason," he answered. "Pals should stick together."

"But you know — seriously — that I am not your — pal!"

The vulgar word passed her lips reluctantly.

"But you are, ma'am; the best I ever had. I guess I could name a dozen instances of it. Want me to go over them? First, there's —"

"You need not. It's too absurd. I shall go at once."

"Not till I go," he told her firmly. "As I was going to say when you interrupted me, ma'am, we'll make a break for the American shore, and as soon as we can get a license and a justice of the peace or minister, why —"

"Stop!"

"We'll get married."

Rosalind turned pale. Truly she was dealing with a madman on this lonely little island!

"Married!"

"Why, certainly! What else? You don't suppose I'm going to lose a pal like you?"

The boatman was so calm that his manner utterly disconcerted her. A rational exterior, she reflected, often cloaked the most dangerous forms of insanity.

"But I have no intention of marrying — anybody."

"That's been the trouble all along," he assured her. "You've had so many offers that you don't take them seriously any longer. But this is different. This isn't an offer, ma'am; it's just a plain announcement of what's going to happen. We're going to be married."

She glanced swiftly through the trees in the direction of the river. There was not a boat within hailing distance.

"It's this way," he went on easily. "You've helped me out of a few tight places. I've helped you once, at least. We're a great team, and there's nothing like teamwork in our business. I don't mind saying I'm strong for you. You have got good nerve; when you make up your mind to anything, you're apt to get it.

"You and I can go a long way together. I'll admit we may quarrel some, but that'll be your fault. You've got a hair-trigger tongue, ma'am. But I won't mind that; I'm getting used to it. The point is, when we get working together we're able to deliver the goods.

"You wouldn't expect me to lose a good pal, would you? Of course not. And I can't see myself doing it, either. It's true that the jig is up here. But it's a wide, wide world, pal. Shall we be going?"

" Do you suppose for one instant," said Rosalind, trying to hide the real terror in her voice, " that I am going to marry — *you?* "

" I'm sure of it," he said confidently. " Why not, ma'am? We won't starve — and I say that without the least idea of tapping your bank-roll. You can keep it soaked away, if you want to. I've got a nice little stake now." He touched the pocket where Morton's check reposed.

" That 'll last us a good while," he continued, " and it's a sure thing we'll turn off some kind of a job before that's gone. Why, just think! With my experience and your social drag —"

" Stop! "

There was absolute desperation in her voice.

" Not much time to lose," he advised, glancing at a nickeled watch. " No telling but that Englishman 'll be stirring up some sort of trouble for us."

Wrath triumphed at last despite Rosalind's efforts to be self-contained.

" You common thief! " she cried, stamping her foot and glaring. " How dare you insult me so? You burglar! You blackmailer! You —"

" Spy and smuggler," he supplied. " May as well get the whole list out of your system, ma'am. I don't mind; I keep my temper better than you do.

" But don't forget that I'm talking facts, while you're just barking at the moon. I hate to disappoint you, in one way; but your scalping days are over, ma'am. You've had your last proposal. I don't doubt you've turned down a lot of pretty good scouts, but you won't turn down any more. That's a cinch, as far as I can see now.

"You had your last proposal — unless there's been one since — when the Englishman got so enthusiastic over you. I heard it, you know. You threw him rather hard. You did the same for Reggy, less than half an hour before. And I understand there's been a long string of them. Well, you're at the end of the string."

He grinned complacently.

"You needn't shout," he added. "You're not getting a chance to turn me down. This is no proposal, ma'am. This is what you might call an order, if I have to speak plain. It don't require any answer. It's not up to you to say yes or no; all you have to do is to come along like a good pal."

Rosalind shrank backward a step. At last she was genuinely frightened, for Sam possessed all the calm of a terrible madness.

"What a fool I'd be to let you go!" he added reflectively. "And — not to flatter myself — what a fool you'd be to miss a chance like this! We've just got to know each other's ways; we're like wheels in the same clock. I need you; you need me.

"I'll admit you don't have to earn your living. But think of the fun you miss when you don't! It gets mighty tiresome, standing on the outside and looking in. What you and I need, ma'am, is excitement — plenty of action — something to keep us on edge.

"You're what I call an emergency pal. You don't really begin to get good until you're in a scrape. It takes trouble to start you going. But when you do get started — if you don't mind my saying it, ma'am — you go to it like the cat to the canary."

She scarcely heard his last words; her mind was

intent on seeking some avenue of escape. Tentatively, she edged toward the path that led to the boat-landing. But the boatman understood and shook his head.

"When we go, we go together," he assured her. "That dress you're wearing looks all right. Whatever you need in the line of clothes we can get when we hit the mainland.

"As far as I'm concerned, all I have to do is to put on my hat. And that's down in the boat, I think; if it isn't, it doesn't matter. We'll start, I guess."

He turned toward the path and beckoned.

"I refuse to stir a foot!" exclaimed Rosalind.

She compressed her lips.

"That means carrying you, then, ma'am."

"You dare not touch me!"

"I hate to, but I'll have to, if you're not willing to walk."

"I will not go! It's — it's insanity!"

The boatman shrugged and advanced toward her. She retreated a pace.

"If you dare —"

"Will you walk, then?"

"I'll find some way —"

"Once and for all, will you walk?"

She searched his eyes for some trace of insincerity or weakness, but found none. A shudder of fear shook her. Then she rallied herself angrily.

"I shall walk," she said coldly.

He nodded contentedly and led the way toward the landing. Rosalind followed mechanically, but her brain was afire with activity. Beyond doubt, the boatman had become insane; if, indeed, he had not been so from the first.

But she realized that at times it was needful to humor an unbalanced mind. For the present, she would accompany him; but surely there would be an opportunity to escape. If she could obtain no aid from a passing boat, at least there would be ample help when they reached the mainland.

" We'll take the old *Fifty-Fifty*," he remarked as he loosed the painter. " It's better than rowing. And if anything goes wrong, why, you're here to fix it. By the way, what do you want me to call you, ma'am, Rosie?"

She glared at him.

" No? Rosalind, maybe? It's a little long; but it'll do, I suppose. It's shorter than saying Miss Chalmers, anyhow. But it's not as short as pal. I rather like that, myself. But you seem to be touchy about it."

Rosalind stepped aboard the launch without answering.

She prayed that the engine might not start; but the prayer was unanswered, for it purred happily at the first turn of the fly-wheel. The launch backed out into the stream. An instant later it described a half-circle, then started eastward.

" We'll hit the trail for Ogdensburg," said the boatman. " Plenty of preachers there."

" Are you aware of the fact," remarked Rosalind, with a sudden smile of triumph, " that before you drag me to a preacher you must drag me to some town clerk or other person and obtain a license?"

To her annoyance, he appeared neither surprised nor dismayed.

" It's just another step in the journey," he said carelessly. " I'll admit that this license game is sometimes a spoil-sport on romance. But you haven't got me there. You'll agree! You'll step right up to the captain's office and take your little oath without saying a word. A good pal never welches."

"I shall most certainly turn you over to the police at the first opportunity."

"No," he said confidently, with a shake of his head; "you won't do anything of the kind. Why, ma'am, you're the pal who keeps me out of the hands of the police! You're an expert at it. I'm proud of you.

"You see, if one of us got pinched, the other would have to go along, too; I'm strong for sticking together. You understand — for better or for worse, ma'am. I think that's the way they say it.

"And if they should happen to pinch you, it would be real embarrassing, I expect. They'd start finding things out, maybe; all about lots of things that have happened to you and me. My, but that would be a piece for the papers! Head-lines and pictures and artists drawing little sketches of Rosalind, the 'Regal Lady,' sitting in a tree and burgling a house and bossing a gas-engine and —"

"Stop!"

"Oh, all right; I'll stop! I expected you to get the idea. You're not much of a hand for getting laughed at, I notice. And folks might laugh if they read the papers. You've got a kind of a long name for a big-type head-line, too; some printer-chap might chop it down to Rosie in order to make it fit."

The boatman grinned and reached over to advance the spark.

Rosalind turned her back upon him — this One-Cylinder Sam who meant to marry her — and gazed despairingly across the water. By sheer perversity of fate, there was not a boat within half a mile. Ogdensburg meant a run of several hours, even at the best gait of the *Fifty-Fifty*. It might be dark when they arrived. She imagined the panic on Witherbee's Island when nightfall came without her.

Sam lighted his pipe and sat hunched over the tiller, smoking thoughtfully. For a quarter of an hour he appeared to pay no attention to anything save the back of Rosalind's head. Then something caused him to glance upward at the sky, then at the horizon that lay behind them. He wrinkled his forehead and put aside his pipe.

It was scarcely mid-afternoon, but daylight was failing rapidly. Rosalind herself, although wholly concerned with her absurd and perhaps dangerous plight, presently noticed the change in the sky. A swift survey of a great bank of black and lead-colored clouds ended with a glance at the boatman.

"Squall coming," he admitted, with a nod.

She experienced a feeling of elation. A squall might mean anything but a license and a parson. It was a storm that saved Britain from the Armada.

Sam, however, made no alteration in his course. Frequently he glanced over his shoulder, but soon this maneuver became unnecessary, for the battle-front of the squall had advanced with such appalling rapidity that it now overhung them, like some monster destroyer of the air. As yet, however, there was no breath of wind.

"You'll make an island?" Rosalind suggested.

"She'll ride it out," he said confidently. "I've been out in 'em before."

Rosalind measured the low free-board of the launch with a doubtful eye. She was still triumphant in what she felt would abruptly shatter the mad plans of the boatman, yet she was sensibly uneasy at the fairly ferocious aspect of the storm.

"Better make a landing," she warned.

"Afraid?"

She turned her back upon him.

Half a mile astern a long, white line extended itself across the river. Beyond it the boatman could not see, for all was murk and grayness and ominous opacity. Then the white line seemed to leap forward at a furious pace. The speed of the launch was as nothing to it.

Suddenly the steersman seemed to awake. He chewed his under lip anxiously as he watched the onrush of the line of foam.

"Worse than I thought," he muttered. "I'm a fool."

A quarter of a mile to his left lay an island, but he knew there was not a chance in a thousand of making the lee of it. Besides, to alter the course meant taking the squall abeam, with a swift ending of the voyage in mid-river.

"Come aft here!" he commanded.

Rosalind turned and studied the white line. It was not more than a hundred yards distant. Without a word she obeyed him.

He motioned her to a seat beside him, and as she sat down passed an arm around her shoulders.

"Sit tight, pal," he said. "And if it gets too bad, there's a life-preserver under your feet."

The change is his tone impressed her for the moment far more than threatened perils. All the banter and sarcasm had vanished from his voice. He spoke gravely, almost grimly.

"I shall not need it," she answered. "I swim."

"We may be in a bad fix," he said, his lips close to her ear. "If it was anybody but you I wouldn't admit it. But you're game. It'll blow hard and get rough. I'm sorry —"

The remainder of the sentence she could not hear, for the white line had overtaken them. The storm-front delivered a blow like a battering-ram, a blow in which wind, hail, sea, and a stifling smother of froth seemed welded into one sinister and mighty weapon. The launch staggered, then leaped forward.

Rosalind felt a cruel beating of ice-shrapnel upon her face, her arms, her thinly clad shoulders. In an effort to give her shelter the boatman drew her head down against his flannel shirt. One hand was needed for the tiller, for the clumsy power-boat was yawing and swaying, and at every lurch struggled, as if with deliberate purpose, to offer her beam to the storm.

He steered wholly by instinct. Every landmark and island had been blotted out as if swept from the surface of the river. Even the bow of the launch was no longer visible.

The boatman sat with his feet braced against a cleat, his body swaying with the roll of the seas. He squinted through half-closed eyes, but saw nothing save a fury of white water and driving hail. Indeed, river and air seemed to have merged into a whirling, stinging, vapory mass, in the grip of which the launch

was flung onward, so that at times she seemed to fly
rather than float.

Rosalind was glad to hide her face, not because
she feared to look upon the fury that encompassed
them, but to shield it from the bitter volleying of
the hail. It seemed not to descend from sky to
earth, but to travel horizontally, with the velocity
and flat trajectory of a rifle-bullet.

Flying water smote her when the wind sliced the
crests from waves and flung them aboard across the
stern of the wallowing launch. The boatman's grip
tightened. Even in the din and ferocity of the storm
she found herself marveling at the power that lay
in his slender but sinewy arm.

His lips were against her ear.

" All right? " he shouted. " Just nod; don't try
to talk! "

She nodded.

Another minute passed. There was no slackening
in the onslaught. Once the tiller was almost
wrenched from Sam's hand by the impact of a sea
that caught the launch a quartering blow. It was
nearly disaster, but he managed to swing the stern
to the wind again. Yet the blow had left its mark.
There was water now above the flooring.

As it swirled about Rosalind's feet she reached
forward to where a tin bucket lay. The boatman
drew her back.

" No use! " he roared. " You can't bail! "

She accepted his decision without question, and
again hid her face against his breast.

" Get the life-preserver! "

She heard the command but dimly, though it was
shouted directly into her ear.

Rosalind shook her head. Of what use was a thing of cork and canvas out there in the white fury?

"Get it!"

Again she shook her head. It was not merely the uselessness of the thing that caused her stubborn refusal. It was the fact — and she was calmly conscious of it, too — that there was only *one* life-preserver in the boat.

Just why this influenced her was not clear in her mind, but she realized with faint surprise that it did. She even found herself pondering over it, telling herself that it was unethical to seize this lone chance that offered itself only to her. Yet she was doubtful, too, that ethics had anything to do with the matter.

The water in the cock-pit was deeper, and there was a growing sluggishness in the movements of the launch that she noted as quickly as the boatman himself.

"Rosalind!"

She lifted her head slightly.

"For Heaven's sake, put it on!"

"No!" she cried almost fiercely.

She felt the grip of his arm tighten convulsively. Something that sounded like a sob came from his throat.

"It's your one chance!" he shouted.

She shook her head.

Then for a brief instant some freak of the gale tore a great rent in the curtain of hail that shrouded them. The boatman's straining eyes had a vision of black rocks fairly in the path of his storm-harried craft. The murk closed in again.

"We're going ashore!" he roared.

Rosalind nodded.

" In half a minute — not more ! "

Again she signed that she understood.

" Listen ! " His lips were bellowing the words into her ear. " I'll steer until we're ready to hit. Then I'll rush you forward and get you ashore somehow. Understand ? "

She nodded.

" Be ready ! "

Now he prayed for another glimpse of the goal that lay ahead, but it was denied him. He could only calculate its nearness; nay, could do little more than guess. Second by second they were closing upon it, yet he dared not release the tiller, for if the launch yawed before she struck she might never strike at all. Safety or disaster lay in the barrier toward which they were sweeping, he knew not which.

But his plans were swiftly made. The woman at his side would have the best chance he could give her.

He tried counting the seconds, but this was useless. If he could but see again for a single instant! It was death to start too soon; death to wait too long. And he could only guess at the moment!

The tension snapped. Why — how — he did not know; the hail still half blinded him. Yet he staggered to his feet, dragging her with him, and rushed forward, knee-deep in the water that filled the rapidly settling launch.

As he neared the bow a black wall sprang out of the gray mist. To Rosalind it seemed to rear itself to an impossible height. The launch lunged heavily toward it.

" Don't cling to me ! " he shouted.

At the same instant she was lifted in his arms. As the boatman stepped out upon the slippery, staggering deck the black wall hung over her.

Rosalind felt herself tossed into the air. For what seemed an interminable period she hung suspended in space. Then something rose to meet her feet with a jarring shock. She was standing on a ledge.

Below her, even above the roar of the wind, came the sound of a heavy, crashing blow. The launch had struck. She knew what that meant. The boatman had given her the one chance!

With a gasping sob she whirled about and stepped to the edge of the rock.

"Sam!"

The hail beat upon her cheeks, but she did not feel it as she stared downward at the frothing water. There was no sign of the launch.

"*Sam!*"

Her voice had risen to a shriek.

Something touched her foot — a hand!

She dropped to her knees and seized it in both hers. He was hanging in mid air, the river lashing hungrily at his feet as his body swayed in the gale.

Afterward he assured her it had been a matter of less than ten seconds. To Rosalind it seemed an eternity. Some of it she achieved herself, although she had no clear recollection as to how.

But he stood at last with the ledge under his feet.

And then, white-faced and laboring for breath, he grinned:

"Good work, pal!"

CHAPTER XXI

NEW LIGHTS ON SAM

FOR a little they stood upon the ledge, the storm beating into their faces. Rosalind scarcely sensed the pounding of the hail. She and the boatman had almost clasped hands with death, and the memory of it drove other thoughts from her mind.

The trivial parts of the affair occupied a curiously exaggerated importance in her reflections. She realized that it was absurdly insignificant, yet she found herself considering chiefly, not the fact that by any effort truly astonishing he had flung her to a refuge far above the boiling river, but the mere incident that while she lay in his arms his scrawny beard, cold and wet, had brushed her cheek — yes, even his mustache. She wondered if he had really kissed her; she was not sure. Nor — and this was another curiosity — did she seem to care.

She remembered, too, the stertorous whistling of his breath as he flung her from him — the queer, Buddhalike appearance of his head, with the hail-stones matted among the hair — the way that his eyes blinked as the water streamed down his fore-head — the rough and sure clasp of his arms — the fact that one of his feet slid several inches along the rolling deck as he gathered himself for the last ef-fort. All the little things were photographed with microscopic fineness upon her mind.

" There must be better places than this," he suggested. " Come on."

He seized her by the arm, turning her toward a rocky slope that led upward from the ledge. She shook herself free with an impatient energy, resolved that she would do something for herself.

They scrambled up the slope and found themselves at the edge of a grove of trees. Here at last was a partial shelter; they went in under the branches.

Rosalind stumbled ahead, her soaked garments clinging to her legs with a persistence that endeavored to trip her. Now and then a branch snapped ominously above their heads, but they paid no attention to these warnings of a new danger. It seemed like luxury to be shielded even imperfectly from the relentless stabbing of the hail.

" Is it an island? " she asked.

" That's sure," said the boatman as they plunged forward through the shrieking gloom.

" The — the boat is gone? "

She knew it without asking, yet the question rose mechanically to her lips.

" Gone for good," he nodded. " That'll save you a whole lot of trouble, I guess. I hated to see her go; you had that old carbureter adjusted to a hair."

Rosalind smiled in spite of herself.

" The trouble was in the air-intake," she said as her foot struck sharply against a root, almost upsetting her. " The mixture was too thin."

" I didn't know what it was. *Ouch!* Caught that branch right in the eye. But it was the new batteries that did the trick most of all."

" And a clean spark-plug," she added as a sudden

gust flung her roughly against a tree. "A dirty one is a crime."

"If I get another launch — I'll get a two-cylinder, and — But then I won't be One-Cylinder Sam, will I?"

"Get a four if you can afford it," she advised, pausing for an instant to free her wet skirt from her ankles. "It'll burn a little more gas, but you'll get more speed and less vibration — Heavens!"

The latter exclamation came as she went headlong over a jutting stone.

He picked her up and steadied her on her feet; then, linking his arm in hers, he urged her forward. The storm roared overhead, but they paid no heed to it.

"Where are we going?" she asked after a little.

"Just going," he replied. "It's better than standing still."

They came to an open space, hesitated for an instant, then plunged out from the shelter of the trees and crossed it. As they neared the farther side a large, dim object barred their way.

"A house!" he exclaimed.

They broke into a run and stumbled up the steps that led to a porch. Rosalind staggered to a willow rocking-chair that was swaying furiously in the wind and sank into it. The boatman looked around him; then grinned broadly.

"Well?" she demanded.

"It's Davidson's!"

The freak of fate that brought her and the boatman to the scene of his escapades impressed her lightly at the time.

"We can get out of the storm then."

" *You* can, at any rate.   Let's see."

He tried a door that stood back of her chair, but found it locked.

" This is the side of the house," he said.   " Let's go around front."

She rose wearily and followed him along the porch.   The front door was locked also.   He bade her wait while he went to the rear, but when he returned it was with the news that all the entrances were fastened.   They tried ringing the bell, but it brought no response save the clanging of a gong.

" Servants must be out," he commented.   " Joyriding in the yacht, I suppose.   Let's have a look at the windows."

They were fastened.

Rosalind began to shiver.   The hail had changed into a downpour of rain, but the wind showed no sign of slackening.

" I guess a locked house won't bother you and me," said the boatman, with a laugh.

He walked to the nearest window, lifted his foot, and sent it crashing through the glass.   Through the opening he thrust an arm, slipped back the fastening, and raised the sash.

" Welcome! " he called, beckoning to her.

Without hesitation Rosalind entered the house by way of the window.   The boatman followed her.

" So long as there's nobody home I'll come in myself," he said.

They were standing in the dining-room; even in the gloom of the interior Rosalind could discern a shining of glass and silverware that stood on a sideboard.   Sam groped along the wall for an electric switch and, finding it, turned on the lights.

" Let's try the library; there's a fireplace there,
he said.

Rosalind remembered how he knew, but she felt
it was not a time for dwelling upon previous house-
breakings. She followed him readily, crossing a
broad hall and entering a room where the floor was
cushioned with thick rugs.

The chimney-place had been set for a fire, but no
match had been applied to the kindlings. He found
one on the center table, and Rosalind, sighing
contentedly, watched the red flames grow and
spread.

Next he pushed a heavy leather chair across the
floor close to the hearth, and motioned her into it.
She sat obediently and stretched her feet close to the
blaze. Without a word, he dropped to his knees
and began taking off her shoes.

She felt too comfortable to protest. Besides, he
did it with the wholly impersonal manner of a sales-
man; also, Rosalind reflected, it was a sensible thing
to do.

After he had placed her damp shoes close to the
fire, at one side of the hearth, he brought her a foot-
stool. Then he disappeared in the direction of the
dining-room. When he returned he was carrying
a tray, upon which were a decanter and two glasses.

" Sherry? " he asked.

" Thank you."

She took the glass that he filled and sipped its contents. The boatman helped himself.

" Still blowing," he commented as he watched the
sparks sucked up the chimney.

Rosalind gave little thought to the tumult without.
She was too thoroughly luxurious. Even though her

gown was wet, she felt that she had been thrust into a wholly sybaritic environment. Lazily she watched two little, ascending volumes of steam as her stockings began to dry before the fire.

" How about eating? " he asked.

" We might," she admitted. " That is, if you know —"

" Been here before," he answered, smiling. " You remember, I guess."

She watched him as he went back to the dining-room, and a minute after that from another apartment she heard sounds, which she judged to indicate the pantry or the kitchen.

It was rather curious to be in a house with a burglar, she reflected. She did not think of it as hazardous, or unlawful, or even improper — merely as curious. Ethics had been knocked out of her adventure long ago. She was thankful for the wine he brought her; she would be glad when the food came. These were material comforts, very real and needful; and her mind for the present was dwelling only upon material things.

It did not seem to her that it was even unusual to break Mr. Davidson's window, to enter his house, to light his fire, to drink his sherry, to eat his food; these were but mere incidents in a necessary proceeding.

Nor did she waste much thought upon the ringleader and companion in the affair. Who or what he was did not matter much — just then; it was what he did that counted. And Rosalind knew, if she had been alone, that she would have done precisely the same thing. She found it rather pleasant to have somebody else performing the drudgery.

He came back with a loaf of bread, some butter, and a can of potted tongue.

"I'm making some tea," he said. "It'll be ready as soon as the water boils."

He carved a slice of bread, buttered it for her, and offered it. She accepted with a nod of thanks, and mentally noted the fact that he knew how to cut thin slices.

The food and wine warmed her; they even thawed her wonted austerity. When he had finished eating, the boatman rummaged some cigarettes. He offered her one; she declined, but with a smile. Had she been alone — well, she might.

Under past circumstances, such an assumption on his part would have roused her to rebuke. But she was in an oddly comfortable mood.

As he settled down in a chair and stretched his long legs toward the fire, she studied him furtively. Particularly she studied his head. So far as shape went, it seemed quite unlike any of the pictures that represented the heads of typical criminals. It was rather well constructed, along conventional and respectable lines.

The beard he wore baffled her somewhat in an attempt to read his face; but that also, she decided, represented a normal average. Rosalind was in no sense a criminologist; yet in outward aspects the boatman had a law-abiding appearance.

He even revealed some traits that she admired. He had courage, for one thing; and resource for another. He had strength, too, which counted for something. In certain things he was rather ingenious, if frankly unprincipled.

Strangely enough, the thing for which she would

have marked him "Excellent," had she been making out his report-card, was the very one that had so frequently lashed her to anger — his absolute lack of servility.

From most persons, and always from her inferiors, servility was something that Rosalind expected — and detested. She took it as her due; yes, even demanded it. But she despised the thing itself.

The boatman had offered her none. This was presumptuous, of course; yet secretly she set it down to his credit. He never groveled; he was rarely deferential. More often, in fact, he was rude and given to mocking. But he inspired in her a sort of wondering and unaccountable respect.

He stared lazily into the fire, as if oblivious of her presence. Without, the storm still ruled, although it had palpably slackened in fury. Sam seemed to be concerned about nothing save his cigarette.

Abruptly Rosalind rallied from her musings concerning him. She had completely forgotten the reason for her presence on Davidson's Island — that she was being kidnaped into matrimony! Her lips tightened, and she glanced at him sharply.

Had he really meant it? He appeared to have forgotten it completely. And if he had meant it, was it a sign of madness?

Try as she would, she could not reconcile the boatman with presumptive insanity. For that matter, she could not reconcile him with much of anything. She never realized until this moment how little she actually knew about him.

He looked up; their eyes met. Rosalind colored faintly. Something shot her thoughts back to the last instant aboard the launch when his wet beard brushed her cheek. She wondered if he really had — there was so much confusion.

" Sam! "

" Yes, ma'am."

" Please don't say ' ma'am ' to me."

" Why not? "

" It's a word you are not accustomed to employing," she answered.

His study of her face was brief yet comprehensive.

" You think so? "

" I know it. It took you a long while to say it without hesitating. And it does not — well, harmonize with other things that you say."

" All right; I'll quit it, Miss Chalmers."

" You helped me out of a rather bad situation a little while ago," she said slowly.

She wanted to thank him, yet felt instinctively that he did not wish to be thanked.

" Well, I got you into it; that was why."

" Yet if I had left your island alone I would undoubtedly have been caught in the same storm."

" Oh, perhaps! "

" I think it was — splendid! "

" Why, thanks, ma — I mean, Miss Chalmers. Only you did the same for me after you were up on the rock. So that makes it a stand-off."

Something in his manner and his speech perplexed her. Always before there was raillery, derision; now he seemed to cloak himself in a grave reserve.

" Sam! "

He waited for her to continue:

" You are not really a — common boatman," she said very positively.

" Sure of that? "

" Quite. But who are you? "

" You know enough, I guess."

" I'm afraid you *are* a burglar."

" It looks like it, doesn't it? "

" Are you a spy? "

" I'm not on the witness-stand."

" Or a smuggler? And before you answer that I don't mind saying that all smuggling is not — wicked."

He laughed outright.

" You certainly want me to confess something, so you made that one easy. Well, if I'm a smuggler I'm not a very good one, I'm afraid. I haven't been able to smuggle you to the American side yet."

Rosalind stiffened in her chair. Automatically she drew her stockinged feet beneath her skirt. If there was to be another battle she felt that there was a lack of militancy about her feet. A lady without her shoes is scarcely girded for combat.

" That of course was an utterly absurd idea," she said firmly. " But I am willing to consider it as a joke, in view — of all that has happened."

" Much obliged. But it wasn't a joke."

" You couldn't have meant it seriously? "

" Absolutely, Miss Chalmers."

" But why? Whatever put such a wild idea into your head? "

" I told you at the time. No use to go all over it again."

" But you must have had some reason."

" Sure. I wanted to marry you. I should say — ' want.' "

" You still —"

"Want to? Oh, yes!"

"And you expect to go on with this impossible — affair?"

This time he merely made a gesture. It might have meant anything.

"Would you marry a woman who hated you?"

He considered this for some time, then looked her evenly in the eyes and answered:

"You don't hate me."

Rosalind flushed, and did some considering on her own account.

"Possibly not," she admitted. "They say it is wicked to hate, so I try not to. But, even if I do not hate you, why should you have the least reason to think I would marry you?"

"Oh, what's the use of speculating?" he said wearily. "Maybe it was because I wanted to put over a stunt nobody else had been able to do — like finding the north pole."

Rosalind rose suddenly and walked toward a window. Her first impulse was to fly into a temper.

A stunt! The task of winning her had become a — stunt! And he had supplemented the insult of comparing her to the north pole!

Yet even in her anger she felt the urging of a desire to smile. Rosalind was a severe and conscientious self-analyst; she harbored few illusions. There was something in the frigid comparison that struck her as rather clever — possibly true.

Perhaps, after all, she mused, it was a rough compliment. To be classed among things practically unattainable implies a certain distinction.

"And you know," drawled a voice from the fireplace, "the north pole was discovered."

She bit her lip and stared out of the window.

The rain had stopped and the wind was flattening. Overhead the racing clouds were being sundered into groups and patches. She could see intervals of blue.

" A boat! " she called sharply. " Mr. Davidson's yacht! "

Sam sprang from his chair and joined her at the window. The yacht was making the wharf.

" Well, I guess this polar expedition has failed," he observed whimsically. " Better luck next time."

Rosalind was thinking rapidly. The arrival of the yacht meant safety — for her. But what of the boatman?

As they watched together a small procession of persons filed out upon the dock and began to march to the house.

" Mr. Davidson! " she exclaimed. " He's back! "

The boatman nodded.

" Mr. Witherbee, Mr. Morton, Mr. Williams — oh, everybody! And they have got — Billy Kellogg! "

She could easily discern the short, stout figure of the young man who had admitted to Polly that he was an impostor. He was walking between Mr. Davidson and one of the men servants, his head bent, his attitude that of complete dejection.

The boatman inspected the group with interest, particularly the stout young man.

" Run! " exclaimed Rosalind, turning swiftly upon him.

" And what are you going to do? "

" I'm all right; *I* can stay. I'll explain — somehow. But you must go. Take the back door, quick!"

"But why should I go?"

"A thousand reasons!"

"So as not to embarrass you," he suggested, watching the oncoming procession.

"I — I didn't mean that. Go, while there's a chance."

"So you don't want me caught?"

"No!"

Still he hesitated. Rosalind gripped him by the arm and pushed him back from the window.

"Hurry!" she commanded. "You have time to get out the back way. Sam — please!"

The boatman smiled.

"All right; I'll disappear," he said. "Maybe I'll see you again, Miss — No; I'm going to say it just once — Rosalind!"

"You said it back in the boat," she reminded him briskly.

"Then I really got away with it — because you heard."

"Yes; you really —'got away with it,' if that satisfies you. Now run! They're on the porch."

He stepped swiftly across the library and into the hall. The sound of Mr. Davidson's key in the lock was heard. With a laughing nod at Rosalind, the boatman turned and ran — up-stairs!

"Sam!"

"S-sh!"

Rosalind faced the door desperately.

"Now I must manage to keep them down-stairs," she muttered.

CHAPTER XXII

FOOTSTEPS ABOVE

AS the door was flung open Rosalind stood with her back against the newel-post of the staircase, braced for defense against an army. Her brain was in a tumult of activity.

"Rosalind!"

It was Polly's shriek. With it she sprang forward. The lady at the foot of the staircase waved her back with a gesture.

"I'm quite all right, thanks," she said coolly.

"You're half drowned!"

"Not in the least; merely a little wet. Don't bother, Polly."

The men were staring as if at an apparition.

"Well, I'll be —"

Mr. Davidson left the sentence unfinished and resumed his incredulous scrutiny.

It was Reggy Williams's turn to make a rush; but, as in the case of Polly, Rosalind wafted him away with a motion of her hand.

"Please don't make a fuss," she said. "No damage has been done whatever — except to a window. I broke it to get in."

"But how? Where did you come from? What brought you —"

The chorus of voices brought a frown of annoyance to her brow.

"I was rowing when the squall came," she observed quietly. "This was the nearest place to land, so I came here. Apparently nobody was at home, so I had to force my way in in order to get out of the storm."

"We — we didn't know what had happened!" exclaimed Polly, her voice trembling. "We thought you might be — lost."

"I took care of myself quite nicely, thank you. I've had tea and bread and butter, and I lighted a fire."

Rosalind's glance scanned the group and rested upon the stout young man. He stood limp and unresisting in the grasp of Mr. Davidson's butler. In the surprise of the meeting he had been forgotten. He seemed quite contented to have it so.

"Well, thank the Lord, you're safe!" said Mr. Davidson heartily. "Glad you made yourself at home; the house is yours. I got your telegram, you see."

He turned to glare at the prisoner, who was bestowing upon Rosalind a look of gloomy reproach. She eyed the young man coldly.

"I thought it was best to send for you," she said.

"Best! I should say it was! You — you impostor!"

The master of the house shook his fist under the nose of the prisoner, who retreated a pace.

"Of course he isn't your nephew?"

"That! My nephew? I should say not!"

The stout young man shifted his feet.

"Once more I'll give you a chance to tell who

you are," said Mr. Davidson as he whirled upon the fellow.

The captive remained dumb.

"See that!" exclaimed Mr. Davidson. "He won't say a word. Hasn't said a word since I got here. We've searched him. And, by George, he's got letters on him addressed to my nephew, Billy Kellogg! And letterheads with the name of ' Hastings & Hatch ' ! I tell you there's something bad here."

" You think —"

" That maybe it's — *murder!* "

Polly suppressed a little shriek, while the stout and speechless young man shook his head miserably.

" Yes — murder! Why not? " demanded Mr. Davidson. " He's probably done away with my nephew, taken his place in New York, and all that sort of thing. I'm wiring for more news now. The scoundrel —"

" But if that's the case," broke in Reggy Williams, " I don't see why he'd want to come up here."

" Perhaps to finish his bloody work — to kill me ! "

The prisoner sagged into the arms of the butler.

" That seems rather incredible," mused Rosalind.

Her observation of the captive had long ago driven her to the conclusion that he was quite harmless.

" Incredible ! " echoed Mr. Davidson. " Everything's incredible here lately. If it's not murder, what is it? Where's my nephew? This man won't tell. He knows; he's simply *got* to know! He hears I'm away and he comes up here posing as Billy.

If it hadn't been for Polly here or Morton he'd have fooled you all."

"But Mr. Morton —"

Rosalind checked herself and glanced at the Englishman. He chewed one end of his mustache, but remained silent. Morton had taken no part in the exposure; on the contrary, he had accepted the impostor.

"Oh, Morton pretended to know him, just so as to be able to watch him better," said Mr. Davidson. "I understand all about that. But what I want to know is, who *is* this scoundrel? Are you going to tell, sir? Who are you?"

The young man remained steadfastly silent.

"Maybe I can make him talk," said Reggy Williams grimly, advancing his huge bulk toward the captive.

It was Mr. Witherbee who remembered first Reggy's heart! Everybody had forgotten it in the turmoil.

"Never mind, old man," he said anxiously, with a restraining hand on Reggy's arm. "Take a chair. Sit down."

Reggy looked at him disgustedly.

"Will somebody kindly explain to me what this take-a-chair game is?" he demanded. "Everybody seems to be crazy on the subject of chairs; everybody wants me to sit down. I don't want to be disobliging; but, great Scott! a man can't sit down all his life!"

Rosalind, still on guard at the newel-post, was chewing her lips.

Polly's eyes were distended with apprehension.

"Well, never mind trying to make him talk now,"

said Mr. Witherbee soothingly. "Just leave it to Davidson."

"I'm going to leave it to the police," said that gentleman. "I've sent for them. We're going to have a few things explained before I get through. First, there's my nephew's murder."

"But you're not sure about that," Rosalind reminded him. "Perhaps he'll turn up all right."

"Perhaps." But Mr. Davidson's tone was pessimistic. "We'll know before long, at any rate. Then there's that boatman who's been hanging around here. I've got men out after him now."

Rosalind breathed softly. She was eagerly yet fearfully listening for some sound from up-stairs.

"What is he wanted for?" she asked.

"Burglary — almost everything! He is in on this; we feel sure of it. Morton tipped me to get him."

Rosalind studied the Englishman swiftly, but his face was impassive. So Morton had turned on the boatman at last! She wondered why.

"Don't forget the smuggling either," said Mr. Witherbee.

"I haven't," answered the master of the house. "I've sent for the customs men. I want them to look this chap over, and also that boatman — when we get him."

"Some of them think the boatman is a spy," Polly reminded him.

"Likely enough. But that's none of my affair. He can spy till he's blind so far as I'm concerned. I want him for housebreaking."

Rosalind experienced a qualm, not of conscience but of anxiety. She felt that her house of cards was about to topple.   If they did get the boatman, what of her?

"Well, no use standing here," said Mr. Davidson. "We can't do anything more, I suppose, until the police come.   Let's go into the library."

"And what'll I do with him, sir?" asked the butler, indicating his prisoner.

"Take him up-stairs and lock him in the attic."

Rosalind's hand went to her throat.   Instinctively she moved to bar the stairway.

"I wouldn't," she advised hastily.   "He might escape."

"Can't," declared Mr. Davidson emphatically. "He's too big to get through an attic window, and if he did manage it he'd drop about forty feet to the ground.   Take him up-stairs, James."

"No," said Rosalind firmly.

Mr. Davidson looked at her in surprise.

"I've a better plan," she continued quickly. "Keep him with us.   Watch him.   Study him. Sometimes they — they betray themselves."

The prisoner regarded her with appealing eyes.

"All right; watch him if you like," assented Mr. Davidson.   "Bring him into the library, James."

Not until the last of them had left the hall did Rosalind desert her post at the foot of the staircase. As she moved to follow she gazed swiftly upward, but the boatman was not in sight.

Her mood was a mixture of alarm and irritation. For the life of her she could not understand why Sam committed the folly of seeking a refuge up-stairs, when there were easy avenues of escape by the rear of the house.   True, he might make his exit by an upper window and across the porch-roof; but it was an extra and a useless hazard. Most amazing was the fact that she did not know whether he was still in the house. She prayed he was not, but feared otherwise. Nobody must go up-stairs until she could be sure.

It did not add to her peace of mind to discover as she followed the prisoner and his captors into the library that she was shoeless. Over by the fire her slippers were still drying. Mr. Morton was staring solemnly at them.

With icy dignity she glided past him and picked them up.

"Ah — allow me," he said, dropping to one knee.

"Thank you, but I always put on my own shoes," said Rosalind.

Damp as they were, she contrived to squeeze into them. They gave her a sense of security.

"You must have been good and hungry, Rosalind," remarked Reggy Williams.

He was examining the tea-tray with its two cups and saucers. She did not at first understand.

"Certainly I was hungry."

"As hungry as two people, evidently."

She colored faintly, but answered readily enough. "Oh! you mean the two cups and saucers. I did it absent-mindedly. I'm not accustomed to lunching alone."

Reggy's finger touched a cigarette-butt that lay on the tray; his glance was accusing.

"I admit it," said Rosalind coldly. "Is there any reason why I should not?"

Reggy made a disapproving gesture, but answered not.

" There are two more on the hearth," she added, pointing.

" But, Rosalind —"

" I am exceedingly fond of them. That is sufficient."

She spoke with a finality that discouraged him, which was exactly what she intended. Mentally she added another mark to the score against the boatman.

The stout young man had been placed in a stiffbacked chair near a window. The butler stood vigilantly at his side, ready to descend upon him if he made a suspicious move. But the prisoner was inert. All volition as well as speech had deserted him.

Mr. Davidson paced the library, talking volubly. Now and then he halted in front of his victim and glowered at him belligerently. That young man was too impassive even to think. He seemed utterly uninterested in his fate.

Mr. Witherbee tried to insinuate a chair under the legs of Reggy Williams, which brought an outraged snort from that gentleman. Rosalind was beginning to feel the tension. Would the boatman never go? Or had he gone?

They pressed her for the story of her own adventures and she supplied it rapidly as she could invent. It was not easy to eliminate Sam from the recital; more than once she checked his name on her lips. Yet she managed a very fair yarn. It filled Polly with thrills of awe and admiration. She could not take her eyes from the narrator.

In fact, so completely did she study the figure of

this remarkable young woman that she was moved to a startled exclamation:

" Why, Rosalind! "

Polly was pointing at Rosalind's left arm. It was too late to hide it; the bracelet was glowing dully in the afternoon light.

" Where on earth did *you* get it? "

Rosalind flushed with anger and dismay. Reggy was staring, also.

" So you do wear it sometimes," he said with a sigh.

" But it's the one we found! " exclaimed Polly, bewildered. " And then we gave it to the sale. And they lost it! And — why, Rosalind! "

The wearer of the telltale ornament was for once speechless. All her resourcefulness was swept away in an instant. Her cheeks were very red, but her eyes were defiant. The look she gave Polly was fairly murderous.

A noise from up-stairs caused abrupt silence in the library. Everybody heard it clearly. It was a footstep!

Rosalind stopped breathing and waited. Mr. Davidson held up a warning finger. The young man in the chair looked expectant.

The first footstep was followed by others. There was nothing stealthy about them; they were frank, careless, and unconcerned. Somebody was walking along the upper hall!

An instant later the footsteps were on the staircase, descending leisurely. The tableau in the library was held without a quiver by its actors. Their eyes were staring toward the doorway that led into the hall. Rosalind was rigid as bronze. She alone knew what the footsteps portended. The game was up!

Very deliberately they came nearer and nearer. She even found herself counting them mechanically. It was like the approach of nemesis. Had the boat-man gone mad again?

The footsteps were in the hall now. Mr. Davidson's stout body began to quiver; he was poised as if for a spring, his eyes ablaze with determination, his hands —

A young man in white flannels walked into the library.

He was slender and tall and immaculate. Under his coat he wore a delicately striped silk shirt. His collar and scarf were beyond criticism. His canvas shoes were spotless.

A casual observer would have noted but one unusual fact; the upper half of his face was deeply tanned, while his cheeks, his lip and his chin were pallid. He was cleanly shaved.

"Hello, folks!" he grinned.

Mr. Davidson made the spring for which he had been poised.

"Billy! You young scoundrel!"

In the same instant he enveloped the intruder with a bearlike embrace.

The young man gazed placidly over Mr. Davidson's head and straight into the eyes of Rosalind Chalmers.

CHAPTER XXIII

UNSCRAMBLING THE MYSTERY

HOT resentment overcame Rosalind — resentment at the boatman's duplicity, at the trick he had played upon her, at her own lack of perception. It was succeeded by a sense of extraordinary humiliation. She felt as if a cross section had been carved out of her life and spread before vulgar eyes upon the slide of an inexorable microscope — for she did not pause to consider that much of what had happened was known only to Sam and herself.

Then came a period of panic. There would be revelations, of course. How far would they go?''

Yet, while her mind was in an agony of agitation, she managed to maintain her poise. Steadily, and without wincing, she stared into the face of Billy Kellogg — and waited.

Mr. Davidson stepped back a pace and surveyed his nephew.

" But — when did you get back? " he cried.

" I haven't been away."

" What! "

William Kissam Kellogg smiled benignantly at his uncle.

" But how — what — where —"

Mr. Davidson paused to recover his breath. The glance of the ex-boatman wandered to other members of the party.

" Hello, Polly ! " he said.

Polly was speechless — unable to answer the salu-tation. She gazed upon Kellogg as she would at some supernatural thing.

" There seems to be a great deal of fuss about nothing in particular," he remarked. " What's up ? "

" Up ! " repeated Mr. Davidson. " Everything's up ! You're alive ! "

" I hope so."

" We — we thought you were murdered," faltered Polly, finding speech.

" Honestly? What put that idea into your head ? "

For answer, Mr. Davidson pointed grimly at the stout young man in the chair.

" Hello, Bob ! " said Billy Kellogg casually. " You couldn't duck it — eh ? "

The prisoner shook his head miserably.

The nephew chuckled as he greeted the captive with a hand-shake.

" Bob's all right," he assured is uncle. " He's a friend of mine."

Mr. Davidson's jaw was hanging.

" But you — you —"

" Why not introduce me, Uncle Henry ? "

The master of the house gulped, and performed the ceremony in a bewildered and perfunctory style. Toward the last he arrived at Rosalind.

" My nephew, Billy Kellogg," he said lamely.

Rosalind bowed almost imperceptibly. Her eyes were hard and questioning. Inwardly she trembled; but she did not flinch. The former boatman studied her with a whimsical glance.

"We've met before, Miss Chalmers," he said, bowing.

"I believe so," she answered briefly.

"You see," said Kellogg, turning to his uncle, "I've had the honor of serving Miss Chalmers at odd times within the last few days. We — Why, hello, Reggy!"

For the first time he appeared to observe Reginald Williams, who had been watching the scene in dumb amazement.

"Bill Kellogg!" he exclaimed. "You mean to tell me that you were —"

Billy nodded and grinned.

"Of course I don't need to introduce Morton," said Mr. Davidson.

Billy looked at the Englishman and nodded coldly.

"No, you don't need to," he agreed.

Mr. Morton preserved a calm exterior. He contented himself with returning the bow.

"Now explain yourself!" ordered Mr. Davidson peremptorily. "When did you quit New York?"

"Haven't been there, Uncle Henry."

"You haven't been at work — at all?"

"Not at the banking-game."

"But how the —"

"Somebody lend me a cigarette," said Billy. "Thanks. I see I've got to tell all."

He cast a swift, malicious glance at Rosalind.

"You see, Uncle Henry," he went on, "it wasn't that I minded banking so much as the fact that I hated to go away and leave this crook here with ten thousand dollars of perfectly good money."

He nodded toward Morton.

"Crook?" echoed Mr. Davidson.

"Sure! Did you think I wasn't wise? I knew it the very night he trimmed me. But he was your guest in *our* house; so what could I say?

"I knew I'd been buncoed the minute I thought the thing over. So I didn't propose to go away and leave him on the job. I decided to stick around and take a chance on getting it back."

Morton was imperturbable.

"And I got it back," added Billy triumphantly, with a fleeting look at Rosalind.

Mr. Davidson turned a questioning glance upon the Englishman, who nodded and smiled faintly. A bewildered look overspread the face of the master of the house.

"I introduced him to poker," explained Billy.

"Introduced — him!" cried his uncle. "Introduced Morton to poker? Why, you young cub, he played poker before you were out of knee-breeches!"

It was the turn of the young man in white flannels to stare.

"He knows more poker in a minute than you do in a month," declared Mr. Davidson contemptuously. "He eats it! And as for being a crook — well, he happens to be the English representative of my own firm; that's all."

Rosalind enjoyed the discomfiture of the ex-captain of the *Fifty-Fifty*. "But, uncle, he —"

"Oh, shucks! You think he trimmed you at bridge, do you? All right; he did. I told him to!"

Billy Kellogg swallowed hard.

"That's what I brought him here for," said Uncle Henry. "You needed a lesson, and there was only one way to give it to you. I told him to come here and skin you alive. I wanted a good excuse to send you to work. I told him to trim you for a year's income if he could. And you did, didn't you, Morton?"

The Englishman shrugged in a bored way.

"It was strictly a matter of business between Morton and myself. You were to get your money back at the end of a year — if you behaved. Why, he told me it was as easy as taking a saucer of milk away from a blind kitten!"

Rosalind smiled and made a motion to attract the attention of Billy. She did not want him to miss the smile. He didn't.

"And now explain where you've been," commanded Uncle Henry.

"I haven't been far," said his nephew in a crestfallen tone. "I went over to the American side for a while and thought it over. I decided I wouldn't be a banker. I made up my mind I'd stay here as long as Morton did and lay for him. But of course I didn't want you to get wise, so I kept out of sight until I could grow whiskers. I'm glad they're gone."

He rubbed his chin tenderly.

"After I got whiskers enough I looked around for something to do. A fellow had a boat cheap and I bought it. I had money enough for that. Then I went to work."

Polly Dawson gasped.

"You — were that boatman!"

The nephew nodded.

"You mean the burglar?" demanded Mr. Davidson, whirling upon her.

"You only thought I was a burglar," explained Billy. "I just dropped in now and then when I needed anything."

" You unprincipled rascal! Do you know the Cain you've raised? "

" Something of it, Uncle Henry. I didn't mean to make too much trouble, of course — not any more than was necessary."

Mr. Davidson suddenly recollected the prisoner, who sat in the chair.

" Who's that, then? " he demanded.

" Oh, he's Bob Murray."

" And who in blazes —"

" An old friend. You see, Bob and I went to college together. Bob's a lot different from me. He likes to work. In fact, he *has* to work. Just about the time you shipped me off to Hastings & Hatch — or thought you did — I heard from Bob. He needed a job. So I gave him mine. I sent him the letter and the full directions. And I understand he's done me credit, too."

" Is this true? " demanded Mr. Davidson, glaring at the captive.

The young man nodded.

" Then why didn't you say so? "

" Because I swore him to secrecy," explained Billy. " I told Bob not to squeal until I gave the word. And he stuck by me."

Uncle Henry only half succeeded in suppressing an expletive.

" Of course, Bob didn't want to come when you sent for me," continued Mr. Davidson's nephew. " But I understand the bank ordered him to come, so he couldn't help himself. He knew I was up here, anyway, and figured that I'd straighten it out for him."

The stout young man breathed deeply and contentedly.

"You're a pair of young fools — and scoundrels!" said Uncle Henry heatedly. "One is as bad as the other."

"Oh, hold on," protested Billy. "Go easy there. Bob's a model young banker. They tell me you've said so yourself; that you were so proud of him you spread the news around."

Mr. Davidson gave his nephew a furious look.

"And to think — none of us recognized you!" exclaimed Polly, staring at the former captain of the one-cylinder launch.

"You were the only one I was afraid of," laughed Billy. "You see, *you* knew me; the rest didn't — except Morton. That's why I wouldn't let you aboard one day after they'd planned to take you. I knew you'd recognize my voice."

"But didn't Mr. Morton?"

All eyes were turned upon the Englishman. He coughed, but said nothing.

"Of course he knew me; but I did not care about him. I knew he would not squeal. You see, I had it on him about the cards — or I thought I did."

Mr. Morton permitted himself to smile in a bored way.

"And now I understand why you were deaf and dumb to me," blurted Reggy Williams with a sheepish flush.

"You see, Reggy and I are old pals," remarked Billy. "I knew he'd never recognize me in my old rig and with the beard; but I didn't dare speak to him. So I played dummy."

Reggy turned an inquiring glance upon Rosalind.

" Was he a dummy when you hired him? " he inquired.

She shook her head.

" But you didn't tell me that! "

The silence threatened catastrophe. It was broken by a strident laugh from Billy Kellogg.

" Oh, I've been having a lot of fun," he said. " Of course I didn't mean to get you all worked up over burglars. Remember the night, Uncle Henry, when you and the help hunted the whole island and then chased me in the launch? "

Rosalind breathed again. The boatman was doing his best to save her.

" Do I remember? " shouted Mr. Davidson. " You bet I do! You young reprobate! I might have shot you; do you know that? And — and who was it that helped you out? "

" Helped me out? " repeated Billy, with an innocent stare and a wrinkling of his forehead. " How do you mean? "

" The other boat — the fellow who boarded you and got your engine going."

The young man in flannels shook his head in a puzzled way.

" No fellow boarded me," he said.

" I tell you we heard him — saw him."

" He didn't come aboard my boat, Uncle Henry. I'll swear."

" Billy, you're lying! "

Mr. Davidson's nephew indicated that he was deeply affronted by the accusation. He gazed solemnly at Rosalind. She was idly turning the leaves of a book that lay on the library table.

"I suppose I must put up with anything," he sighed.

"After what you've made us put up with I should say yes!" snorted Mr. Davidson. "But there *was* somebody else; we've got evidence. It was the other man who tried to rob Witherbee's — the same night! You've been keeping bad company, young man."

Billy glanced again at Rosalind, but her face was averted from him.

"And, Morton, I'm surprised at you," continued Mr. Davidson. "If you really knew him, why didn't you tell me?"

"Um — ah! But — don't you see? —it would have been hardly sporting. Oh, not a bit!"

"And you deliberately let me go on making a fool of myself!"

The Englishman shrugged.

"And it was you who sent the customs men to look up Morton, I suppose," added Mr. Davidson, turning again to his nephew.

"I'm sorry I did that; it was just an impulse. I only wanted to bother him some."

Uncle Henry made an exasperated gesture.

"Well, you're disgraced, and so am I," he growled. "You're a worse scapegrace than I believed. You've made a fool out of everybody, including Miss Chalmers, who I understand has been employing you."

Rosalind looked up from the book and shook her head.

"Billy didn't make a fool out of me," she said.

The ex-boatman blinked.

"You see, I knew him from the first," she added.

" In fact, I've known him a good while. But — although perhaps it wasn't very considerate of the others — I didn't say anything because —. Well, for the same reason that Mr. Morton gave. It hardly seemed sporting."

Billy bit his tongue savagely; but he could not hide the little wrinkles at the corners of his eyes.

" What's she up to now? " he thought.

" So I just let the joke go on. If it was wrong, I'm sorry," concluded Rosalind.

" And you mean that you two have known each other all the time? " cried Polly, staring from one to the other.

" All the time," confirmed Billy. " Why, I've known Rosalind since she was a tomboy and — and climbed trees."

Rosalind flushed, but she nodded what was interpreted as a confirmation.

" Well," demanded Mr. Davidson, after a pause, " what am I going to tell the police when they come? "

" Try to head 'em off," suggested his nephew.

The master of the house accepted the suggestion and moved toward the telephone. As he lifted the instrument the bell began ringing.

" Well? " he asked, the receiver at his ear. " Yes, it's Mr. Davidson. What? Say it again. Richardson? Who — Oh, yes. I understand — yes.

" Tried to get Witherbee? Yes, he's here; we're all here. Yes, Mr. Morton is here, too.

" What's that? Well, what do you know about that?

" Huh? Sure!

"What? Yes; I'll tell him.

"Oh, certainly! It'll be all right. Glad you got him. Congratulations! Yeh — fine! Uh-huh! All — right!"

He replaced the instrument on the table.

"Customs men," he explained. "They wanted to apologize for bothering Morton the other day. They've got their man."

"Who?"

"Fellow that's been smuggling diamonds. Got him with the goods only an hour ago. A chap named Schmidt."

Rosalind and Billy exchanged swift looks.

"Why, that's the man they thought was a spy!" cried Polly.

"Well, he wasn't. He was just a plain smuggler."

"But, Billy, he used to hire your boat."

The ex-boatman made a weary motion with his hands.

"It's getting too many for me," he said. "He told me he was a grain-broker. A right decent sort of cuss, too."

"So you've been aiding and abetting a smuggler," remarked Mr. Davidson slowly as he glared at the boatman. "That's fine business for a nephew of mine. What else have you been doing? Any murders or embezzlements, or anything like that? Any highway robberies? Or maybe you were a pirate — eh? Well, why don't you answer?"

"What's the use? You're covering all the main points, I guess. I can't think of anything else."

Uncle Henry abandoned in disgust the task of cataloguing the probable misdeeds of his nephew and turned to the telephone in an effort to head off the police.

"Well, I suppose we may as well be going back," observed Mr. Witherbee. "There doesn't seem to be anything more to find out."

That reminded Polly.

"But the bracelet!" she exclaimed. "Rosalind! How in the world —"

Polly broke off abruptly and looked about the room.

"Why, where is she?"

Rosalind had disappeared.

CHAPTER XXIV.

CURTAIN !

TRUST Billy Kellogg to find her! He did. She was down in the boat-house, trying to smash a padlock that detained one of Mr. Davidson's skiffs. There was no doubt she was tremendously anxious to leave the island.

At his approach she looked up defiantly.

" Well? " she demanded.

" I did my best," he said contritely.

It was impossible to miss the resentment in her eyes.

" Your best! "

" I didn't tell any more than I had to," he explained. " You see, Rosalind —"

" Mr. Kellogg! "

" Oh, well! You called me Sam not so very long ago. And only a few minutes back I was Billy — and you said you had known me a good while."

" In self-defense."

" I don't see how —"

" It forestalled endless explanation," she said in a chilled voice.

" But you don't suppose all the explaining is over, do you? " objected Billy. " Polly was still asking about the bracelet when I left."

Rosalind sat on a nail-keg and stared at him combatively.

" I hope you are satisfied after having disgraced me," she said.

" I got your bracelet."

" And made a fool of me from beginning to end! "

" You dared me."

" I? "

" Yes — ma'am."

He smiled in a way that merited annihilation.

" Of course you dared me," added Billy. " Everything you did or said was a dare. Every time you were so scornful and so superior it was a dare. Why, I couldn't have helped it if I'd tried. And I didn't try, as a matter of fact."

Rosalind was in a strange plight of mind. She tried to summon haughtiness, but the mood would not respond. Her armor seemed to have fallen from her.

" You — you were brutally insulting," she faltered.

" I suppose I wasn't very polite," he admitted. " Nevertheless, you'll have to admit you weren't very polite to me. Let's forget the whole business."

" Forget? "

" Why not? What's the use of rehashing it? "

" You expect me to forget — after what has happened? The tree — and the water — and the por — portrait! "

" It wasn't a portrait," he said mildly. " I made a mistake. As for the telegram — Bob misunderstood when I wired him. I only wanted to be sure who you were. I wasn't bidding. At first I thought it wasn't a bad picture. But I found out I was wrong."

She looked up at him.

"Why, that portrait didn't begin to resemble you — ma'am."

"Please — I asked you!"

"Not to say 'ma'am.' I remember now. But it's so hard not to say 'Rosalind.'"

She made no answer to that.

"I wish you'd lash out at me just as you did when I was a boatman," he went on. "I was getting used to that."

Still Rosalind had no answer. She was groping blindly for her old footing, but could not find it. Everything had gone in the crash.

"Please unfasten the skiff," she said after a pause.

"What for?"

"I — I wish it. I'm going home."

"In a skiff?"

She met his glance with a flash of her old disdain.

"I'll go if I have to swim," she said. "Haven't I undergone enough? Haven't I been humiliated and made ridiculous and —"

"Not necessarily. It all depends on whether we're going to confess the whole business or stand on our constitutional rights. They don't know a tenth of it — yet. Why should they? We told 'em we'd known each other a long time. Why not play the hand out?"

Rosalind's eyes questioned him.

"I mean, why not resume the voyage — for Ogdensburg?"

She gasped.

"Certainly; why not?"

She rallied swiftly from the shock of the proposal.

"I think you forget yourself," she said sternly.

"Not a bit." He shook his head. "I haven't forgotten anything. On the contrary, I'm remembering all that happened and all that was said. I'm remembering about our being pals. You needn't jump at that. It's not a bad word, after all — pals. I say, let's go ahead."

"Mr. Kellogg!"

"Make it ' Billy.' "

She shook her head.

" ' Sam,' then."

She remained silent.

"I suppose I ought to apologize for a lot of it," he muttered. "But somehow I can't. You know as a matter of fact you deserved most of it."

Rosalind sat very straight on the nail-keg.

"Yes; you did. You were so all-fired scornful of everybody and everything — particularly me. You rubbed it in. You just carved me into slivers every time you spoke — and I guess you thought I wasn't even good enough to furnish slivers.

"I'll admit I'm not much use in the world; I'm about as useless as the first six rows in a movie house. But that wasn't any reason for climbing me every time I did something or said something. So far as usefulness goes I'll stack up with Reggy, anyhow.

"Wait a minute now. I'm not going to hurt your feelings. That was just a preface. Here's the rest of it: All the time you were carving me and climbing me I was strong for you. That's Gospel. I just had to be. You bullyragged me into loving you.

"Perhaps that doesn't sound quite right. I don't mean that you tried to. But I mean that every time you clouted me I loved you some more.

"Wait — please wait! We'll cut out the trip to Ogdensburg. I see you're not ready for that — yet.

"Yes; I said, 'yet.' I'm filing a claim. Some day I'm going to take it up, perhaps after we've known each other a conventional time.

"I'll admit it may not seem very promising now. But the gold's there, Rosalind. I *know* it. You may have hidden it from a lot of other people, but you can't hide it from me."

Rosalind's nineteenth — or was it the eighteenth, or twentieth? — proposal bewildered her.

"So remember! It stands this way: I love you, and some day I'm going to marry you. I'll wai. — but I won't quit."

He paused and watched her for some sign, but she was mute, motionless. Suddenly his voice changed.

"Oh, if you'd only let yourself go, Rosalind! If you'd only throw off the mask! You nearly did, back in the launch, when it was all touch and go for a few minutes.

"I don't love you because you're brave or capable or wonderful. That's only part of you — the part everybody sees. But there's a lot more than that. You've tried to bury it out of sight in your woman's heart, but it won't stay there always. It's the real *you* — and I'm going to have it!"

There was a moment of silence. Then Kellogg spoke with his old briskness.

"Well, let's see if we can get the skiff loose. You want to get over to Witherbee's a soon as possible, I guess. Your gown isn't dry yet."

Rosalind nodded. She watched him as he fumbled with the padlock. She had the sensation that something extraordinary was happening to her — a sort of transmigration from one existence to another.

Her mind was not working very clearly; it groped. Through it all ran a faint and vague whisper of alarm. She wondered if she was losing her sure and steady grip on Rosalind Chalmers. It was so absurd, too; so unthinkable — so —

" Funny about Schmidt, wasn't it? " remarked Billy, still struggling with the lock. " I never had the least idea. Did you? "

She shook her head mechanically and without the least thought of the boatman's patron.

I'm getting Uncle Henry to fix things up for Bob," he went on. " He's going to keep the banking-job. Poor devil! He's been scared stiff for the last two days. What did you think of him, anyhow? "

This time she did not hear his question at all.

The padlock came loose in his hand, and he unchained the skiff.

" All ready," he said. " I'll row."

But Rosalind did not take the hand that he reached to steady her. It was busy, unclasping the bracelet on her arm. An instant later she flung the golden treasure far out into the river.

" Rosalind! "

She looked at Billy with a smile of contentment.

" There goes the last of my lies," she said with a luxurious sigh. " I've told so many that I'm completely ashamed of myself. And most of them were all on account of that."

She pointed to where the bracelet had disappeared forever.

"It seemed to chain me to so many things I want to get rid of," she added thoughtfully. "It was not only the lies — it was almost everything. And I simply had to do something physical to break away."

The incompetent boatman nodded to signify that he understood — but he didn't. Something in her eyes baffled him.

"Well, hop in," he said shortly, breaking the tension.

Rosalind drew back a step from the skiff.

"I object to being ordered to do things," she said firmly.

"I beg your pardon. I meant —"

"You mean to ask, of course," she broke in.

"Yes; certainly."

"That's better," she said softly. "It is very much nicer to be asked."

She was about to embark when he gripped her suddenly by the shoulders and stared into her face.

"What did you mean by that?" he demanded, shaking her gently. "Am I dreaming — or crazy? 'Nicer to be asked!' Rosalind! Why — I'm a fool! Did you mean —"

"Ask me."

He got his answer, too, even if it was slightly muffled.

In the latest print of Hamersly's "Social Register" there is a cross-index on a certain page among the C's that refers the reader to a certain other page among the K's; or if you happen to hit the K page first, an equally obliging cross-index will send you back to the C's, if you are at all curious. If you look under "Sam," you'll find there's nothing at all. It is because of that very omission that two certain persons have agreed that Hamersly's is trashy, unreliable and incomplete, and have canceled their subscription.

THE END

www.ingramcontent.com/pod-product-compliance
Lightning Source LLC
Chambersburg PA
CBHW030342020726
47493CB00003B/640